She'd n... the pictu... eyes now.

She barely noticed the motorcycle; all she could do was stare at the man astride the low-slung, snarling beast.

He was dressed like a walking advertisement for some rebel motorcycle gang, and he looked like the personification of everything she'd been fascinated by as a girl, but had been too terrified to go near. That hadn't changed much, she thought, as she became aware that her heart was racing in her chest.

He didn't seem to fit in here in Santiago Beach; this was a sun-and-surf town, and he was a splash of the wild side.

The wild side.

Suddenly she knew. With an instinctive certainty she couldn't question, Amelia knew.

Luke McGuire was back in town.

Dear Reader,

The 20th anniversary excitement continues as we bring you a 2-in-1 collection containing brand-new novellas by two of your favorite authors: Maggie Shayne and Marilyn Pappano. *Who Do You Love?* It's an interesting question—made more complicated for these heroes and heroines because they're not quite what they seem, making the path to happily-ever-after an especially twisty one. Enjoy!

A YEAR OF LOVING DANGEROUSLY continues with *Her Secret Weapon* by bestselling writer Beverly Barton. This is a great secret-baby story—with a forgotten night of passion thrown in to make things even more exciting. Our in-line 36 HOURS spin-off continues with *A Thanksgiving To Remember,* by Margaret Watson. Suspenseful and sensual, this story shows off her talents to their fullest. Applaud the return of Justine Davis with *The Return of Luke McGuire.* There's something irresistible about a bad boy turned hero, and Justine's compelling and emotional handling of the theme will win your heart. In *The Lawman Meets His Bride,* Meagan McKinney brings her MATCHED IN MONTANA miniseries over from Desire with an exciting romance featuring a to-die-for hero. Finally, pick up *The Virgin Beauty* by Claire King and discover why this relative newcomer already has people talking about her talent.

Share the excitement—and come back next month for more!

Leslie J. Wainger

Leslie J. Wainger
Executive Senior Editor

Please address questions and book requests to:
Silhouette Reader Service
U.S.: 3010 Walden Ave., P.O. Box 1325, Buffalo, NY 14269
Canadian: P.O. Box 609, Fort Erie, Ont. L2A 5X3

THE RETURN OF LUKE McGUIRE
JUSTINE DAVIS

Published by Silhouette Books
America's Publisher of Contemporary Romance

For the girls who, like me, always fell for the bad boy…
and were lucky enough to marry a reformed one.

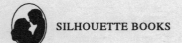 SILHOUETTE BOOKS

ISBN 0-373-27106-9

THE RETURN OF LUKE McGUIRE

Copyright © 2000 by Janice Davis Smith

Visit Silhouette at www.eHarlequin.com

Printed in U.S.A.

JUSTINE DAVIS

lives in Kingston, Washington. Her interests outside writing are sailing, doing needlework, horseback riding and driving her restored 1967 Corvette roadster—top down, of course.

A policewoman, Justine says that years ago, a young man she worked with encouraged her to try for a promotion to a position that was, at that time, occupied only by men. "I succeeded, became wrapped up in my new job, and that man moved away, never, I thought, to be heard of again. Ten years later he appeared out of the woods of Washington State, saying he'd never forgotten me and would I please marry him. With that history, how could I write anything but romance?"

IT'S OUR 20th ANNIVERSARY!
We'll be celebrating all year,
Continuing with these fabulous titles,
On sale in October 2000.

Desire

 #1321 The Dakota Man
Joan Hohl

#1322 Rancher's Proposition
Anne Marie Winston

#1323 First Comes Love
Elizabeth Bevarly

#1324 Fortune's Secret Child
Shawna Delacorte

 #1325 Marooned With a Marine
Maureen Child

#1326 Baby: MacAllister-Made
Joan Elliott Pickart

Romance

 #1474 The Acquired Bride
Teresa Southwick

#1475 Jessie's Expecting
Kasey Michaels

#1476 Snowbound Sweetheart
Judy Christenberry

#1477 The Nanny Proposal
Donna Clayton

#1478 Raising Baby Jane
Lilian Darcy

#1479 One Fiancée To Go, Please
Jackie Braun

Special Edition

 #1351 Bachelor's Baby Promise
Barbara McMahon

#1352 Marrying a Delacourt
Sherryl Woods

#1353 Millionaire Takes a Bride
Pamela Toth

#1354 A Bundle of Miracles
Amy Frazier

#1355 Hidden in a Heartbeat
Patricia McLinn

#1356 Stranger in a Small Town
Ann Roth

Intimate Moments

#1033 Who Do You Love?
Maggie Shayne/
Marilyn Pappano

#1034 Her Secret Weapon
Beverly Barton

#1035 A Thanksgiving to Remember
Margaret Watson

#1036 The Return of Luke McGuire
Justine Davis

#1037 The Lawman Meets His Bride
Meagan McKinney

#1038 The Virgin Beauty
Claire King

Chapter 1

It wasn't nearly as tough being a bastard as it used to be.

Luke McGuire knew that, knew that if he'd been born a hundred, or even fifty years ago his life would have been a much bigger nightmare. But the unexpected letter he held made long-buried memories rise again, memories of the nightmare his life had indeed been.

He stared down at the scrawled lines that filled the page of three-hole notebook paper. He glanced again at the envelope, addressed only to his name and the small town of River Park; if Charlie Hanson didn't know everybody in town, he might never have gotten it.

He wasn't sure he didn't wish Charlie had never heard of him.

He shoved a hand through his wind-tangled hair, pushing it back from his forehead. He was going to have to cut it or start tying it back soon; the thick, dark strands were getting in his way. Not that seeing any better changed the plea the letter contained.

He could just toss it, he thought. After all, if River Park

had been a little bigger, or Charlie a little less efficient, it could have wound up in some dead letter file, since there was no return address on the envelope. So he could throw it away and go on pretending blissful ignorance.

Except he'd read it. He'd read it, and he didn't know if he had it in him to ignore the plea it contained.

His little brother was in trouble.

Little Davie. The child who had been the only good thing in his life so long ago, the only person who ever looked at him with pure, honest love shining in his eyes.

Little Davie?

Luke caught himself with a wry chuckle as the math hit home. Eight years. David would be fifteen now. Hardly the wide-eyed, innocent child he remembered.

Especially the innocent part, he thought with a grimace as he read the letter once more.

Guilt rose up, sharp toothed and ugly. He'd known what he was leaving David behind to face. He'd hoped the fact that his brother was the wanted son would make things different for him, that having a father there to defend him would make it all right.

Maybe it had only gone sour in the six months since David's father had died. That made sense; their mother would never be openly cruel to him while Ed Hiller was alive. Not when he was her meal ticket. But she had a thousand ways to be quietly, subtly cruel, covering it with feigned concern, even wearing the mask of affection to hide the emotional whip.

He felt a flicker of sympathy for the man who had been as much of a father as Luke had ever known. It had been Ed who had lectured Luke—gently—on not living up to his potential, Ed who had told him he was smarter than his grades were showing, Ed who, seeming to sense Luke was on the verge of bolting, pressed him hard to finish school. Ed hadn't loved him the way he loved his blood son, but he'd been kind, and fair, which meant more to Luke than

Ed Hiller could ever have known. He felt a brief flicker of regret that he had never told the man he was grateful.

And now that man's son was crying out for Luke's help. Wanting, of all things, to come and live with him. And Luke had done enough running of his own to realize that David was in full stride.

He got up and walked to the window of his cabin. It was the smallest of the five on the property, but Luke had taken it eagerly. It also had the best view of the river. At night he could hear the rush of the water and pretend he could hear the rough and tumble of the rapids just downstream. It was all he needed. It was all he wanted.

He heard the crumple of paper and realized he was clenching his fist around David's letter. It wasn't his problem, he thought. He didn't have to deal with it. Which was a good thing, since he'd sworn to never set foot in Santiago Beach again, and nothing had happened since he'd left to change his mind.

He would just throw the letter away. Pretend it had never reached him.

He finished crumpling it up, feeling the oddly sharp dig of one of the corners of the envelope against his palm.

Not for anything or anyone would he go back to Santiago Beach. Not even for the boy who had made those last years survivable.

"Hey, McGuire! You comin' or what?"

The voice of his friend and partner Gary Milhouse was a welcome interruption.

"Yeah," he called out. "On my way."

Good idea. Half a pizza and a beer or two, and he would forget all about it. There wasn't a damn thing he could do anyway.

He stuffed the letter in his pocket and walked right past his wastebasket. He would burn it later, he thought. That way it wouldn't be lying around to taunt him.

Maybe three beers.

* * *

Amelia Blair watched the gangly boy heading toward her bookstore. His hair moved loosely on top of his head, where it was long and bleached a white blond. A darker, medium brown showed beneath, where it was shaved short. A baggy shirt and baggier pants flapped as he crossed the street. He was walking—almost strutting—in that self-conscious way teenage boys had when they were trying to be adult but were still in the imitation stage, before it came from the inside.

She knew she tended toward worry anyway, but she was certain her concern about her young friend was warranted. He'd changed so much from the open, natural boy she'd met when he'd first come into her bookstore four years ago. And the change had not been for the better.

The buzzer on the door announced David's arrival in the cultured tones of Captain Jean-Luc Picard; she'd adapted the sound effects from *Star Trek* and rotated them daily. They were a big hit with her younger customers—some of whom stopped in daily to see who would be talking—and even made the older ones smile.

"Hey, Amelia."

He sounded normal enough this morning, she thought. "Hello, David. How are you?"

He shrugged. "Hangin' in."

Amelia nodded, knowing he usually wanted to leave it at that. She couldn't blame him; the subject of his father's recent unexpected and sudden death in an accident was still new, and he was still raw and aching.

He made a show of looking at the books in her front display rack, but since his taste ran more to science fiction, she doubted he was really interested in the bestsellers and her own personal choices. She knew it took him a while to work up to really talking to her, and she'd found the best approach was to just welcome him and wait.

After a moment he stopped fiddling with the latest political exposé and stepped over to the counter. He leaned his elbows on it and finally looked at her. "How was kickboxing today?"

She smiled. "Tiring. We're working on punch-kick combinations, and it's tough."

"Bet it'll take out a bad guy."

"That's the idea, anyway," Amelia said. She'd signed up for the classes three years ago in the hope they would help her feel less…timid. She was at home in her world here, amid her books, but outside, she was never quite sure of herself. She had resigned herself at twenty-five to being forever a mouse, with mousy brown hair to match, but now, at thirty, she was determined to at least be the bravest mouse she could be.

As a side benefit, it had impressed David, who had decided she had to be fairly cool to be taking kickboxing. After that, the relationship had grown rapidly.

"I wish my mother would change her mind and let me take lessons," David said.

Amelia hesitated. She doubted that was likely. Jackie Hiller seemed to run her son's life with a heavy hand, allowing him only the extracurricular activities she approved of.

Of course, she also doubted Mrs. Hiller knew about the new friends David had acquired. Loud, obnoxious, frequently nasty and purposely intimidating, the group of about five boys had already gained an unpleasant notoriety in Santiago Beach. From what Amelia had seen they were all hotheaded, which unfortunately made them very attractive to a boy still angry about his father's death.

"Maybe if you got a part-time job and offered to help pay for the lessons?" she suggested, thinking that something physical, like kickboxing, might be just the thing David needed to release some of that anger. And the part of the program that dealt with mental and emotional control couldn't hurt.

But David snorted aloud. "It's not the bucks. Hell, she

spends it like crazy. She just wants me to do wussy stuff like piano lessons. And during the summer, too!''

''Well, even Elton John had to start somewhere.''

David looked at her blankly. ''Who? Oh…he's that old guy from England, right?''

She smothered a sigh and nodded, wondering how a boy only fifteen years younger could make her feel ancient. ''He's lasted in the music biz for decades now because he can play the piano.'' Well, that was stretching it a bit, but it made her point. And she liked Elton, even if he was more of her parents' generation.

''Yeah. Well. I still hate it.''

She grinned at him then. ''So did I.''

He blinked. ''You did?''

''Yep. My mother made me practice for two hours a day, then I had to play for my father when he came home.''

''Bummer,'' David said with an eloquent shiver. ''But I won't have to do it much longer.''

''Talk your mother out of it, did you?''

''Not exactly.''

Something about the way the boy said it set alarms off in Amelia's mind. ''What, exactly?''

David looked at her, then looked away, then looked sideways back at her again. Her worry increased, but she reined it in, telling herself to remember that he had to take his time, but he eventually opened up.

''I'm going away,'' he finally blurted out.

''Away?''

''To live somewhere else.''

This startled her, but she knew if she peppered him with questions he would clam up. So she settled on one thing she knew was true. ''I'll miss you,'' she said simply.

He looked startled, then pleased, then he blushed. She knew when he felt his cheeks heat, because he lowered his head again.

''Where are you going?'' she asked, careful to keep her tone casual.

He didn't raise his head. He tapped his fingers in a restless rhythm. Took a deep breath, let it out.

''I'm going to live with my brother,'' he said in the same kind of rush.

''Your brother?'' She was genuinely startled now.

''Yeah. Luke. Luke McGuire. My half brother, really. You don't know him, he was gone before you came here.''

No, she didn't know him. But she knew *of* him. It was hard to live in Santiago Beach and not know of the town bad boy who had departed the morning after the high school graduation he'd barely achieved and never been back. Luke McGuire might have been gone for better than eight years, but his reputation had lingered.

''I didn't realize you were in touch with him,'' she said carefully. ''You never mentioned him before.''

''He'll be coming to get me soon,'' David said.

Amelia noticed he hadn't answered her directly, but didn't belabor the point. ''When? Do I have time to get you a going-away present?''

Again the boy blushed. ''I...don't really know. Not yet, anyway. But he's coming. I know he is.''

For a moment David sounded like a child waiting for Santa Claus, and she wondered if the arrival of the brother was as much a fantasy. She also wondered, as she had before, if the phantom brother wasn't part of David's problem, if because some people expected him to be just like his troublemaking brother, it had become a self-fulfilling prophecy.

David met her gaze then, his jaw set and his chin up. ''You'll see. So will my mom. She can't keep him away, even though she hates him.''

Amelia considered that. Ordinarily her response would have been something soothing, assuring the boy his mother surely didn't really hate his brother. But she had met David's mother, knew that Jackie was very conscious of appearances and hated to be embarrassed. Given Luke's reputation and what the woman had no doubt gone through raising him, she could easily believe there was no love lost between the two.

"It must be difficult, if he and your mother don't get along, but you want to go live with him."

"She doesn't know about it. Yet," he added, his expression turning mutinous.

"Does she even know you've been in touch?"

"No. Yes."

Well, Amelia thought, there's a teenage response for you. She waited, knowing David would explain if she just waited.

"I mean she knows I wrote to him, but she stole my first letter before the mail lady picked it up. I found it in the trash."

Amelia smothered a sigh; she couldn't think of anything more likely to make an already resistant teenager downright stubborn. But it wasn't her place to pass judgment on his mother's parenting skills.

"So you wrote again?"

He nodded, a little fiercely, the blond hair flopping in time with the movement. "Couple of weeks ago. And I took it to the post office myself. I even bought the stamp myself, 'cause I know she started counting the ones in her desk. She puts a mark on the next one on the roll. She thinks I'm too dumb to figure that out."

Amelia couldn't imagine living that way. Her parents might have been older and a bit fussy in their ways, but she had never had to live with this kind of subterfuge and mistrust.

"And what did your brother say?"

"He hasn't answered. Yet." This time the "yet" was in an entirely different tone, one of stubbornly determined hope. "I think he's just gonna come and get me. He doesn't have time for writing letters."

"He doesn't?"

''Nah, he's too busy.''

''Doing what?''

''I'm not sure, but cool stuff. He'd never have some boring job or wear a tie or nothing like that.''

''But you don't know what he does do?''

''No. But he's not in jail, like my mom says!''

Amelia's breath caught. ''Jail?''

''She just says that. She's always said it, that he was probably in jail somewhere. She's always sayin' bad things about him.''

Amelia felt an unexpected tug of sympathy for the absent Luke McGuire. ''You were young when he left, weren't you?'' she asked gently.

''I was almost eight.'' He sounded defensive. ''I remember him really good. He was really cool. He used to take me with him places, unless he was with some girl. And sometimes at night, you know, when I was real little, when I couldn't go to sleep, he'd sneak in and read to me.''

And there it was, Amelia thought. The birth of a reader. Somehow she never would have expected the inspiration to be the disreputable Luke.

Primed now, David kept on, extolling the virtues of his long gone half brother.

''And he'd bring me stuff, not stuff you buy, he didn't have much money, but stuff like a neat rock, or a feather, that kind of thing. I'd put it away in my special box—'' He stopped suddenly before adding sourly, ''Before my mother found it and threw it all away.''

Amelia sighed again. She herself had had a collection of leaves she had pressed and dried, all the different ones she could find. Her mother hadn't liked having them around, she thought they were dirty, but Amelia loved to look at them, and that was all that had really mattered; the collection had stayed.

Thanks, Mom, she whispered silently, as she often did to both the parents she still missed so much. And never had it mattered less than it did at this moment that they hadn't been her biological parents.

"People say he was kind of a...troublemaker," she said carefully; she didn't want to join a chorus, but she did want to know if David was utterly blind to any faults his brother had.

"Yeah, he got in some trouble." The boy said it with a kind of relish that made Amelia nervous; she wondered if this was the key to David's new friends, who seemed to find—or make—trouble wherever they went. "He was no nerd like my mom likes, he had fun, he went out at night, hung with his buddies, and they did whatever they felt like. Didn't pay any attention to stupid rules."

Or laws? Amelia wondered. She tried to remember any specifics she'd ever heard about the wayward Luke, but all she could call up was the general impression of a teenage boy gone wild. What she did know was that David appeared to be heading in the same direction; there was far too much of a gleam in his eyes when he spoke of the older brother he clearly admired. And while she could appreciate—indeed, she'd been pleasantly surprised and touched by—David's childhood recollections of another side of his brother, she was afraid it was the wild side he was trying to emulate.

Perhaps his mother had the right idea, after all.

"—window broken out, and some of that disgusting graffiti sprayed all over!"

"How awful," Amelia agreed as she rang up Mrs. Clancy's gardening magazines.

"Those boys are getting out of hand," the older woman said ominously. "It was bad enough when they would harass people on the street, blocking the sidewalks, riding those awful skateboards so fast they could kill a person if they knocked them down, which they nearly did many times. But now this...somebody should do something!"

Somebody being somebody other than herself, Amelia

guessed. Mrs. Clancy was of the speak-loudly-and-let-someone-else-carry-the-stick school. She was a formidable, large woman in her late sixties, with silver hair she was proud of saying hadn't been cut since she was sixteen, and if she had ever known what it was like to be young and bored in a small town, she'd clearly forgotten.

Diplomatically, Amelia changed the subject to one she knew the woman could never resist. "Going for that prize-winning rose again next year?"

The woman's eyes lit up. "I'll beat that Louise Doyle yet, you just wait and see."

Mrs. Clancy chattered on as Amelia slipped the magazines into a bag. "I wish you luck," she said as she handed them over with a smile. "I always love walking by your garden."

That much, at least, was true. And Mrs. Clancy left the store happy, and would return next month as usual. Amelia had once wondered why she didn't subscribe and save herself the trip, but soon figured out that this was the only time the poor woman had away from the recently retired Mr. Clancy, and she wasn't about to give it up.

Amelia glanced at the clock; she was five minutes past closing. Not unusual for her, but tonight she was a bit tired; she'd had her kickboxing class early this morning, and this afternoon she'd gotten in several shipments of books to be shelved, and handling it all herself was getting wearing. But she wasn't sure she wanted to hire someone, she liked her quiet times in the shop when she could actually read herself—it was hard to recommend sincerely a book you hadn't read—and she was getting by on only Sundays off, even with the long hours. By opening at ten and staying open until eight, she managed to serve everyone fairly well and had enough down time during the ten hours the store was open to get some other things done, although she still came in an hour or more before opening to deal with things that took uninterrupted concentration.

But dealing with those heavy cartons of books was a different matter than mental exercise, and tonight she was tired.

She went through her closing up ritual quickly and almost thoughtlessly; she'd done it so often she thought she could do it in her sleep. The register was totaled out and locked, the back door closed and secured, and she decided to put off cleaning the restroom until tomorrow morning. She picked up her small purse, flipped out the lights and made her way to the front door.

She was turning to lock it from the outside when she heard the sound. A low, throaty growl that sounded almost more animal than mechanical. She chalked that bit of anthropomorphism up to her weary state as she turned to look; it was a motorcycle, that was all.

All?

The word echoed in her mind as she stared. A motorcycle, yes. But she'd never seen anything like the picture that greeted her eyes now, riding out of the twilight. The bike was big and sleek and shiny black, but she barely noticed it as it cruised past, growling as if in protest at the slow pace. All she could do was stare at the man astride the low-slung, snarling beast.

He was dressed like a walking advertisement for some rebel motorcycle gang, except that the declarations of affiliation were missing. Plain, unmarked black leather jacket and boots, black jeans, and a pair of wraparound, black framed sunglasses with mirrored lenses. She thought she caught a glint of gold at his left earlobe. His hair was nearly as dark as the bike, and more than long enough to whip back like a mane in the wind of his passage. His face was unshaven, but not bearded, and beneath that his skin was tan, as if he spent a lot of his time outdoors. Probably on that monster, she thought a little numbly.

Instinctively she drew back in some alarm; she didn't want to draw the attention of this intruder. He looked like the personification of everything she'd been fascinated by as a girl but had been too terrified to go near. That hadn't changed much, she thought, as she became aware that her heart was racing in her chest.

She noticed a duffel bag fastened to the rack behind the seat of the bike. Was he traveling, then? Did he just travel about the country as the spirit moved him, like some fictional character in a weekly action show or something? She nearly sighed aloud.

She caught herself and smothered the familiar yearning to be something other than what she was. The words to an old song came to her, something about a man who was the wrong kind of paradise. This man would be just that for a woman. For this mouse of a woman, at least, she admitted, knowing herself too well to think she could ever even begin to handle a man like that.

As he went past the store she saw a helmet—also, of course, gleaming black—hooked to the back of the bike, and wondered if he ever bothered to wear it, or if he just carried it in the hopes of talking himself out of a ticket in this mandatory helmet state.

She thought she saw his head move slightly, but if he glanced her way at all, she couldn't tell behind the mirrored glasses. She doubted it; there was nothing to draw his attention. She couldn't imagine what it would take to interest such a man. The bike had California plates, but he didn't seem to fit here in Santiago Beach. This was a sun and surf town, and he was a splash of the wild side.

The wild side.

Suddenly she knew. With an instinctive certainty she couldn't question, she knew.

Luke McGuire was back in town.

Chapter 2

Santiago Beach hadn't changed a bit, Luke thought. Oh, there was some new development around the edges, some new houses and the occasional strip mall, but the downtown district hadn't changed at all. It was still the quaint, villagelike, tourist-attracting place, the main drag with the incredibly hokey name of Main Street, that had bored him to distraction. Everybody seemed to think living near the beach was the dream life for any kid, but it hadn't been for him.

No, it hadn't changed much at all. He had, though. He had to admit that. Not, he amended with an inward grin, that he resisted gunning the Harley's engine on occasion, just to break the smothering quiet. That it also turned heads, made people either gape at him or eye him suspiciously—or even with shock, like the woman outside the bookstore—was just a side benefit.

But down deep, he was no longer the kid who had done that kind of thing just for thrills, just to build on the reputation that had already begun to snowball. Now he did it for...what? Nostalgia?

Lord, nostalgic at twenty-six, he thought with a rueful twist of his lips. *Back then, at eighteen, you thought anybody on the far side of thirty was decrepit, and now you're thinking people can still be young at forty.*

He wondered if at thirty he would push that back to fifty, then at forty to sixty, continually pushing the boundaries back so that they were a safe distance away.

And he wondered if just coming back here was making him lose his mind. He never thought about this kind of thing at home. Of course, at home his thoughts were focused mainly on how to keep himself and everyone else alive through the next adventure. He rarely thought about Santiago Beach at all; in his mind, his past consisted of the last eight years.

But it was amazing to him how quickly he relapsed, just from seeing the old, familiar things, all in their old, familiar places. The faces might be different—although some had looked familiar—but the effect they had on him was the same. He immediately felt cramped, trapped, and he found himself wondering if his favorite secret hideout, the place no one had ever found, was still there.

The urge to turn the bike around and head for the high country was tremendous.

But he couldn't. He had to find Davie first, make sure he was all right. He'd wrestled with it for days, but now that he'd decided, now that he'd arrived, he wasn't going to turn tail and run until he'd done what he'd come here for. He really wasn't that kid anymore, desperate and weary of fighting a battle he could never, ever win.

He'd learned well in the past eight years. He'd learned how to depend only on himself, learned how to take care of himself, and most of all, he'd learned how it felt to win. And he liked it.

He wasn't going to let this place beat him again.

She wouldn't have sought her out, Amelia thought, but now that Jackie Hiller was right here, she should say something. She would never betray David's confidence, but she was worried. Especially if she was right about that dark, wild apparition she'd seen riding down Main Street.

The image, still so vivid in her mind, gave her a slight shiver. She knew she'd grown up within the boundaries of a strict childhood and been further limited by her own natural shyness; men like the one on that motorcycle had had no part in her life. But if that were indeed Luke McGuire, Amelia could easily see how David had built his half brother up into an almost mythological being in his mind.

She shook off the odd feeling. Jackie was coming out of the community center, and Amelia wondered if she had been giving one of her speeches. That was where Amelia had first met her a couple of years ago, at a meeting of the local Chamber of Commerce, where the woman had earnestly, passionately, almost too vehemently, pitched her views on the problem of teenage pregnancy. For a decade now she had been giving lectures at local schools and communities on the subject, and from what Amelia had heard, she was quite zealous in her crusade.

The woman was dressed impeccably, as usual; Amelia didn't think she'd ever seen her without perfect makeup, tasteful gold jewelry and medium heels. Her dress was tailored yet feminine, and looked very expensive. Her hair was perfectly blond, exquisitely cut and looked equally expensive. In all, a package Amelia doubted she could ever put together; she had the money, but not the time. Not time she wanted to spend on that kind of production, anyway.

But that wasn't what she was here for. Steeling herself, she waited until Jackie finished speaking to a woman outside the doors of the center, then approached.

"Mrs. Hiller?"

Jackie turned, an all-purpose smile on her face. It changed slightly when she saw Amelia, apparently recognizing her as someone she had met before.

"Amelia Blair. Of Blairs' Books."

"Ah, of course!" Her greeting was effusive and, for all Amelia could tell, genuine. "How nice to see you again. I've been meaning to stop in and see you."

Amelia blinked. She had? As far as she knew, the woman had never set foot in the store before; whatever her reading tastes were, if any, she satisfied them elsewhere.

"I wanted to talk to you about carrying our new news-letter," Jackie went on. "I understand you have several teen-agers who come in regularly?"

"Yes," Amelia said, recovering. "Yes, I do."

"It's free, of course. And I'm sure you'll want to help in getting out such an important message."

Amelia couldn't argue about the importance of the mes-sage, but she didn't like the assumption that she would agree, sight unseen.

"I'll be happy to take a look at it and get back to you," she said, refusing to be swept up by the woman's polished energy. She might be a mouse, but she could be a stubborn one if she had to be.

There was only the most minuscule of breaks in the woman's demeanor, as if she'd heard a tiny blip she hadn't expected. But she went on as if nothing had happened. "Fine. I'll get one to you. I'm sure you'll be able to find space for it."

Jackie turned to go, as if assuming Amelia had only ap-proached her because she had willed it. As if Amelia couldn't possibly have had a reason of her own.

"Mrs. Hiller, I needed to talk to you."

She turned back. "Oh?" Not quite looking down her nose, she waited.

"About David."

Jackie smiled. "Of course. I've also been meaning to tell you I appreciate the way you've encouraged him to read. I don't approve of some of the things you've picked, but I suppose reading anything is better than nothing."

How on earth, Amelia wondered, did she make an expression of thanks insulting?

"You're right, it is better," she said, carefully picking her words. "It's important that kids learn to love reading, and the only way that happens is for them to read things that interest them."

She could see the disagreement rising to the other woman's lips and continued quickly to forestall it.

"But what I wanted to talk about is not David's reading. It's…his brother."

The practiced smile faltered. Something hot and annoyed flickered in the cool blue eyes, and Amelia wondered rather abruptly if the man on the motorcycle had blue eyes, too.

"Why on earth," Jackie finally said, "would you ask about *him?*"

"I just…" Amelia stopped, wishing she'd thought this through before she'd done it; it was going to be very difficult not to give away David's secret. But she didn't have to; Jackie was on a roll.

"That boy," she said firmly, "was a hellion from the day he was born. I tried my best, but I've never seen a child who got into so much trouble so often and so young. I couldn't turn my back for a minute or he'd be into mischief. And later it got worse. He became incorrigible. It's a miracle we all survived."

"I see," was all Amelia could manage.

"Oh, I know what David's probably told you. He's built Luke up into some kind of idol, and he won't see reason about it. I've had to be extra hard on David so he doesn't turn out like Luke did."

"And how is that?" Amelia asked, curious to see how much truth there was to David's assumption that his mother hated his brother.

"Useless, troublesome, wicked and hideously embarrassing," Jackie said baldly. "But he's my cross to bear, much as I would like to deny he exists. And the sooner David gets over this silly moping around and mooning over a brother who isn't worth it, the better.''

Well. That answers that, Amelia thought. And felt another pang of sympathy for the much-maligned Luke. "I'm sure a lot of David's mood is because of his father," she said, purposely changing the subject.

"It's been six months," Jackie said. "It's time to move on.''

Startled at the woman's bluntness, Amelia said cautiously, "I don't think that's something you can put a timetable on. Everyone has to grieve in their own way."

If this was Jackie Hiller's way of grieving, Amelia thought as the woman abruptly remembered an appointment and stated she had to go right now, it was rather odd. And the woman seemed to have no idea how deeply David felt the loss of his father.

Amelia acknowledged the hasty goodbye and the promise to drop off the newsletter, and only after Jackie had taken a couple of steps did she think to call out to her.

"Mrs. Hiller? What does Luke look like?"

The woman's expression was nothing less than sour. "He looks,'' she said, "like his damned, black-Irish father."

The woman turned on her Ferragamo heel and walked swiftly away, as if in a hurry to leave the topic behind her in more ways than one.

His damned, black-Irish father...

The image of the man on the motorcycle came back even more vividly now. It all fit.

As did something else. That man had been at least in his mid-twenties. Jacqueline Hiller looked to be in her late thirties, although she could be a well-maintained forty-something. Not that she would want to hear that, Amelia was certain. But that meant that if the man on the bike was indeed Luke McGuire, he must have been born when Jackie was very, very young. And that he'd still been at home when Jackie had begun her crusade.

She wondered how it must feel to be the reason your mother campaigned like a zealot against teen pregnancy.

"Look, Davie, I'm really sorry about your dad. He was a good guy."

David nodded, his mouth tightening.

After one of the longest nights of his life, when his gut had tried hard to convince his head he should go home, Luke had waited down the street from the old house this morning until David had come out. And he had to admit, the boy's joyous greeting had been gratifying. He'd barely recognized his little brother, but the boy had had no such problem. He supposed it was because he'd already been eighteen when he'd left and hadn't changed all that much, whereas David had gone from small child to teenager.

"He liked you," David said.

"I liked him, too."

"He never said bad things about you, even after you left. Not like Mom."

Luke sighed. "I've been gone eight years, and she's still riding that old horse?"

"Sometimes I tell her to shut up."

And I'll bet that goes over like a busted paddle. "Hey," he said aloud, gripping his brother's shoulder, "don't make trouble for yourself. You don't have to defend me. Not to her."

"But if I don't, nobody else will," David said. Then, brightening, he added, "But you're here now. *You* can tell her to shut up."

Luke laughed. "Yeah, I suppose I could." He wouldn't— it wasn't worth it—but it seemed to make David feel better. "But if you don't mind, I'll wait a while. I'm not sure I want her to know I'm here yet."

"I didn't tell her," David said. "I didn't even tell her you were coming."

"Were you so sure I would?"

The boy nodded. "I knew you'd remember what it was like here. I did tell some people, though."

"Oh? Who?"

"My friends, some of them. Snake, anyway."

"Snake?"

"Yeah, like in the movie about New York being turned into a prison, remember?"

"Yeah, I do."

"And Amelia."

Luke lifted a brow. "Amelia? Who's that, your girl-friend?"

David blushed. Luke's mouth quirked; *that* was a stage he was glad to be long past. "Nah," the boy said. "She's too old. She's thirty, I think."

Ancient, Luke silently agreed with a rueful smile; his own thirtieth wasn't all that far away.

"She's a little quiet," David went on. "You never know what she's thinking. But she's cool. Even takes kickboxing lessons. She runs the bookstore downtown."

A memory flashed through his mind, of riding down Main Street last evening, just as it was starting to get dark. And of a woman, almost huddled in the doorway of the book-store, as if she feared he would ride right up onto the side-walk and grab her. That surely couldn't be the "cool" Amelia....

"What happened to old man Wylie?"

"He retired. Amelia's folks moved here and bought the store, and she worked there. Then they died, and now it's hers. She's cool," he repeated. "She gets me good stuff to read, not that junk they make you read at school. You can talk to her, about anything and she really *hears*. And she talks to you, not *at* you."

"Definitely cool, then," Luke agreed; there had been a time in this town when he would have been pitifully grateful to find someone like that.

"She lets me talk about Dad," David added, looking

away and taking a surreptitious swipe at his eyes that Luke
pretended not to see. ''Mom doesn't want me to ever bring
him up. But Amelia says I should talk about him, that it'll
help.''

Another point for her, Luke thought. A big one.

David looked at his brother hopefully. ''Want to meet
her? I told her you'd come, but she wasn't sure.''

Luke wasn't sure he wanted to meet anybody in Santiago
Beach, but the cool Amelia had a few things in her favor.
She apparently listened to David, something their mother
never did; he doubted that had changed much. She had acknowledged his right to grieve for his father, something else
he apparently wasn't getting at home. And most of all, she
hadn't lived here when Luke had, so she didn't know him.

''All right,'' he agreed at last, and David yelped happily.
It was fairly close so they walked, although Luke guessed
David was itching to ask for a ride on the bike. Later, he
thought; that would be just about right to send the old lady—
Lord, she had always hated being called that—over the edge.

David was so excited he couldn't just walk; he ran ahead,
heedless of the people dodging out of his way. Luke watched
his not so little brother—the wiry David was only about four
inches short of his own six feet—with a wry amusement.
Once he'd been the same way, in a hurry in a slowed-down
place. And if people had stared at him, or yelled at him, so
much the better.

Nobody yelled at him today. No reason to; he was stroll-
ing along at the same snail's pace as everyone else. But they
still stared. About half of them, anyway. He'd shed his riding gear for an unobtrusive pair of jeans and a blue T-shirt,
so he knew it wasn't his clothes. And he didn't recognize
them all, the gapers, although some of them brought back
flashes of unwelcome memory. But then, he supposed a lot
more people in Santiago Beach had known him—or of
him—than he'd known himself. It had been one of his mis-
sions in life back then, to make sure of that.

''C'mon, Luke! Hurry up!''

He watched as David waved him on, trying to get him to pick up his pace. He did, slightly, but these days he got most of his need for speed taken care of elsewhere.

He'd caught up to David when they reached the bookstore. He noticed the display in the front window: a beach scene with real sand, a surfboard propped in one corner, a towel, a bottle of suntan lotion, sunglasses and, of course, a book open beneath a small umbrella, with others stacked beside it. As if the reader had just paused for a cooling dip in the ocean.

He barely had time to admire the cleverness of it before David yanked the door open, and before even stepping inside, he was yelling.

''Amelia! He's here! I told you he'd come, I told you!''

The woman behind the counter turned just as Luke stepped inside. It was her. The frightened rabbit of a woman who had been so intimidated by his mere presence last night.

Several things registered at once.

She wasn't old.

She was average height, maybe five-five.

Her hair was an unremarkable medium brown, cut short and tucked tidily behind her ears.

She was dressed plainly, in black slacks and a white blouse with black piping, with a simple gold chain at her throat.

She had the biggest eyes he'd ever seen, the same medium brown as her hair.

And those eyes were staring at him as if he were some kind of apparition.

''It *was* you,'' she whispered, in a voice so soft he was sure he wasn't supposed to have heard it.

She'd known who he was last night? How?

Before he could ask, David had. ''Whaddya mean?''

''I saw…him last night. On a…motorcycle.''

''Isn't it cool?'' David enthused.

"I suppose," the woman said cautiously.

"I want to ride on it," David said with a sideways glance at Luke.

"I'll think about it," Luke said, never taking his eyes off the woman who was looking at him with such...trepidation. There was something familiar about her expression, but he couldn't put his finger on what it was. "If you remember why we're here and introduce me."

"Oh! Sorry. This is Amelia. Amelia, my brother, Luke." Then he looked at Luke, puzzled. "Why'd I have to do that if she already knew who you were?"

"Because it's good manners," Amelia said. David grimaced.

"Because," Luke said, "it shows you're an adult, not a kid."

"Oh." That explanation clearly appealed to him. "Okay."

"Amelia Blair, I presume," Luke said, turning his attention back to her.

"I...yes."

She lowered her eyes, sneaked another glance at him from beneath her lashes, then looked away. And suddenly he had it; she was looking at him like the good girls used to in high school, half-scared, half-fascinated. They had seemed to fall into two categories back then: those who were both frightened and intrigued in varying ratios, and those who simply looked down on him from the lofty height of their uprightness.

He'd tried to avoid all of them, although those who were intrigued had been, on occasion, persistent. But even then, he'd known they were after him for all the wrong reasons. He'd had his own battles to fight and had no interest in being a pawn in someone else's.

Not, he thought as she stole another sideways look at him, that that would be a problem with the quiet Ms. Blair. She looked more likely to run *from* him than *after* him. Once he'd taken a twisted pleasure in the effect he had on good girls. Now he wasn't sure how he felt. It was hard, he realized suddenly, to think that way again. To put himself back in the place he'd once lived, in the mind-set he'd once developed to survive. Maybe he'd come further than he'd thought.

Ms. Blair was too tense and far too serious. But she got points from him for caring about David and for thinking David needed more attention to his grief than he was getting.

"David's been...telling me a lot about you," she said, sounding more than a little awkward.

"Has he?" Luke said, wondering what the boy could possibly have said, after eight years with no contact at all between them.

"He told me you taught him to like to read."

Startled, Luke looked at his brother. "You did," David said. "When you used to come in and read to me. I read every night now."

Reading had been his favorite—and sometimes his only—escape when he'd been under his mother's roof. He'd tried to pass that along to David, but he'd had no idea it had worked so well. "I...that's good," he said, not sure what else to say.

"Amelia gets me the best books," David said, smiling at her. "Sometimes she even loans her own to me, if I can't buy them."

"Speaking of which," Amelia said, sounding glad to be back in familiar waters, "the newest in your science fiction series came in. I just put them up."

"Cool!" David raced toward the back of the store without another word.

"So," Luke said when David was out of earshot, "has David been the only one telling you about me?"

"I... What do you mean?"

He shook his head. "I'm disappointed, Ms. Blair. You mean I'm no longer the hot topic in Santiago Beach?"

She seemed to consider that. Then she surprised him, a tiny grin lurking at the corners of her mouth as she said, "I'm afraid you've lost a bit in the gossip standings after eight years."

So the mouse had a sense of humor, he thought. But before he could comment, David was back, his book clutched in one hand, a crumpled five-dollar bill in the other. Amelia gave him his change and offered a bag, which David declined, stuffing the book in a pocket of his baggy pants.

"Come on, Luke, I want my friends to meet you."

Luke, who was still looking at Amelia, noticed something change in her expression, saw two worry lines appear between her brows. Afraid he would be a bad influence on David's friends? he wondered. If she was, she was also no doubt too polite to say so.

As David dragged him away, Luke found himself wondering just what his brother had told her about him that made her look so relieved as they began to leave. There had been a time when he had reveled in rattling the cages of people like the quiet, reserved Amelia Blair; now her wariness simply bothered him. He'd gotten out of the habit of dealing with it, and he didn't like the idea of having to relearn how.

David kept up a steady stream of chatter as they walked down the street. Luke tried to pay attention, but it was hard, back here in the place where so much of the history he'd thought was well behind him lay in wait to ambush him around every turn.

But when they encountered a group of five boys who looked about David's age, maybe a little older, he gave himself a mental slap; there was something about this group that warned him to be alert. Not that there was anything particularly different about their looks—the haircuts, the pants like David's and the reversed baseball caps were omnipresent these days—but there was something about the way they walked, the way they whispered among themselves, the way they looked him up and down so assessingly, that made him watchful. And also made him wonder again just what David had been saying about him.

Somehow he doubted it was that he'd taught his little brother to love to read.

Chapter 3

Amelia shelved four copies of the latest courtroom thriller, the last books in the box. That left her only two boxes to go, she thought as she stretched her back.

The door buzzer announced a customer, and she stepped out from behind the rack of books. Her heart leapt, then stilled, and for a moment she didn't know why. When she realized it was because the man who had come in was dressed all in black, she blushed in embarrassment. When she saw that it was eighty-year-old, silver-haired Mr. Hodges, her color deepened. Thankful she could pass it off as exertion, she went to great him, wondering how on earth one sighting and one brief encounter with a man could have such an effect. This just wasn't like her; she'd gotten over her fascination with bad boys long ago. She had taken her mother's warnings to heart and had thought herself the better for it.

She got the autobiography Mr. Hodges had ordered from her office, where she'd set it aside when it had come in.

"Looks like a good one," she said as she rang it up. "But

I still think you should write your own, Mr. H. Nobody could top your adventures.''

She meant it, too. The man had been a bona fide World War II hero, medals and all, and after the war had become a stunt pilot of some renown. She'd seen photographs of him in his younger days, and he'd been quite the looker, in his flying jumpsuit, boots and a daredevil grin that still appeared on occasion.

''Ah, nobody's interested in the ramblings of an old man like me.''

''That's not true!'' she protested. ''I would be. Lots of folks would. I bet even Hollywood would be interested.''

Mr. Hodges chuckled. ''You're a sweetheart, Amelia. And named after one of my childhood heroes. If I were twenty years younger…''

She laughed, as the ongoing joke between them required. But there was, as always, that tug of…not sadness, but a sort of wistfulness that she had been named after the adventurous, if reckless, Amelia Earhart, yet had none of her nerve or courage.

It wasn't until after he'd gone that Amelia wondered if it had been something more than the black clothing that had put her in mind of Luke McGuire. If perhaps that daredevil grin, and the reckless glint in the eye that went with it, hadn't been part of it, since Luke had his own lethal version of both.

And his eyes, while blue, weren't at all like his mother's. Where hers were a pale, icy color, Luke's were deep and rich and vivid, the color of water reflecting the sky on a crystal clear day. And the scar beside his left eye only added to his daring appeal. As did the earring he wore. He was—

She cut off her own thoughts, stifling a tiny shiver, irritated with herself for feeling it. David's brother was simply a man who rode a motorcycle. He'd been dressed perfectly normally when they'd come in yesterday.

And he'd still set her pulse off on a mad race, she admitted ruefully. As if the normal clothes were a disguise, one that she could see through, down to the leather-clad biker he really was.

She wondered if Jackie Hiller had known something David didn't when she'd told her son his brother was probably in jail.

He shouldn't have come.

He'd suspected he would regret it before he'd even left River Park, but he hadn't thought it would happen quite this soon.

Now that he was here, David had apparently broadcast it to the entire town. He couldn't get angry with his brother, he hadn't told him not to say anything, simply because he hadn't thought of it. He was too long out of that kind of thinking.

But he was learning again fast. Every time he ventured out, he was the focus of far too many eyes. He'd dodged his mother so far, didn't know if she even knew he was here yet—but he was sure someone would tell her soon enough, if they hadn't already.

Heck, Mrs. Clancy had probably been on the phone immediately after this morning, he thought as he sipped at his coffee.

Just down the block from the single motel in town, where he'd taken a room, was a doughnut shop. He'd never been in there as a kid—candy had been his sugar hit of choice— so he'd hoped it might be a reputation-free zone. And it had been; the owner didn't seem to recognize him when he ordered a simple black coffee.

And then Mrs. Clancy had arrived. Of all people.

It had taken her a moment, but he knew the instant she put it together by the way her brows lowered sharply and she pulled down her glasses to peer at him over the frames.

"You!"

He thought about trying to deny it, but it seemed pointless with David telling the world he was here.

"Good morning, Mrs. Clancy. Nice day."

"Don't you nice day me, you...you hooligan!"

That's me, Luke-the-hooligan-McGuire, he thought wryly.

"What are you doing here?" she demanded.

He kept himself from making a comment about it being a free country, knowing it would only aggravate her. Funny, once that would have been his highest goal, to aggravate this particular woman.

"Getting coffee," he said instead.

It seemed to aggravate her just as much. "Don't be flippant, you know perfectly well what I meant."

"I came to see David."

The brows lowered even farther, and the glasses went back on her nose. "Does his mother know you're here?"

Interesting phrasing, Luke thought. And he said with intentional emphasis, "I have no idea if *my* mother has any idea I'm here."

"She isn't going to like this."

"That's her problem. If she stays out of my way, I'll stay out of hers."

The woman's mouth tightened, although he'd thought it was already about as sealed as her mind. "So where are you causing your trouble now? Or have you been in jail where you belong?"

Startled, he nearly splashed hot coffee on his hand. Seconds later he told himself he shouldn't be surprised at all; what else would they think, this town that had been so damn glad to see him leave?

"I think it would take prison to satisfy you," he said, unable to keep the edge out of his voice. "You buying doughnuts, or just entertaining the staff?"

Only then did she seem to notice the shop owner and his assistant watching them with great interest. Flustered, she gave her order and told them rather sharply to step on it, she didn't approve of who they allowed in here. Luke turned to make his escape but stopped at the door and looked back at her. He wasn't quite sure why he said it, but it was out before he could stop it.

"You know, you're one of the few people in this town who has real reason to hate me, and I'm sorry for that."

For an instant she looked taken aback, but the frown reappeared quickly. "Just leave," she said. And with a shrug, he did; he hadn't expected anything else.

He started down Main Street, and by the time he'd finished his coffee, it was clear that anybody who recognized him was of the same mind as Mrs. Clancy; they remembered only the worst about the kid he'd been and assumed that he'd either ended up in jail, or should have.

At first he laughed it off, but when he finally tossed his empty cup in one of the plentiful trash containers that were new since he'd lived here, he was feeling a bit beleaguered.

So let them think what they want, he told himself. *They will anyway. What do you care? It's not like you give a damn about any of them.*

And the next person he came across, he would just let them think the worst. Maybe he would even help them along, fulfill their grim expectations. It was probably the nicest thing he could do for them, let them be so utterly smug about how right they'd always been about that McGuire kid, how they'd always known he would come to no good.

He heard distant chimes and reflexively checked his watch. The clock on the tower at the community center and library had been chiming the hours away for as long as he could remember. It was just after nine, and he wasn't supposed to meet David until ten, so he continued his stroll down the street he had admittedly terrorized on occasion. He'd raced his old, beat-up Chevy up and down, radio blasting, just to see the heads turn. He'd set off cherry bombs to watch people scatter and done his share of spray-painting graffiti here and there. It all seemed pretty tame now, but fifteen years ago it had been rowdy stuff.

By Santiago Beach standards, it probably still was, he thought. What would blend into the bigger picture in a big city stood out glaringly here in the sleepy seaside village the Chamber of Commerce kept touting.

Of course, he'd taken the blame for a lot of things he hadn't done, too, but nobody believed that. Even his mother. Especially his mother. He'd finally given up on proclaiming his innocence to her when he realized it didn't matter what he said, that he was guilty before he even knew what he was accused of.

He shook his head sharply, trying to rid himself of the unwanted memories. He hadn't come here for this, to wallow in old misery. He'd given that up long ago. He was here to help David, if he could. And that was what he should be concentrating on.

He just wasn't sure how to go about it. There was no point in trying to talk to his mother; she'd never listened to him in her life. But he had to know just how bad things were for his brother.

He saw the bookstore up ahead and wondered if he'd subconsciously been heading there all along. It did make sense, he thought; the tidy Ms. Blair seemed to be the adult whom David was closest to.

Except that the store wasn't open yet. The lights were on, but he couldn't see anyone inside, and the sign said ten o'clock. Right when he was supposed to meet David.

He turned to look out at the street where it curved to head down to the beach and the pier, thinking. He should have asked her yesterday, except that David had never been far away. Maybe he should have set up a time to talk. Assuming she would be willing, he amended; just because she hadn't lived here when he had didn't mean she was immune to the horror stories that apparently were still being told about him. She might not want to—

"Luke?"

He spun around on his heel, startled. Amelia stood in the doorway, looking at him questioningly. And with only the barest trace of the apprehension he'd seen yesterday.

"You're here," he said, rather lamely.

"I come in about an hour before opening to get set up," she explained. "Did you...want something?"

"Yes," he said, oddly disconcerted. "You."

She drew back slightly, her eyes widening. They weren't just medium brown, he saw now in the morning light, they were a sort of golden brown, rimmed strikingly with darker brown. And he realized suddenly what had rattled him; she was wearing black and white again, as if it were some kind of uniform, but this time the pants were snug black leggings, and the white was in the form of a lightweight cotton sweater that clung gently to curves he hadn't noticed in the tailored blouse of yesterday.

"Me?"

Her voice had a hint of a gulp in it, and he registered what he'd said. "I mean, I wanted to talk to you," he said hastily.

"Oh," she said, still looking and sounding a bit wary.

"About David."

"Oh." There was understanding in her tone this time, and he could almost see her relax slightly. "Come in, then."

He did, noticing that she didn't change the sign to Open but also that she didn't lock the door behind him. He wasn't sure if she just hadn't thought about it, or it had been intentional. The latter, no doubt, he thought wryly. It probably meant she wanted to be able to get out, or wanted somebody else to be able to get in. In case the terror of Santiago Beach went postal on her or something, he supposed.

"I have coffee in my office," she said as she led the way.

"Thanks," he said, ready for the jolt of a second cup; it had been a rough morning so far. "Black," he added as he stepped in after her.

She fussed a bit with the coffeemaker on a table in the small, windowless office, which gave him a chance to look around. The place was as tidy as he would have expected, not an easy task in a small space that had to serve various functions, he guessed. The desk was small, and after placing the phone, some in and out trays, and a computer on it, there was barely room for a writing space. There were two file cabinets behind the desk, leaving the wheeled chair a bit cramped for turning room.

But the decor was a little surprising, bright with color from various prints and posters on the walls. He would have expected book-related things, and there were a couple, but there were many more adventurous themes—skiing, mountain climbing, hang gliding—all presented in a very adrenaline-inducing way.

When she turned and handed him a mug of steaming coffee, he indicated the posters with a nod. ''What you do in your spare time?''

She looked startled. ''Me? Oh, no. Never.''

''Then why the wallpaper?''

''To remind me that other people do those things. I admire courage.'' She said it, he realized, as if it were something to be found only in those others.

''Some would say foolhardiness,'' he said; he'd heard it often enough aimed at himself.

''Yes. And I suppose sometimes it's true. But the exhilaration must be worth it.''

''Until something goes wrong,'' he said.

''Yes,'' she answered simply, and glanced at the wall behind him. He turned and saw, in a direct line of sight from her desk chair, a large photograph of Amelia Earhart.

''So,'' he said, turning back to her, ''you're a namesake?''

''Yes. She was a heroine of my mother's. The name hardly fits, but it gave her pleasure to honor a woman she admired. Now, about David,'' she ended briskly, clearly changing the subject. ''Why don't you sit down?''

He took the chair she indicated, an antique-looking wood affair of the kind it made him nervous to sit on. But it was surprisingly comfortable, and had a spot to set down his coffee mug on the wide, wooden arms.

''I know David wrote to you,'' she said, forgoing any niceties.

He appreciated the leap, since he hadn't known quite what to ask. ''I didn't even know he knew where I was.''

''He told me you sent him birthday cards.''

Luke nodded. ''But I never put an address on them. I knew my mother would throw them away.''

She didn't react, didn't look shocked or surprised. He wondered if it was because she already knew his mother's tricks, or maybe she didn't find them presumptuous. ''He must have guessed from the postmarks,'' was all she said.

''That's how he addressed it, just to me in River Park. If the place was any bigger, I might not have gotten it.''

''Where's River Park?''

''In the Sierra foothills. Near the gold country.'' He studied her for a moment. ''How bad is it?''

She didn't pretend not to understand; he appreciated that, as well. ''He's horribly unhappy over his father's death. It's so devastating to lose a parent at that age. And for a father and son who were so close, it must be even worse.''

''I wouldn't know, I never met mine,'' he said casually. ''I don't even know what he looked like. My mother isn't one for family photos.''

It didn't really bother him anymore. There had been a time when it had almost made him crazy, but that was long ago. He—

''He looks like you.''

He stared at her. He slowly set his coffee mug down. He shifted in the chair. ''What?'' he finally said, certain he couldn't have heard her right.

"Or you look like him, I guess is more accurate."

"And how the hell," he said slowly, "would you know that?"

"Your mother told me."

He'd made a big mistake, a huge mistake. There was no way he would get a reasonable answer about David from someone close enough to his mother that she would even speak of the loathsome Patrick McGuire. He set down his mug and stood up.

Her brows furrowed. Unlike Mrs. Clancy's, they were delicately formed and arched. "What's wrong?"

"When you report back to my mother, give her my love," he said sarcastically.

"Report?" She looked genuinely puzzled. "I barely speak to her. Why would—" She broke off, as if suddenly understanding what he'd meant. She stood up, meeting his gaze steadily. "Luke, I'm not a close friend of your mother's. I've only even spoken to her a couple of times. After I saw you that night, when I didn't know it was you, I…asked her what you looked like, that's the only reason she mentioned your father."

It was you….

He remembered her saying it, and now this explained it. She'd somehow guessed his identity with that glimpse. He wasn't sure how that made him feel.

"I only spoke to her this time," she went on, "because I was worried about David." Her mouth twisted. "She didn't seem to care."

"Now that's the mother I know and love," he quipped.

She cocked her head sideways as she looked up at him consideringly. "You don't sound at all bitter."

"I'm not. Not anymore. I don't have time."

"David said you were busy."

He blinked. "He did?"

"I thought it was just…little brother talk about a big brother he idolizes."

"Idolizes? He doesn't even know me anymore."

"But he's built you up into an idol of mythic proportions in his mind. You're his hero, Luke. Especially, I'm afraid, for all the trouble you got into here."

Luke sank back into the chair. "Damn," he muttered. That wasn't what he wanted to hear. Nobody knew better than he how hard it was to get off that path once you'd started.

"He's taken up with some new friends since his father died. They're…"

"Troublemakers," he supplied when she stopped. "Like me?"

"I don't know exactly what kind of troublemaker you are," she said, "but I do know that these boys are getting worse. They haven't physically hurt anybody yet, but it's only a matter of time. And David's starting to think like them."

He didn't bother to disabuse her of the notion that he was still a troublemaker. He'd vowed to let the people in this town think what they would about him. It was David who mattered now.

"He gets too far down that road, it'll be hard to stop him."

"It's a self-destructive path," she said. "Who knows where he'd end up."

Luke propped his elbows on the wooden chair arms, steepled his fingers and looked at her over the top of them. "In jail? Or worse? I believe that's the assumption. And I should know."

For a moment he thought she was going to ask him what he should know about, jail or assumptions. But she didn't, and he figured she'd decided for herself. And although her quiet, reserved expression never wavered, he had little doubt as to what she'd decided, just like everybody else in Santiago Beach.

"What are you going to do?" she asked.

"Do?" *How about rattle that restraint of yours?* he thought, and blinked in surprise at himself.

"About David."

He steered his attention back in to the topic at hand. "I don't know. Talk to him, I guess."

She looked about to speak, then hesitated. He waited silently, wondering if she would have to be coaxed, or if just setting the lure of silence would be enough.

It was. Finally.

"I...it's hard to get kids his age to buy 'Do as I say, not as I do,'" she said, watching him warily.

Think I'm going to jump you for painting me with this town's brush? he wondered.

And yet, he had to admit it stung a little, that she assumed along with the rest of Santiago Beach that he'd continued to be up to no good since he'd left. He opened his mouth, ready to tell her that he'd changed, that he wasn't the same reprobate kid he'd been, that he'd made something of his life, that he'd—

The next person he came across, he would just let them think the worst...fulfill their grim expectations. It was probably the nicest thing he could do for them....

His own vow came back to him, made just minutes ago. And he shut his mouth. Let her think what she obviously already did. Why should she be any different?

He leaned back in the chair. Steepled his fingers again. "I'll take that as evidence you don't think he should come live with me."

"Is that really what he wants?"

He shrugged. "It's what he said in his letter. He hasn't mentioned it since I got here."

She studied him for a moment, still giving nothing away. Then she said quietly, "Do you want him to?"

He expelled a long, slow breath and jammed a hand through his hair. That was an answer he didn't have. "I don't know. Davie...well, he's about the only good memory

I've got from here. I don't want him to go through the hell I did, but...my life isn't the best for a kid. Especially a screwed-up one. I'm gone a lot, days at a time.''

If she wondered what he did that called for that, she didn't ask. ''You...could change that. Couldn't you?''

There was something about the way she was looking at him that prodded him to say flippantly, ''Go straight? Perish the thought.'' Oddly, for a split second she looked hurt, and he regretted the jibe. ''Look, I'm worried about him, but...''

''You don't want the responsibility?''

She didn't say it accusingly, merely in the tone of a normal question. Which he supposed it was. ''I don't know if I'm ready for that kind of responsibility.''

''Then why did you bother to come?''

''Not,'' he said sourly, ''to be reminded at every turn what a total waste my life has been.''

''It can't be a total waste.'' Her voice was unexpectedly gentle, and it seemed to brush away his irritation. ''You have a brother who adores you. That's worth a lot.''

He couldn't deny that.

He couldn't deny the odd feeling that having those eyes of hers look at him with softness instead of suspicion gave him, either.

Luke walked out her door at five to ten, and Amelia was glad she had at least a few minutes before she had to open. She was going to need every one of them to recover.

She was exhausted. Just sitting there talking to Luke McGuire, pretending it was a casual conversation between two people with a common concern, had worn her out. It wasn't her shyness, after years of work she'd overcome that to a great extent. But never in her admittedly sheltered life had she ever talked at length to a man like this one, a man with a reputation, a man with a *past.*

A man who was worried about his young brother, she corrected herself. A man who was honest enough to admit he wasn't prepared to take that brother on, yet cared enough to come some distance to find out how bad things really were.

Perhaps she needed to reassess her opinion of him.

Perhaps, she thought wryly as she forced herself to get ready to open, she shouldn't have developed an opinion of him at all before she'd met him. Although, if she'd waited until she'd first seen him, riding down the street last night, who knew what kind of opinion she would have formed.

Speaking of honesty, if she was going to match his, she had to admit that when she'd been younger and under the watchful eyes of her parents, it had been easy to suppress any of the more turbulent urges she might have had. Such as those brought on by the wilder boys in school. She was finding it much harder now to deny she found bad boy Luke McGuire fascinating and unsettlingly attractive.

But he still frightened her. In a way that was so bone deep she didn't even know where it came from. It was more than just the warnings her mother had given her, more even than trying to avoid trouble. It was something, she supposed, based in whatever quirk it was that made her an introvert rather than an extrovert.

But whatever it was, it kicked into high gear around Luke.

She tried to stop thinking about it; she didn't usually dwell on her shortcomings in dealings with men. But this morning she hadn't even managed to finish writing one check to her distributor, and now it was time to open. She put her pen down to mark the page in the notebook-style checkbook, then walked across the store. She flipped the sign in the front window to Open and went to unlock the front door, only to find that she'd never relocked it after letting Luke in.

Rattled? Not me, she muttered to herself.

She'd barely made it back to the checkout counter when the door announcement sounded. She'd forgotten to change it; it was still Captain Picard, when today was supposed to be Data. She pulled herself together, put on her best helpful smile and turned to greet her customer.

Her smile wobbled.

David's friends. All five of them.

And one of them had a knife.

Chapter 4

Luke had watched the five boys strut away, recognizing the cocky walk and the smart mouths all too well. Those guys were trouble waiting to happen, and they were going to suck David down with them if things kept on.

The group had come upon them as they were about to sit down at one of the picnic tables in the park by the pier to eat and watch the ocean. By now Luke had a pretty good idea of how much—and in what way—David had talked him up to them. On this second encounter they were still assessing, calculating, silently asking just how tough he really was.

He had their number now, and he had shifted his stance slightly, just enough to signify readiness for anything. He had selected the obvious leader, the one they all watched to set the tone, to make the first move. The one who, Luke noted cautiously, had his right hand buried in the pocket of his baggy cargo pants. Some kind of weapon, Luke was sure, and hoped it wasn't a gun. He had kept his gaze steady, level, and his face expressionless. And he stared him down. Not in a way that made it a threat the boy would have to respond to or lose face, but in a way that said, "It's up to you how this goes."

At last the boy had backed off, although Luke wasn't sure it was for good, and had led his little troop away.

"Nice guys," Luke muttered now as they sat down.

"They're my friends," David said, jaw tight with a stubbornness Luke recognized; it was like looking at the face in the mirror when he'd been that age.

"What about your old friends?" Luke asked, knowing he had to tread carefully here.

"They're boring, man. They don't do anything cool."

"Mmm."

Thinking, trying to decide what to say to that, Luke selected a French fry with great care. When he'd offered an early lunch, David had wanted fast food, saying his mother didn't allow it very often. And he got so tired, David had added, of the stuff the cook fixed.

The cook. And, according to David, live-in help as well. His mother had obviously gotten where she wanted to be. He wondered cynically if Ed Hiller's life insurance paid for it.

"It's hard to keep good friends," he said finally. "But it's harder to find good new ones, because you just never know about people at first."

"You still have friends from school?"

Zap. He'd missed the jog in the river on that one.

It's hard to get kids his age to buy "Do as I say, not as I do...."

Amelia's words came back to him then, and for the first time he realized what a genuinely untenable position he was in with his brother. How could he tell him what to do when, at the same age, his own life had been such a mess?

"No," he admitted. "But most them weren't real friends. I mean, they were buddies, guys you hang with, do stuff with, but...that doesn't necessarily make them friends. Not real ones, good ones."

David frowned. "What's the diff?"

At least he was listening, Luke thought. Now if only he could think of what to say. "Friends help you out. They don't try and make trouble for you, or suck you into any. They don't rag on you if you don't want to do something."

David was watching him, his expression changing, a hint of disappointment coming into his eyes. "You sound like Mom, always lecturing me."

Luke sucked in a quick breath; *that* was not a comparison he relished. His mouth twisted. "Whew. Nice shot."

"I was waiting for 'Friends don't let friends drive drunk,'" David quoted.

"Well, they don't, but I'm sorry, Davie. I didn't mean to lecture you. I used to hate it when she did it to me."

David smiled fleetingly at the old nickname that only Luke had ever used. "I know. I remember you fighting with her. I could hear you after I went to bed."

"I'll bet. It got loud sometimes."

"I hated it." David lowered his eyes and picked at the sole fry left in his meal. "Sometimes...I hate her."

Again, Luke didn't know what to say. It hardly seemed right to encourage that, but how could he blame the kid when he felt the same way? "I understand," he said finally. "But I think...she does love you. She's just no good at showing it."

"I don't think so," David said solemnly. "She just hates me less than she hated you."

That was such a cogent assessment that Luke couldn't counter it, wasn't sure he wanted to. David lifted his gaze, his eyes, so much like his father's, deeply troubled.

"I can't take it much longer, Luke," he said, sounding much older than his fifteen years. "Everything's falling apart since Dad died. He was what kept her from being really bad, but now she's worse than ever, almost like she was right before you left."

Luke expelled an audible breath. "Is it all her, Davie? Or

is she worried about you, what you're doing these days, those new friends?''

''She just doesn't like them.''

''Who does?''

''Huh?''

''Besides you, who does like them?''

David looked puzzled. ''I don't know. Why?''

''Just curious.''

Silence reigned for a few minutes, and Luke let it, hoping the boy might be pondering that. But it seemed a lost cause when, after downing the last of his soda, David merely looked at him and said, ''I like your earring. Wish I could get one, but Mom'd never let me get pierced, not even just an ear.''

Luke fingered the small gold paddle that dangled from his left lobe. ''This is about as far as I go. I'm a wuss about needles.''

''You?'' David said, clearly disbelieving. ''You're not a wuss about anything.''

''Oh, yeah, I am. I'm no hero, bro.'' He glanced at his watch. ''It's nearly eleven. Aren't you supposed to be somewhere?''

David swore, crudely. ''Stupid drawing lesson. Like a teacher's gonna make me be able to draw when I can't.''

''Pretty bad, huh?''

''I suck,'' was the succinct answer. ''And I hate all this stuff, drawing, piano, what a waste of a summer.''

''Could be worse.''

''Yeah? How?''

''I don't know. Ballroom dancing? Accordion lessons?''

David laughed and for a moment was the boy Luke remembered. Luke smiled as he stood up. ''Go. Don't get me in any more trouble for making you late.''

David got up, too, but hesitated, then said simply, ''She knows.''

''She does?''

"Old lady Clancy called her."

"Figures."

"I don't think she's figured out yet that…you're here because I asked you."

"Take my advice, don't let her," Luke told him. "Tell her I got…nostalgic."

David nodded slowly. "She said this morning that after my summer class I have to sit through her stupid lecture, waiting so she can drive me home. Like I can't walk or ride my bike eight blocks." He gave Luke a sideways glance. "I think she just doesn't want me to see you, so she's keeping me too busy. But I'll dodge her somehow. I can't be in any more trouble with her than I already am."

Luke considered that. "I think you probably can be," he said frankly. But then he grinned at his brother. "But I can't. Maybe we'll just have to make it my fault."

David brightened considerably at that, then took off running toward the community center where summer classes were held. Luke thought about how his mother had never bothered with those for him. He'd told himself he was glad to have his summers free, to have a mother who didn't care where he went or what he did as long as he didn't cause her any problems.

He sat there, staring out at the water, at the picturesque cove that had such appeal for people from all over but had never been anything to him except a place to hide in a crowd. He'd always enjoyed watching the surf, had been drawn to the water, but something had seemed missing to him. He'd kept coming back, because it was so close, but the sea and sand and surf just missed reaching that deep, hidden place in him.

He wondered if David had such a place, a place he kept buried and safe, afraid he would never find what it was in the world that made his soul answer.

He wondered if their mother would smother that place in him before the boy ever had a chance to even look.

* * *

Amelia tried to contain her nervousness, but she was afraid she wasn't doing a very good job. She tried to give them the benefit of the doubt, but her idealism couldn't quite stretch to the idea that these new friends of David's were here to pick up some summer reading.

Especially given the way they strolled around the store not looking at any of the books, but just her. Especially given the way the one in the cargo pants with all the pockets flipped that knife around. A butterfly knife, the kind where the handle flipped closed around the blade, then reopened with a flick of the wrist, becoming deadly once more. She'd read about them when researching martial arts before deciding on kickboxing.

Open and closed, he flicked it back and forth, with the appearance of idle habit and a smoothness that spoke of long experience. And if she confronted him, she was sure he would smile innocently and tell her it was just that, a habit, that it didn't mean anything, and why was she so nervous?

She gathered her nerve and tried to think. God, she hated being such a coward. The boy was back near the children's section now, while the others were at various places, almost as if taking up stations. Almost as if they had a plan...

She glanced at the phone. She could pretend to be making a call and dial 911 instead. But they really hadn't done anything yet, although she was sure waving that knife around was against some kind of law. But it wasn't like he'd threatened her or anything, she told herself; it was only because she was so spineless that it seemed threatening.

Besides, they were David's friends, even if she didn't care for them, and he might never speak to her again if she called the police on them.

The one with the knife turned and headed back, flipping that blade as if it were a part of him.

It struck her then that perhaps she should try to treat these boys like she did all kids who came into her store. She could find the courage to simply do that, surely?

She drew a deep breath. She picked up the cordless telephone, thinking she would pretend to be calling a customer about a book if she had to, just so she wouldn't seem so alone. She walked out from behind the counter, trying not to look at the boy who had taken up a position there. She glanced at the boy with the knife. Braced herself. And spoke.

"Did you know your knife is a Balisong?"

The boy looked startled; he must have thought she was too afraid to speak. She prayed he didn't know how close he was to being right.

"You talkin' to me?"

"Your knife. It's called a Balisong. And that move you're doing is sometimes called the ricochet."

He looked down at the blade in his hand as if he'd never seen it before. Amelia walked past him to a book bay a couple of rows back. She hoped she could find it; she thought she'd seen it the last time she'd straightened this shelf.... And then she had it, the book on ancient weapons used in the various martial arts. She was sure this was it; it covered even the most obscure practices.

She found it quickly, held the page with the photo out for him to see. "Isn't that beautiful? Look at the dragon design etched into the handle. This guy's collection is worth a lot of money."

The boy's eyes flicked from the photo to the simple stainless steel model he held, then to her face.

"Nobody seems to be sure if they originated there, but it was in the Philippines that they were first incorporated into martial arts. That's where it got the name."

His expression was unreadable, and she wasn't sure if she'd made things better or worse. Nor was she sure encouraging this was a good idea, but he already had the blade, and she doubted he would give it up because she—or anybody else—said so.

"There are several Web sites on the Internet about them. Even more photos of some really beautiful ones."

Something like curiosity flickered in his shuttered eyes, as if she had done something unexpected.

Suddenly he turned on his heel and walked out. Without a word, the others followed, only one of them glancing back over his shoulder at her.

Amelia closed the book. Her hands were shaking. So were her knees. She sank down on the footstool she used for shelving books.

She hated being afraid.

But she was very much afraid she hadn't seen the last of them.

Moments later the door opened again. God, they were back. They'd decided to come back and…who knows what. She glanced at her office, with the safety-promising lock on the door, but knew there wasn't time. She reached for the phone she'd set on the shelf. The book slipped off her knees and fell to the floor with a thud.

"Amelia? Are you here? Are you okay?"

The phone followed the book; it was Luke. She recognized his deep voice, although there was a different note in it now. A touch of anxiety, she realized with a little jolt of shock. As if he were worried.

"Back here," she managed to say, using the shelves as a prop to stand up, until she was sure she was steady enough to do it on her own; she would hate for him to realize what a coward she was, that five young boys had managed to terrorize her without doing a thing.

He came at a fast trot, only slowing to a walk when he saw her upright. "I saw those kids coming out from up the block," he said as he came to a stop. "I just ran into them with David a while ago, and they weren't my idea of kids with nothing on their minds but playing on a summer day."

"One of them…had a knife." She managed to suppress

a shiver; in front of this man, apparently her pride out-weighed her fear.

"The one with all the pockets?"

She nodded.

"Snake, David called him."

"How…appropriate," she said faintly.

"Too many movies," Luke retorted.

She smiled, hoping it wasn't as shaky as she felt. Her toe hit the book she had dropped, but before she could pick it up Luke was reaching for it. He glanced at the title, then at her, brows raised.

"I…was trying to divert him. Showed him pictures of knives like his, only fancier ones, worth a lot."

"You deflected a hotheaded, knife-wielding teenager with a book?"

"I didn't know what else to do."

"How about calling the cops?"

The notorious Luke McGuire, suggesting she call the police? "They weren't really doing anything."

"How about waving around a weapon I'm pretty sure is illegal in this state?"

She didn't understand this; this was hardly what she expected to hear from him, this championing of law and order. "I didn't want to make things harder on David. They know he comes in here a lot."

"Oh." He seemed to consider that. Then, handing her the book, added, "I guess I shouldn't argue with success. They left, after all."

Amelia blinked. She hadn't thought about that. It might have been a desperate ploy on her part, but it had worked. "Yes. Yes, they did."

"And you look like you could use a stiff drink. But since it's not even noon, how about another cup of coffee?"

"I…yes. That sounds good. But I'll have to make fresh."

"Don't bother. How about next door? They have something you like? Can you take a break?"

She hesitated, although the coffee bar next to the store

made a latte she was fond of. Finally she gave in; she could afford a short break, and from the right table next door she could see any customers who might arrive anyway.

Moments later she was cradling the rich drink, thankful for the warmth despite the fact that it wasn't the slightest bit cold out.

She looked across the table at him, intending to thank him, but her breath caught in her throat. He was leaning back in his chair, out of the cover of the table's umbrella, and his hair gleamed almost blue-black in the sun. The glint of gold she'd seen that night—and had barely noticed in their first encounter—turned out to be an earring in the shape of a tiny boat paddle, although she supposed it must have some other significance she wasn't aware of; she couldn't quite picture him doing anything as mundane as rowing a boat around, or paddling a canoe. She found she liked it, although her mother had always decried the trend of men wearing earrings. Amelia found it rather rakishly attractive...if the man wearing it could carry it off.

Luke could definitely carry it off.

He was dressed today in jeans and a T-shirt with the logo of what seemed to be an outdoor equipment company. But the simple clothing did little to lessen his impact, and she realized the black leather had only emphasized what was already there. No matter what he wore, this man would never look quite...tame.

He was staring down Main Street, and she was thankful that he'd left off the concealing sunglasses, so she could see where he was looking. And so that she could quickly avert her gaze when he turned his attention back to her.

"David says you moved here when your folks bought the store," he said conversationally. It seemed odd to her, sort of anticlimactic after the high drama she'd imbued the last few minutes with, to have a normal conversation. It took her a moment to gather her wits and answer.

"Yes. My father was a university professor. He retired to

write a book and ended up owning a bookstore instead.''
She smiled. ''Which, not coincidentally, was what my
mother had always wanted.''

''So she pushed him into it?''

Amelia laughed. ''No. Neither one of my parents ever
pushed the other one to do anything. They never had to. All
either one had to do was say they wanted something, and
the other one would move mountains to make it happen.
They were crazy about each other.''

Luke didn't react for a minute, and Amelia realized he
was absorbing what she'd said as if he had to translate it
into a language he understood.

''That must have been…nice,'' he said at last, but she
could see he was floundering, unable to relate this to anything he understood. And Amelia felt a sudden, sharp tug of
sympathy for him, that something so basic and normal and
necessary to her was so foreign to him.

''It was,'' she said softly. ''And sometimes I forget how
special and rare.''

''Was?''

''My mother died four years ago. My father was lost without her, and within six months he was gone, too.''

''I'm sorry,'' he said, and there was no floundering this
time; he might not know what it was like to live with such
love, but he understood grief. ''That must have been tough,
losing them both like that.''

''I loved them dearly, but they would have wanted to be
together. And they'd had very good lives.'' She took a sip
of her latte. ''They were a bit too protective, I suppose. I
was pretty sheltered. But I think that comes with being the
only child of older parents.''

''So you were a late arrival?''

''Sort of. They adopted me when they were in their forties
and realized they weren't going to be able to have a biological child.''

He blinked, setting down his own cup of simple black coffee. "You were adopted?"

She nodded. "But they were the best parents I could ever have had. The always made me feel special. Chosen. I can't imagine a biological child feeling any more loved than I was."

"You were lucky." His voice was a little tight.

"Yes, I was. Whoever my birth mother was, she did the best thing for me she could ever have done."

"Gave you to parents who could love you."

"Yes."

There was no denying the taut emotion in his words. It struck her suddenly that she had indeed been lucky, luckier than some children who stayed with their natural parents. She wondered if Luke had ever wished his mother had given him up, given him a chance at loving parents. And then she wondered how could he not; it would almost have to be better than living with a mother who, to judge by her speeches, blamed his existence for ruining her life.

"I think," she said softly, "I was even luckier than I realized."

He looked at her for a long, silent moment. He didn't pretend not to understand what she meant. "My mother had her reasons."

"But none of them were your fault."

His eyes narrowed. "Just how much do you know?"

She wished she hadn't said it; the way he was looking at her, it was all she could do not to dodge his gaze. "I've heard your mother speak about the disaster teenage pregnancy can make of a life. I've seen you both, close enough to guess at ages. And—" she took a breath before finishing "—I can do math."

He sat back. His mouth twisted up at one corner, and the opposite dark brow rose. "Clever girl."

She bit her lip; she *knew* she should have kept quiet.

She'd meant to express compassion and had only antagonized him.

"I only meant that…she's wrong to blame you. It's not like you had a choice."

"When I'd been away long enough, I realized she probably didn't have much choice, either."

"But she could have given you up to someone—" She stopped as he lifted a hand.

"She couldn't. Her mother wouldn't allow it."

"Your grandmother?"

He laughed. "Not if you asked her. She died when I was thirteen, and she never once acknowledged I was connected to her in any way. I wasn't her grandson, I was her daughter's punishment."

There hadn't been a trace of anger, self-pity, or even regret in his tone. He had clearly dealt with all this long ago. But it made Amelia shiver. "My God. How did you stand it?"

"I didn't. Not very well, anyway. I went a little crazy. But then, you know that."

She shook her head. "I don't know why you didn't burn the entire town to the ground."

He stared at her for a moment, then gave a sharp shake of his head. "What I don't know," he said, sounding surprised and more than a little rueful, "is why I told you all that."

He drained his coffee, got up and tossed his cup in the recycle bin left out for the purpose. The conversation, it seemed, was over. She got to her feet, a little surprised that she was fairly steady; being with Luke was, in its own way, as unsettling as her encounter with David's friends.

When he walked her back to the store, she was surprised to see half an hour had passed; it had seemed only minutes. Then he turned to face her and put his hands on her shoulders as he looked at her seriously.

"Are you all right now? You were pretty shaky."

So he'd seen, Amelia thought with a smothered sigh. She should have known he would. She supposed fear like hers wasn't easily hidden. "I'm fine."

"Next time Snake comes in waving that knife, call the police."

Something about the proprietary way he said it stayed with her long after he'd gone. It warmed her, in a strange, unfamiliar way.

But that feeling soon vanished with the realization that she had actually carried on a conversation, twice, with the notorious Luke McGuire. And even more shocking, she had *enjoyed* it, right down to the nervous hammering of her heart. It had been...exhilarating. Liberating, somehow.

And frightening.

She just wasn't sure what she was frightened about: his presence, or her own reactions.

And she wasn't sure she wanted to know.

Chapter 5

Luke stood outside the community center, pondering. He'd already gone up to the bulletin board and read the notice, so he knew today was one of the days his mother was giving her fire-and-brimstone sermon.

He walked toward the small meeting room. It only held about fifty people, and if he remembered right, there were windows on either side of the main doorway, allowing a view of the back few rows of seats. And if he was guessing right, in the back would be where David was, no doubt sulking at being forced to sit though this yet again, just so his mother could be sure he wasn't out doing evil with his no-good half brother.

He went to one of the windows and looked in. No sign of David. He went to the other side and tried it from that angle. He could just see the top of someone's head in the last row. The hair was bleached and long on top, shorter below.

Bingo, he thought.

He stood outside the door for a moment, pondering if he wanted to do this. It didn't take him long to decide.

She expects the worst, doesn't she? Don't want to disappoint her....

He slipped on the black leather jacket he'd been carrying because it was really too warm to wear it. But it was effect he was after now, and he knew the jacket completed the picture the black jeans and motorcycle boots began. He reached up to the hair he was now glad he hadn't gotten cut and pulled a couple of the strands he was always pushing out of the way down in front of his face. She'd always hated that.

He yanked open the door and strode in.

"—all over the county. Children barely old enough to take care of themselves having children of their own."

His mother's voice rang out strongly. It was a message kids needed to hear, he admitted. He just didn't like being this close to her particular message. She looked...polished, a carefully burnished version of the woman he remembered, smoother, more studiedly elegant; she'd finally reached the perfection she'd always wanted.

"The tragedy of teenage pregnancy, the ruination of young lives, you have no idea what it's like until it's too late, until it's happened to you, until you have an unwanted child weighing you down, crippling you—"

She'd spotted him. For the first time in his life, he saw his mother looking too shocked to speak. She stood there with her mouth open; she would have a fit if she realized she looked like a goldfish, he thought.

David spotted him then and leapt to his feet, a huge grin on his face. The rest of the attendees were starting to turn now, to see what she was gaping at. They'd probably never seen the polished Jackie Hiller rattled, and he took a perhaps petty satisfaction in being the one to have done it.

"Hi," he said cheerily to the room at large. "I'm the visual aid."

''You,'' she breathed, only the microphone on the dais enabling him to hear the furious word.

''Yep, me.'' He glanced at the rest of the group. ''I'm the reason for all this. You know, the tragedy, the ruination, the weight. Or, if you like it more bluntly, I'm the unwanted bastard child that started this campaign.''

Whispers started around the room, coupled with darting glances at the elegantly dressed woman at the lectern.

''Get out!'' He didn't need the microphone to hear her this time.

''Hey, Mom, just trying to help. I mean, if looking at me doesn't scare them, what will?''

Luke heard a peep of laughter he knew had come from David. He gave his little brother a crooked grin. Then he jerked his head toward the door he'd come in. David jumped up, grabbed his backpack and started toward him.

Their mother was still yelling at them when they went out the door.

''—the time the clock tower was painted black? I just know that was him.''

''I always suspected as much. And when the entire fleet of school buses had their tires slashed that time, you know who was behind that.''

''Oh, I'm sure he was. He got away with so much.''

''Except for Marie Clancy. He's lucky she only hit him with her rake.''

''If I were him, I'd steer clear of her. I don't why he dared to show his face in Santiago Beach again anyway.''

Not for any reason you three would believe, Amelia thought as she put down the cantaloupe she'd been considering and hastily pushed her cart away from them.

She'd been there a few moments before she'd realized what the two men and a woman were talking about. Once she had, she'd been oddly frozen, unable to do anything but listen. By the time she'd been able to move, she'd heard way too much.

There was no way, she thought, that one lone teenage boy could possibly have been responsible for everything they'd talked about. They talked as if he'd run a one-boy campaign to bring Santiago Beach to its knees.

But she also knew that where there was this much smoke there was generally at least a match burning. So Luke was no angel, but he was hardly the devil incarnate, either.

But still, it bothered her that she had taken so much pleasure in talking to him, that she had found being with him so exhilarating. Was there something wrong with her, that she was still so…tempted by a man like that? Her parents would have been scandalized. And Amelia had never, ever done anything remotely scandalous.

She stopped at home—the small house bought by her parents despite its dark, dreary look and turned into a light, airy cottage—to put her groceries away, then headed to the store. She usually walked, since it was only about three blocks away and she told herself she needed the exercise, and rare were the days when the weather was bad enough to keep her from it. Sometimes she wondered what it would be like to live in a place that actually had weather, instead of this perpetually sunny land where most of the time the only difference between seasons was in degrees of dryness.

As the day passed she caught herself looking up eagerly every time Lt. Worf sounded a warning, then feeling a bit let down when one of her regulars walked in. She chastised herself mentally, telling herself she was acting irrationally, downright silly. But still, when Worf boomed out a another welcome, she looked.

"You know," Jim Stavros said with a grin as he walked in, "you got me watching that show on the reruns, because of that silly door thing of yours."

Amelia laughed. Jim was one of her best customers. He

read across the board and was always willing to try a new book on her recommendation.

Jim was also a cop. Had been for twenty-five years. She usually didn't think about that, except for the occasional reminder when he refused to read a new police procedural that had come in, saying it made him crazy to see mistakes.

Jim had been a cop, although not the sergeant he was now, in Santiago Beach when Luke had been here.

She told herself not to ask; she chattered about other things, asked him about his wife, Joann, a nurse at the local hospital, and their kids, anything to keep from having a gap in the conversation, and then, when he stood at the register, wallet in hand, it slipped out.

"Luke McGuire? Oh, yeah, I knew him. All of us knew him. Heard he was back in town."

It seemed pointless to dissemble, so Amelia just nodded.

"Hell on wheels, that boy was. Still is, I hear. Already been stopped once on that bike of his."

Amelia went still. "Stopped?"

Jim nodded. "For speeding, on the canyon road. Same place I used to nail him. I'm surprised he hasn't gotten himself killed. He did crash once, back then. Lost it on that same road and flipped that old Chevy he used to drive."

"Was he hurt?"

Jim frowned. "Yeah. Kid broke an arm and a couple of ribs. For a while they thought it was worse. Joann was working that night, and she made the call to his mother. Woman didn't show up until late the next morning."

"Her son was in the hospital injured, and she didn't even come?" Amelia couldn't say she was surprised, not after what she'd learned, but it still seemed awful.

Jim nodded. "Joann said she wasn't surprised. She had just started at the hospital back when the kid was born, and it was the talk of the place then that the old lady, the grandmother, was one of those judgmental fanatics, ashamed of having an unwed mother as a daughter. That she ordered her to keep the baby, even though she didn't want it.''

"As punishment?" Amelia asked, remembering Luke's words.

"Yeah. Crazy, isn't it? Always felt kind of sorry for the kid, in a way. I mean, it's got to be tough to have a mother who doesn't even care enough to give you a name.''

Amelia winced. "Then who did name him? The grandmother? I'm surprised he didn't end up as Cain or something equally pejorative.''

"I think that's what the nurses were afraid of. So they named him. That's why he's Luke.''

"Why he's—" Amelia broke off as it came to her. Of course. The hospital was St. Luke's. "What a lovely start in life," she said, sounding more bitter than Luke ever had.

"Yeah. Guess it's not a surprise he ended up like he did. We kind of hoped things would change when she married Ed, but by then maybe it was too late. Ed tried, though. He was a nice guy. Too nice to have been married for his money.'' He looked at her thoughtfully. "What's all this interest in Luke McGuire?''

"I…'' She scrambled for an explanation that wouldn't make her sound like a total fool. "His brother. He comes in here a lot. So I was just…curious.''

"Well, you take my advice, don't get tangled up with that boy. He's pure trouble.''

"But it's been eight years…maybe he's changed.''

"It would have to be a heck of a change, and I'm not sure he had that kind of character.''

She wanted to defend him, to tell Jim that at least he had cared enough to come back to the place he hated—with reason, she was beginning to see—to see if his brother needed help. But she was fairly sure that would just net her an even stronger warning, and she didn't want to hear it.

Why she didn't want to hear it was something she didn't dare think about.

But at least something had been explained, she thought after Jim had taken his books and gone; if Jackie had married Ed Hiller only for financial security, then it would explain the woman's lack of empathy for her son's raging grief.

Or it could simply be that she didn't give a damn about either of her kids. Some people just weren't cut out to be parents, Amelia thought. She just wished more of them knew it and eschewed the task.

What Jim had told her, and Luke's casual, even laughing references to his mother's coldness and his grandmother's viciousness, ate at her all morning. Thinking of the differences between how they were raised caused her a pain that was almost physical. She tried to ease it with work, straightening shelves, checking the inventory and placing reorders. And when, just before noon, she looked up from the back of the store at the sound of the door and this time he was really there, she felt her eyes begin to brim just looking at him.

Quickly she blinked away the moisture, knowing she would never be able to explain. But apparently she wasn't quite successful, because his first words when he reached her, accompanied by a frown, were, "You didn't have another visit from those charmers, did you?"

"No," she hastened to assure him.

"Then what's wrong?"

"I...nothing." When his expression turned doubtful, she added, "Just a sad story I heard, that's all."

For a moment he just looked at her. "Do you cry at sappy commercials, too?" It could have been a nasty dig, had it not been said in the gentlest of tones.

"Yes," she admitted, her chin coming up, determined not to be ashamed of it, even if her pulse was racing with trepidation.

"Soft heart," he said.

But again, he said it so gently it was impossible to take

offense. And then he reached out and brushed the backs of his fingers over the chin she'd raised to meet an expected threat. It was the merest feather of a touch, but it seared like flame, and Amelia felt her breath catch in her throat, as if her body had forgotten how to go about the process of breathing.

He pulled his hand back and looked at his fingers. He curled them into a fist, then ran his thumb over them, as if testing to see what had happened.

That his actions meant he'd felt it too didn't register with Amelia for a moment. When it did, her breath came back in a rush that would have been a gasp if she had not been able to muffle it.

Say something, she chided herself. Don't just stand here like some drooling fool of a woman who can't say two words to someone just because he happens to be an attractive man. A dangerously attractive man. In more ways than one.

But the only thing she could manage was the well-worn query that made her wince even as she said it. "Can I help you?"

He looked at her oddly for a moment, then gave a half shrug and said, "I need a book."

As reasonable as that sounded in a bookstore, Amelia was still startled. "You do?"

"Looks like I'll be here longer than I thought, and I don't have anything to read."

He said it as if that were a considerable problem, as if reading was an integral part of his life. Apparently his teaching David to love reading had come from a genuine love of his own, and that hadn't changed. She should have realized, she thought belatedly.

"What were you looking for?" she asked in her best professional manner.

He grinned. "Something violent. Got any nice, bloody mysteries?"

She didn't know if he was serious or just teasing her about

his reputation. With an effort she nodded toward the mystery rack and asked neutrally, "How bloody? Just a dead body to start, or do you prefer a string of them, complete with gore?"

His grin widened as she spoke. "You don't get rattled, do you?"

So he had been teasing, she thought. But that didn't change the answer to his question. "Not here," she said simply. Books were her world, her passion, and she was at home among them as she was nowhere else.

He walked over to the mystery bay, picked up a volume and turned back to her. "Is this the latest one? I've lost track of what letter she's on."

"Yes, that's the latest." Curious, she asked, "You like those?"

"Yep. She's one of my favorite detectives." He grinned again. "Besides, I like the glimpses into the workings of the female mind."

Right now, this female mind was barely working at all, Amelia thought ruefully. Because only now did she really focus on what else he'd said. He was going to be here longer than he'd thought.

"You're not getting anywhere with David?"

His mouth twisted. "I'm not getting much chance to try. All of a sudden his mother's keeping him very busy. And I stole him out from under her nose this afternoon. I don't think she liked that."

Amelia's eyes widened. "No, I can imagine she wouldn't."

"We didn't get too far before she caught up with us. Told David if he didn't come with her right then she was calling the cops on me."

"Oh, Luke…"

"I tried to tell him they couldn't do much to me, but he's pretty intimidated by her," he said, sounding the tiniest bit weary.

She sat down on one of the chairs she kept for browsers and gestured to him to take the other. He seemed to hesitate for a moment, then sat. After a moment of choosing words, she spoke.

"Have you asked her about seeing him? I mean, whatever the feelings between you, you are sort of on the same side in this. Neither of you wants David to get hurt."

"I haven't spoken to her in eight years, and I have no plans to start now."

Amelia drew back slightly. "But you said you stole David from under her nose...."

"Out of one of her speeches. She was making him wait there for her so she could keep an eye on him and then drive him home."

Amelia stared. "You marched into one of your mother's lectures and carted off your brother?"

He shrugged. "Seemed like a good idea at the time. Now I'm not so sure. She'll be watching him even closer."

"Then what will you do?"

He sighed and ran a hand through his hair. Amelia watched, fascinated, wondering what the thick, shiny strands felt like. "Give up, maybe. I'm not sure I could get through to him anyway."

"The way he idolizes you, if you can't get through to him, no one can," she said, trying for an encouraging tone.

"I think I'm half the problem." The weariness was even more evident, and she noticed then his eyes were slightly shadowed, as if he hadn't been sleeping. "He's got this set idea of who I am, and that he wants to be like me. So he's doing his best to walk that same road, and he's going to really screw up his life."

"Can't you just tell him that? He might listen to you."

"I doubt it." He leaned forward, rested his elbows on his knees, letting his hands dangle. Strong hands, she thought. Scarred here and there, and calloused on the palms. Hands that were used. Whatever he might be, he was no stranger to some kind of regular work, it seemed.

She realized he was looking at her look at his hands and fought not to blush. She didn't think she was successful, but he didn't seem to notice.

"You were right about that," he said. "He isn't going take my word for it, that he shouldn't do what I did."

"Ironic, isn't it?" she said. "He's idolizing you for all the wrong reasons, but those wrong reasons are the only thing that would make him listen to you."

His mouth twisted down at one corner. "And I don't know how to get through to him."

"Could anyone have gotten through to you?"

His expression changed then, and a small smile curved his mouth. "I—"

Lt. Worf cut him off as the door opened, and Amelia silently wished whoever it was could have waited just another minute. She got to her feet, and when she saw it was Mrs. Clancy, she redoubled her wish.

"Hello, Amelia," the woman called. "I was hoping that new book on roses had come in. There's a procedure I want to—"

She broke off the instant she saw Luke. Her smile vanished, to be replaced by a glower that would have alarmed someone even less timid than Amelia. But somehow, knowing that the woman's antagonism was aimed at Luke made her more determined to deflect it.

"Amelia," she said icily, "you should be more discriminating about your clientele."

"Oh, dear," Amelia said, purposely misunderstanding, "I could never discriminate. That's against the law."

Mrs. Clancy gave her a sharp look, as if she was fairly certain Amelia was too intelligent to have missed her meaning, but not sure enough to call her on it.

"Do you have any idea who this is?"

Luke stepped forward then, as if to put himself between

the two women. He leaned a shoulder against a bookshelf and crossed his ankles nonchalantly.

"You mean that I'm the devil's own spawn, Mrs. C.? I don't think my mother would appreciate that assessment, given the inferences."

"Your mother is a fine woman. She made something of her life after her one youthful mistake."

"While I've been off doing more of the same, no doubt adding to my illustrious police record, doing a little jail time and other things you'd expect of a troublemaker like me, right?"

"Exactly!" Mrs. Clancy nearly spat it out, sounding even more upset that Luke had robbed her of her tirade against him.

"Luke, please," Amelia began.

Mrs. Clancy turned on her. "You be careful, child. He's nothing but trouble, always has been."

Images of the child he must have been, unwanted, unloved, even his name chosen by strangers, boiled up in Amelia until she couldn't stop herself. "What on earth did he do to you?"

"That's an easy one." To her surprise, it was Luke who answered. "I was sixteen, mad at the world, and took it out on Mrs. Clancy's garden, because it was handy. I didn't think about it, about how it would hurt her, about what I was really destroying. I only knew she didn't like me anyway, so I just did it."

"You have no idea what you destroyed," the woman said, nearly trembling with a fury that looked as real now as it must have been then.

"Oh, I do," he said, very softly. "Now. Years of work, of loving care. Plants you'd babied and tended like most mothers tend children. And worse, that rosebush that had been your mother's. I didn't know what that meant then. I've learned since."

Amelia's throat tightened at the raw emotion in his voice. But Mrs. Clancy didn't hear it, or didn't care.

"So I'm supposed to believe that and forgive you now, is that it?"

Luke sighed. "No. I can't, so why should you?" He reached into his pocket and pulled out a couple of wadded bills. He separated a ten and handed it to Amelia. "I'll get the change later. I'm sure Mrs. Clancy would prefer it if I left."

He did, without another word or a backward glance. Amelia wanted to say something, anything, to him, but couldn't get out a single word.

When she looked at Mrs. Clancy's satisfied, slightly smug expression, she decided it would be best if she kept it that way.

Nearly midnight, and Amelia lay awake in her brass bed, staring at the patterns thrown on the ceiling by the brilliant moonlight coming through curtains moving softly in the slight breeze. She left that window open in the summer, since it was on the ocean side of the house, and too far up for an intruder to reach easily. She loved the faint scent of salt air that came her way when the breeze was right, and fancied sometimes, just before falling asleep on quiet nights, that she could even hear the sound of the surf, although the beach was a good mile away.

But tonight she hadn't fallen asleep at all. Her mind was too jumbled with images, her emotions too tangled.

Luke had never come back for his change. Not that she blamed him, after the blistering Mrs. Clancy had given him. And it had continued after he'd gone; once rolling, the woman had to tell her the entire story of her destroyed garden, every precious plant that had been trampled, ripped out, or cut off at the roots. Her words painted a very unpleasant picture.

But she didn't think she would ever forget the sound of

Luke's voice as he'd admitted what he'd done to the crotchety old woman. If she'd ever heard true regret from someone, she'd heard it then. And even Mrs. Clancy had said, although it had clearly made little difference to her, that Luke had worked in that garden every day for months to pay for the damage; he'd only done it, she had said with a sniff, to keep himself out of jail.

With a sigh Amelia turned over, settling her head on the pillow, trying to find the perfect position that would let her go to sleep. She found it and was nearly there when the phone jangled her back to half awake. She pulled herself up onto one elbow and reached for the receiver.

"Hello. Amelia?"

"Yes," she said, brows furrowing as she tried to place the feminine voice.

"This is Jackie Hiller. I got your number off my son's bulletin board."

She remembered giving David her home number after his father had died, in case he ever wanted to talk. When he had never called, she'd figured he'd tossed it away; somehow, knowing he hadn't warmed her. And then the juxtaposition of the late hour and the call jarred her fully awake.

"Is something wrong with David?"

"That boy, I swear, he lives to aggravate me. I thought I heard a noise, but by the time I went to look, it was too late. Next thing I know, the police will be calling me."

Amelia sat upright in bed. "What is it?"

The answer was short, sharp with irritation. And devoid of concern.

"He's gone."

Chapter 6

Luke was engrossed in his book, the body found, the hunt begun, when a noise pulled him out of the story. Frozen, still holding the book upright, he cocked his head to listen, not sure what exactly he'd heard. He had the window open; it was a warm night, and he liked the occasional whiff of fresh air, although he wasn't used to the road noise. He might not have heard the sound at all if the window had been closed.

Then he heard voices coming from outside the next room, and he relaxed. Somebody with a visitor.

But now that his attention had been drawn away from the story, his mind shot back to the same place it had been inhabiting any time he wasn't concentrating on something else.

Amelia Blair.

He wasn't sure why. He would say she wasn't his type, except that he didn't think he had a ''type'' in the usual sense of the word, a physical type. Unlike some of his friends, he didn't look only at blondes, or have a fixation with breasts or long hair. He supposed the closest he came to specifics was he liked long legs, but that was more because of the way they made women move; he liked that long, graceful stride.

No, his "type" was more a personality thing, he thought, scratching his bare chest idly. He was drawn to women who had that sparkle in their eyes that said they liked to have fun and whose appearance convinced him they could do so without worrying every second that they would break a nail, or their hair would get mussed, or their makeup would run.

Amelia's nails were short and neat, her hair the same, but if there was any fun-loving sparkle, she kept it too well hidden behind that reserved demeanor for him to see. She—

The noise again. Closer this time.

He rolled off the bed and padded barefoot across the room. He was about to reach for the curtain at the window beside the door when there was a tentative knock. Wary, as he had been ever since he'd returned to Santiago Beach, he lifted the blackout drape and looked out.

David.

He glanced at his watch as he went for the door. When he saw it was midnight, tension spiked through him.

"I thought you were next door. Your Harley's parked there."

"The other spot was full," Luke answered as the boy stepped in and quickly shut the door behind him.

With an effort, he held back his questions, stuck his hands in the pockets of the jeans he'd pulled on after his shower and waited for his brother to speak first.

David stood awkwardly, glancing around the room. It was a typical motel room, in decent shape if a bit cramped, and decorated in a cool green and blue scheme Luke found fairly inoffensive. His duffel bag was on the luggage rack; he hadn't unpacked it except to pull out his shaving gear. He'd brought nothing worth hanging up anyway. His boots were under the rack, his leather jacket slung over a chair, his tennis shoes on the floor beside the bed. Not neat as a pin, but not a mess, either.

David's glance fell on the bed, and the book he'd left open and face down. Then he looked at Luke and spoke at last.

"You still read late."

Luke nodded. "Can't go to sleep if I don't."

David nodded. "Me either." He smiled, briefly. "Amelia says it's the best routine there is, reading before bed."

"Won't get any argument from me."

David walked over to the bed and sat on the edge of it, fingers toying with the book. "Is it good?"

"So far."

"You like mysteries?"

Luke nodded. "They appeal to my need for order in the universe."

David blinked, as if startled by his words. He was silent for a moment before saying, almost shyly, "I used to like it when you came in and read to me, when I was little."

"So did I, Davie. We had some good times, huh?"

The smile came back, stayed longer this time. "Some of the guys think it's a waste. They think only nerds or freaks read if they don't have to."

"Not true."

"I know." David looked at him pointedly. "I mean, you read, but you never let anybody push you around. You're tough, tougher than Snake even. Back in school, everybody knew you were smart. Dad always said you were, but you didn't go all wimpy and get straight A's or anything. You stayed cool."

Luke looked at his brother for a moment. "You mean I got myself a police record."

"Well, yeah. I mean, nobody messed with you, not even the grown-ups. They were all afraid of you."

"And you think that's cool?"

"Well...sure. You're still a legend around here." David

sat up straighter. "I'm going to be like that, somebody people *know* about, somebody they respect."

Luke suppressed a sigh. "David, don't ever confuse a bad reputation with respect. Oh, it's great when you're trying to impress kids, but sooner or later you're going to grow up, and then a bad rep impresses nobody worth impressing."

David frowned. "That's not what you used to say."

"I know. That was before I spent a damn long time trying to get out from under the rep I'd built, trying to convince the world that I didn't belong locked up somewhere for good."

He walked over to one of the chairs beside the small table under the window, pulled it out and put it down in front of his brother, then sat down in the other. When David sat down, Luke took a deep breath, then went on.

"Being locked up might seem now like a good way to show you're tough, or seem kind of exciting, even glamorous. It's not, Davie. It sucks, in a very big way."

"But...you were never locked up for very long. Just two days, that time over the car."

This was going to be the hard part. "I was, Davie. After I left. For almost two months. It was the worst time of my life, worse than anything our dear mother ever threw at me."

David's eyes widened, and Luke hoped he'd gotten through with that one; nobody knew better than David the hell he'd gone through at home.

"What for?"

"It doesn't matter now," Luke said, not wanting to give David any further inspiration down that particular road. "Just trust me, it was hell. And you do *not* want to go there."

David shifted tacks then, a persuasive note coming into his voice, and Luke knew it was finally coming. "I don't really want to end up in jail," he said. "But if I stay here..."

He wanted to say yes. Just say "Sure, bro, pack up your stuff and let's go." But he'd learned long ago that wishes alone weren't worth much. He understood David's desperation to escape all too well. But he also understood something else, and there was no easy way to say it.

"I know what it feels like to need to get out so badly, Davie. And I wish I could just say yes. But she'd never let it happen. You know that. She'd never let you go with *me,* of all people."

"Then I'll just run away. She wouldn't have to know I was with you!"

"It'd be the first place she'd look."

"But I *can't* stay here. I can't! She doesn't even miss my dad. Sometimes she acts like he was never even here. I want to be like you, free and on my own, without her breathing down my neck every second."

He had no answer for David's feelings about his father, so he tried to focus on what he did know.

"I'm nobody to emulate, bro. She may not be the best mother around, but I wasn't worth much then, either."

"But she made you be that way, she was such a bitch to you!"

Luke was touched at his brother's passionate defense, yet felt like he had to keep on, to make him see that the Luke McGuire he was talking about was nobody to model himself on.

"She won't even let me talk about him," David blurted out, hiccuping on the last word. Luke sensed he was close to tears and knew it would humiliate the boy for him to see that. So he leaned back in the chair, lifted one foot up to rest it on his knee and studied the frayed hem of his jeans as David went on.

"She says she's tired of hearing it, that it's time for me to get over it and grow up. But I miss him. I miss him so much…."

Something hard and painful wrenched loose inside Luke. "Damn," he muttered. "You're right. She *is* a bitch." He'd hoped, truly hoped, that she would be different with David.

That because he was legitimate, her husband's son, it would be better for him. But now he wondered if what he'd suspected then was true, that David had been merely insurance, to be sure his wealthy father was nailed down tight.

"See? I told you she was. I want to come with you, Luke. Please? I won't get in the way, I promise, and you can teach me stuff, like how you hot-wire a car, and—"

"Whoa, there!" Luke held up a hand. Clearly he had a lot more convincing to do. "Look, she may have treated me like crap, but I made my own decisions back then. Most of them bad ones. I'm not saying things might not have been different if she'd been different, but they were what they were, and I made the worst of it instead of the best."

"But—"

"Listen to me, Davie. I was a royal foul-up. I made a major mess of most of my life. You want somebody to be like, pick your dad, not your screwed-up brother. He was a great guy, and he deserves to have a son who grows up like him."

David went very silent. And in that silence, the tap on the door seemed much louder than it probably was. Luke got up, wondering if, with the window open, they'd gotten loud enough to disturb someone. But when he pulled open the door, he just stood there staring in shock.

Amelia.

For a long moment she simply stared back, and he was suddenly aware that he had nothing on but a pair of very worn jeans. Even in the yellowish glow of the light outside the door, he could tell she was blushing. Finally she lowered her head with a sharp little jerk, as if yanking her gaze from him.

"Hi," he finally said, and it sounded lame even to him.

"Hi," she answered, still not looking up. "I'm sorry to interrupt, but…"

Luke drew back sharply then, wondering how long she'd been outside, how much she'd overheard. She stopped speaking and still wouldn't—or couldn't—meet his eye, which made him guess she'd heard quite a bit.

"Amelia?"

David's question came from over Luke's shoulder, and he thought he saw relief flash through her eyes. "May I come in?" she asked.

Luke was fairly sure it would be the dumbest thing he'd done all day, but he stepped back and held the door. Besides, what could happen with David there?

"Hello, David," she said as she stepped into the room.

The boy got to his feet. "Hi." He frowned suddenly. "How come you're out so late?"

"I could ask you the same thing," she said. "And probably should."

David's chin came up. "I wanted to see Luke. I got a right to see my own brother, don't I?"

"I would think so," Amelia said easily.

"Damn right," David said, sounding as if he were trying to convince himself as much as anyone. "I don't care what she says. I won't hate him just because she does."

"That's never a good enough reason for anything," Amelia agreed, her tone still light, nonchalant. "But I'm not sure sneaking out is the answer."

"How else am I supposed to see him? Besides, she'll never know."

Amelia put a gentle hand on the boy's shoulder. "I'm afraid she already does. Why do you think I'm here?"

Good question, Luke thought, and was more disappointed than he wanted to admit that apparently she was here only to look for David. And that realization made him very glad they were carrying on this conversation without him; who knew what he would be stupid enough to say if he opened his mouth.

"You're...lookin' for me?" David asked.

Amelia nodded. "Your mother called me."

David swore, and Luke felt the urge to tell him to watch

his mouth in front of her. She just had that effect, with that quiet, good-girl demeanor of hers.

"She was...worried."

"Yeah. Right. Pissed, you mean."

"That too," Amelia admitted. Luke supposed it must have seemed pointless to her to deny it to the two people who knew the woman best.

David's eyes widened suddenly. "You're not gonna tell her, are you?"

"If you go home, I won't have to."

"But I'm not going home. Not ever. Well, maybe to get my stuff, but then I'm going with Luke."

Amelia's gaze flicked to Luke. His mouth tightened, and he gave an almost imperceptible shake of his head, hoping she would understand that it was David saying that, not him.

"You've worked that out with your mother?" Amelia asked.

For the first time since she'd known him, David flared up at her. "I'm just going, and don't you tell her!"

"She'll find out, David. The law is on her side."

"I don't care. I want to live with Luke! Don't I get a say about my own life?"

Luke took a deep breath. "She's right, David. Your mother will find out, and when she does, she'll take you back. And if you don't cooperate, she'll send the cops to get you. And me."

"But...can't you be my guardian? You're an adult now, you could go to court or something, couldn't you?"

Luke rammed a hand through his hair. What had been merely an effort to take himself off that cracked pedestal David had him on became something much more painful in front of Amelia. But it had to be done; he couldn't save his pride at the risk of his brother's future.

"Remember that reputation of mine you're so proud of?" he asked the boy.

"Yeah," David said slowly, warily.

"That's the very reason no court in the world would trust me with you. No way they'd even considered releasing you to me, not with my record."

Watching his younger brother's face change, watching his hopes crumble into anguish, was one of the hardest things he'd ever done.

"It's not fair!"

"Life ain't," Luke said, bitterness creeping into his voice, feeling like he'd somehow let down this boy he hadn't seen in eight years.

David looked at them both a little wildly. Then he bolted and had the door open before either Luke or Amelia could move. She was closer and started toward him.

"David, wait!"

He was gone, racing down the long walkway in front of the motel. Amelia stepped outside quickly, starting after him.

"Amelia, stop."

She looked back over her shoulder at him.

"Let him go."

He caught up to her just as she said, "No! He's too upset."

The moment the words were out, a look of surprise crossed her face, as if she couldn't quite believe she'd said them. Was it so rare for her to disagree with someone?

"I know you want to help, but going after him now will only make it worse," he said.

"But it's the middle of the night. He could get in trouble."

"Right now he's going to be looking for someplace to hide, where he can be alone, where he won't have to talk to anyone."

"But—"

Luke reached out and gently took her shoulders. "Trust me on this. I've been where he is. He needs to be alone for a while."

She looked at him for a long, silent moment. Then, under

his hands, he felt the tension seep out of her. But still she expressed concern. "What if he runs away?"

"I don't think he's quite ready for that yet. He's on the edge, but he's not ready to jump."

She looked up at him very intently. "And if you're wrong?"

I'll slit my throat, Luke thought. "If I'm wrong, I guess my reputation around here as a screw-up gets enhanced." He lifted one shoulder in a half shrug. "I'm probably getting credit for Davie getting off track anyway."

She lowered her gaze, and he knew he was right. He'd figured as much, that the gossip would be that David was turning out just like his brother.

"I don't know how they can blame you," she said softly. "He was only seven when you left."

"But I left him a fine, grand image to live up to, now didn't I?"

She seemed to consider that for an inordinately long time before saying, "Do you believe in genetic memory?"

He blinked. As a non sequitur, that one would be hard to beat. "What?"

"Genetic memory. That you can have ideas or thoughts that don't come from your own personal experience but from the common experience of your ancestors."

"I'm sure," he said slowly, "that there's a reason you brought that up just now."

She gave him a sideways look. "You said you never knew your father. But just then you sounded as Irish as they come."

He blinked again. "I did?"

"The way you phrased that reminded me of a colleague of my father's who visited us from Dublin once."

The idea that he carried some innate habits that might have come directly from the father he'd never known startled him. For a moment he just stood there, toying with the idea, wondering how he felt about it. It wasn't until Amelia shifted her feet, as if tired of standing, that he realized how long he'd been lost in that reverie.

"Sorry. I know it's late," he began.

She nodded. "I should go." All of a sudden she sounded nervous again, like she did so often. He wondered what he was doing that set her so on edge.

He didn't want her to go, he realized. He wasn't sure why; he just knew that, unlike his brother, he didn't want to be alone right now.

"The coffee shop here is open twenty-four-seven," he said before she could turn away. "Would you like something? Before you go, I mean?" She hesitated. "Maybe we can think of something to do about David. And I'm sure they have decaf," he added.

She smiled at that and finally nodded. "All right."

When they walked into the small café, he thought the waitress looked at them rather intently, but Amelia didn't seem to notice anything amiss. Although her mind was obviously elsewhere, because she glanced at the pay phone just inside the door and said, "We should call...David's mother."

"Afraid she's worried? Don't be," Luke said shortly.

"No," Amelia said, surprising him yet again. "More afraid she's called the police by now."

She had, he had to admit, a point. "You'd better call, then. The last thing David needs is for her to know he was with me."

She nodded, and he waited as she made the call. It was strange to think it was his mother she was talking to, when he himself hadn't spoken to her—except for that mocking exchange at the community center—since the day he'd walked out for the last time. Strange, but not painful; there wasn't a doubt in his mind that his decision had been for the best. His only regret was that he hadn't done it sooner. But he'd stayed to finish high school, more for David's father than anything; it seemed one small way to acknowledge the man's efforts to treat him well.

Whatever the waitress had been speculating when they'd come in, apparently she'd set it aside. In less than a minute they were seated in a booth with rather unsettling olive green vinyl cushions, had cups in front of them and the place to themselves.

And after a moment he found he couldn't resist the urge to pick up where they'd left off, and somehow he knew that he wouldn't have to explain who he was talking about, that she would understand.

"You know," he said, "I don't even know if he knows I exist. I could never get my mother to tell me if he ever knew she was pregnant. She wouldn't discuss him at all, and all her mother ever said was that he seduced and abandoned her."

"I think," Amelia said softly, "that you should assume he never knew. That if he had, he would have come back."

His mouth twisted. "That's a kid's fantasy."

"Every kid should have one."

"Did you?"

She took a sip off her coffee. "Of course."

"What was it?"

"I'm not sure I'm ready to share that," she said honestly.

He leaned back, the vinyl creaking. "Fair enough," he said, knowing he wouldn't really want to share his own, either. It would be far too pitiful to admit that all he'd ever wanted as a kid was for his mother to love him. "I wonder if David has one," he said almost idly.

Her silence was almost pointed, as was the way she stared down at her coffee cup. He was just noticing that her lashes were rather amazingly long and soft looking when it hit him.

"I get it," he said, a little harshly. "David's fantasy was that his big brother would come back and save him, right? And I just blew that all to hell."

"Luke—"

He cut her off with a sharp, disgusted exhalation. "I can't win in this town. I never should have come back."

"Yes, you should have," Amelia said, so positively that puzzlement took the edge off his anger.

"Why?"

"Because later, when he's calmed down, it will matter to David that you came. Even if you couldn't do what he wanted you to do."

"Right." He knew he sounded surly, but he couldn't help it.

She looked at him then. "Would it have mattered to you if your father had come back, even if he couldn't have taken you with him?"

I'd have lived on it the rest of my life.

The words came out of nowhere in his mind, startling him. He'd never thought of himself as fixated on the father he'd never known, but apparently it was closer to the surface than he'd realized.

"Yes," he finally managed, his voice a little tight. "It would have mattered."

She nodded. "And someday it will be important to David that you cared enough to come."

"You mean the older we get, the less we settle for?"

"I suppose you could put it like that. I like to think it's more learning how to make the most of what we have instead of wasting energy and effort on things we can't change."

He ran a finger up and down his coffee cup, the inexpensive, thick ceramic insulating him from the heat of the beverage. "Is that the voice of experience?"

She took another sip of coffee, then set down her cup. She stared into it for a long moment, as if the answer were in there. "In a way," she said finally. "That...that fantasy you asked about? I wanted to be Amelia Earhart. A risk-taker, a daredevil. I wanted to go faster, higher.... But I never will. I'm...not brave, not adventurous, the exact opposite in fact. I'm just me, and I've learned to be content with that.''

Luke stared across the table at her, a bit taken aback at her unexpected confession and oddly stung by her rather biting self-assessment. Especially coming from the woman who had diverted a knife-wielding kid named Snake with a book.

"You know, Ms. Blair," he said at last, "I think you might be just the tiniest bit wrong about that."

She looked up at him. "About what?"

"The risk-taking part."

Her brows furrowed. "Hardly. The biggest risk I've ever taken was going to college a hundred miles from home."

"And," he said, gesturing at their surroundings, "sitting in a public place in the middle of the night with the scourge of Santiago Beach."

She looked up then, sharply, and he grinned at her.

Slowly, like the dawn breaking over the rim of a canyon, a smile spread across her mouth.

"There is that," she said.

And Luke felt like he'd worked a very small miracle.

Chapter 7

By noon the next day Amelia was thinking that Luke's joking words had been truer than she would ever have guessed. Apparently a simple cup of coffee, taken with "the scourge of Santiago Beach," was one of the bigger risks she'd ever taken. At least, judging from the reaction.

She supposed the waitress must have recognized them; she had looked vaguely familiar. And she had apparently wasted no time in spreading the news that the respectable bookstore owner had been out with the highly unrespectable Luke McGuire, at a very suspicious hour, in a coffee shop. A *motel* coffee shop. And most of the people she'd told seemed to have decided it was their duty to stop in and ask Amelia what on earth she thought she was doing.

At first she'd reacted viscerally, wanting to defend Luke. After all, she was the one who had heard him tearing himself down to his brother, trying to destroy the heroic image the boy had built up, trying to convince David he wasn't worth imitating, that, as a role model, he was a lousy choice. He'd been brutally, painfully honest, and she knew it hadn't come easily. But he had done it—for his brother's sake.

But no one here would understand that. They probably wouldn't even believe it if she told them. They had made up their minds long ago about Luke, and she, the relative newcomer, wasn't going to be able to change them. She had to accept that.

What she couldn't accept was the rest. The fact that when she explained that they had been talking because they were both concerned about David, she got only looks ranging from doubt to outright disbelief. She was not used to being thought a liar, and it made her angrier than she could remember being in a very long time. And gradually she became defensive, deciding that if they wanted to believe the worst, let them.

A thought struck her then that this was what Luke must have gone through every day of his life here. That he must have constantly faced the blank wall of preconceptions, the smug certainty of minds already made up, closed and locked. No wonder he'd given up trying to change anyone's perception of him. And she thought, not for the first time, that for all the problems it caused, her parents had had only the best intentions in keeping her in their protective shell.

Maybe, she thought after the worst of them all, Mrs. Clancy, had warned her in a very stern way that she would ruin what was so far a good reputation if she kept on, she would make up a good story. If they wanted something juicy, maybe she would just give it to them. Tell them she and Luke were plotting some nefarious crime, or that she was involved in a hot, torrid, passionate affair with him.

Her body cut off her thoughts with a burst of sudden heat that startled her.

A hot, torrid, passionate affair with Luke.

With a tiny sound she hated to admit could have been a moan, she pressed her hands to her face, the heat of her cheeks making her fingers feel almost icy.

The very idea was absurd. The idea of her having a hot, torrid, passionate affair with anyone was absurd; she just didn't have it in her. But the idea of having it with Luke, well that was just—

Breathtaking. Stimulating. Titillating.

Arousing, she said to herself, making herself face the fact inwardly, even if she couldn't out loud.

Was that what this was, this sudden rush of heat at the mere thought? Her experience was so limited: one high school romance that had ended before it had really begun, when she'd refused to leap into bed with him; one in college that had crumbled when an ex-girlfriend had returned; and the last one shortly after her father's death, when she'd been feeling vulnerable and had tried to find something to fill the sudden void in her life in the bed of a man who, while nice enough, hadn't been looking to cure a member of the walking wounded.

But never had she ever experienced anything like this wave of sensation at just the *idea*....

Luke McGuire...and her? Quiet, meek, timid Amelia Blair? It was impossible. Worse, it was absurd. No wonder people were going into shock.

I think you might be just the tiniest bit wrong about that....

Luke's words came back to her then, along with the memory of the teasing glint in his bright blue eyes. And the grin he'd given her. Lord, they should make him give some kind of warning before unleashing that grin.

To distract herself, she tried calling Mrs. Hiller again. And again she got the answering machine. She had gone by the house this morning and run into the woman, dressed impeccably as usual and carrying a briefcase, and clearly heading out for the day. Amelia had breathed a sigh of relief; David must have come home. She was taken aback when Jackie had said no, there had been no sign of him, but she had no more time to sit around and wait, she had appointments to keep.

"Since you saw him last night, he's obviously still in town. He'll turn up when he's ready, and then I'll deal with him." She had brushed past Amelia and only as an afterthought had turned and said, "Thank you for your call, by the way."

"You're welcome," she'd said rather lamely, unsure of what else to say in the face of such monumental unconcern.

"However," Jackie added in formal tones, "I do not approve at all of my son associating with Luke. I'd appreciate it if you didn't encourage contact between them."

For the first time in her relatively placid life, Amelia wanted to slap someone. The woman spoke as if Luke wasn't connected to her at all, as if he were just some stranger "her son" had taken up with.

It had taken a good hour of physical work at the store to take the edge off her anger. Then, after she opened, the parade of self-appointed watchdogs had begun, and now she was fully out of sorts. Not to mention that her worry about David had returned full force; if he'd been out all night, who knew what might have happened.

She gave herself a shake, then started back into her small storeroom. She still had a couple of cartons of books to unpack and a dump to set up for the front of the store. She grabbed her box opener, and for a moment her gaze lingered on the razor-sharp blade.

Good thing I'm not one for mayhem, she muttered to herself. But then again, she amended as she attacked the first box, maybe she could learn.

Luke awoke slowly, knowing how deeply he'd been asleep by how long it took him to surface. Even though he was used to being up late, frequently going for restless walks at night, last night had been a long one. He'd lain awake until dawn, unable to find the switch to turn off his racing mind.

He had—successfully, he'd thought—given up on guilt a long time ago. But it was making a powerful comeback at the moment; he felt as if he'd betrayed the only person who'd really cared about the kid he'd been. But he just didn't see any way around it. What he'd told David was all true; their mother would never stand for it, and she had all the cards: biological, financial and twenty-six years of public making up for her single mistake—him. Even if he thought he could handle it, there was no way somebody with his history would be entrusted with a teenager already headed down the same path.

That would have been enough to drive away sleep, but then there had been the sizable distraction of Amelia to add into the mix.

He didn't know what it was about the quiet, reserved woman that kept him thinking about her; he only knew it happened. And he couldn't quite convince himself it was solely because she cared about his brother. That had brought him to her in the first place, but it hadn't been the reason he kept going back. Or the reason he'd blurted out that invitation for coffee last night, before he even realized he was going to do it.

He'd been surprised when she'd said yes. She'd been so nervous he thought she would bolt just as David had. She always seemed that way, tense underneath that reserved exterior. Unless she was wrapped up in her concern for David. And sometimes, it seemed, even concern for him.

He sat up slowly, blinking bleary eyes as something David had told him came back to him. *She's a little quiet. You never know what she's thinking.*

Well, he sure did. She seemed on the verge of running at some point during every contact he'd had with her. Every time he saw her, there was at least one moment when she seemed to draw back from him warily, when he had the idea she was looking for an escape route.

He rubbed at his eyes, but stopped midmotion when another thought came to him. Maybe it was the other way around? Maybe she was only rattled enough to let it show when he was around?

That made him smile. He couldn't deny he liked the idea of shaking her out of that reserve, just on general principle. Maybe that was why he was so drawn to her.

Or maybe, more simply, he thought as he dragged himself to the shower, it was that she was one of the few people in town who didn't remember him from before, one of the few he could talk to and not be certain they were always thinking of his rowdy past. Not that she didn't know about it, obviously she did, but she didn't seem to dwell on it. She hadn't seen it firsthand, so it wasn't emblazoned on her memory the way it seemed to be with everyone else around here.

It wasn't until he got out of the shower and caught a glimpse of himself in the mirror that another possibility hit him. His gaze strayed, as it often did, to the crooked, white scar that wrapped around the right side of his rib cage. His mother had never known about that one; by the time he'd gotten that slice in a knife fight at David's age, he'd known better than to expect any help from her, even if he was bleeding. He'd disinfected it as best he could, fighting not to make any noise at the pain and wake her up, bandaged it lopsidedly, and the next day had smuggled his bloody shirt out to throw it away in a Dumpster on the other side of town. The wound had been slow to heal, because he kept tearing it open, but eventually it had healed.

He stared at it now and wondered if Amelia was nervous around him because she was afraid of him.

Once the idea of people being afraid of him had had great appeal; at least it meant he mattered in some way.

Now... Well, now it just made him uncomfortable. Or, at

least, the idea of Amelia being afraid of him did. And he hoped he was wrong.

He tossed the towel over the shower rod and walked out into the room. He was going to have to do laundry soon; he'd only brought three extra shirts and one extra pair of jeans. He pulled out the clean clothes he had left, thinking that there was a Laundromat just off Main Street. True, there was also one just down the street from the motel, but the other one was right around the corner from Blairs' Books. He could start his clothes washing, then head over there. He doubted anybody would make off with his meager wardrobe; that kind of thing just didn't happen in Santiago Beach.

At least, not since *he'd* left, anyway, he amended with a grin as he dressed quickly.

It wasn't a pretend grin. Most of the time he was able to mean it when he thought of his life here. But always underneath he knew how lucky he was to have escaped as lightly as he had; he'd been headed for much worse.

Soon all his clothes were sudsing away, and he was astride his bike and on his way around the corner; his trust of crime-free Santiago Beach didn't run to the Harley.

He'd never spent so much time in a bookstore, he thought as he set the kickstand and dismounted. He'd loved to read—which would have surprised anybody in town, including his mother, since he went out of his way to hide the fact from her, afraid she would try to stop that, too—but he hadn't had money to spend on books. So he'd spent lots of time in the library, which had set him up for ribbing from his friends, but he'd bluffed his way out of it, saying it was the perfect place to hide out and not get hassled by anybody.

Besides, he had a perfectly legitimate reason to be here now; Amelia might have heard something about David.

She was behind the checkout counter as he neared the door, and for a moment he stopped outside, watching. He knew the door alarm—whoever it might be today—would alert her the minute he opened it, and he wanted a minute to watch her first.

She was bent over what looked like a magazine, reading intently. She had a pen in one hand, which she was tapping rhythmically against the glass countertop. The other hand came up and pushed a straying lock of hair neatly behind her ear. It was an unconscious move, she never looked up, but it was graceful and somehow extremely feminine. As was the hand that did it, and the delicate ear she tucked the strand behind.

The haircut suited her, he thought. Sort of pixieish. And, he thought as he finally reached for the door, he'd never realized before how darn sexy the nape of a neck could be.

He stopped, fingers already curled to grip the handle, as he realized what he'd just thought.

Sexy?

He looked up again; now she was biting her lip, as if deep in thought, and damn if that wasn't sexy as hell, too.

She made a note on a pad of paper beside her, then flipped the magazine closed. Luke knew she would look up any second, and he hastily tried to shove aside his unexpected reaction. He yanked open the door a little quicker than he'd meant to and nearly jumped when the voice of the Enterprise computer welcomed him.

What is wrong *with you?* he asked himself sharply.

And then Amelia looked up and saw him. And the shy smile that curved her mouth drove everything else out of his mind.

"Hi," she said, in a tone that matched the smile and made his chest tighten oddly.

"Hi," he returned. So much for witty conversation.

For a moment he just stood there in awkward silence. So did she, although he didn't know how awkward she might feel.

"Come back for your change?" she finally asked.

"No, I had to do some laundry," he finally said, "so I thought I'd come by while it's washing."

If she realized he'd gone out of his way from the motel to do it, she didn't say so. "You weren't expecting to stay this long, were you?"

His mouth quirked. "No. But then, things in Santiago Beach never do go quite like I expect."

Boy, isn't that the truth? he added silently as he noticed again the spiky length of her lashes. They had to be real, he thought; she just wasn't the type for tons of makeup. Something to make them darker, maybe, but that was it. And her nose had this cute little tilt to it.

Yanking himself back to the matter at hand, he said in a rush, "I thought you might have heard if David turned up at home."

She frowned then, which made him notice the full softness of her lower lip. With an effort, he focused on what she was saying.

"—she didn't seem worried. I tried calling the house just a few minutes ago, but I didn't get an answer. Of course, David could be there and just not answering. Maybe if you called…"

He shook his head. "He's still pretty peeved at me, I'd guess. And I sure don't want to end up with my mother on the phone, if she's back by now."

"He'll get over it," Amelia said, as if she thought he needed assurance.

Or comforting. And before his mind darted to all the ways he'd suddenly realized he would like to be comforted by her, he shrugged. "Maybe. Eventually. He's got no reason to really trust me. Just some old memories."

"But they're mostly good ones," she countered. "And when he's over his anger, he'll realize you coming here at all is a very big reason."

Luke shook his head. "You're an optimist, Amelia."

This time she shrugged. ''Not really. But I'm not a pessimist.''

A fine line, but he supposed it was a line. A silent moment spun out between them, and this time it was she who seemed in a hurry to break it. ''How's your book?''

''Good, so far. I was up too late with it, though.'' He'd been fighting a yawn, and better she think that than the truth, that she'd been a big part of his sleeplessness, he thought.

''I didn't sleep much, either,'' she said, and then, as if she'd said something inappropriate, looked quickly away. For an instant Luke wondered if she'd been *thinking* something inappropriate.

I can but hope, he thought with an inward grin. And then wondered if he meant it. If she had been, what would he do about it? It wasn't like he planned to stick around here any longer than he had to, and good girls like Amelia didn't indulge in short flings with visiting troublemakers. Not that he wouldn't like to try and change her mind....

The computer voice sounded again, and they both automatically turned to look.

It was David.

The boy's head was down, and he was scuffing his shoes as he walked, looking as downcast as it was possible for him to look. He was still wearing what he'd had on last night, so he apparently hadn't been home. But he was here, and that was a good sign.

He had nearly reached them when he finally looked up. There was a split second delay while he realized Amelia wasn't alone, and another while he realized who was with her.

He stopped dead. His eyes narrowed, and he glared at his brother as he started to back away.

''Still ticked at me, huh?'' Luke said.

''I trusted you, counted on you to get me out of here.''

''Didn't your mother tell you I couldn't be trusted?''

David stopped backing up, surprise showing on his face.

Luke sensed Amelia go still, sensed her getting ready to speak, but made a subtle gesture to her to wait.

"Yeah, but I never listen to her," David said.

"Guess now you think she's been right all along, then."

David's brow furrowed. His gaze shifted to Amelia, his expression changing to one that was almost pleading. Luke realized that right then Amelia had a much better chance with David than he did.

"I've got laundry to finish," he said to her, and the nod she gave him told him she understood he was leaving so she could talk to David, who hopefully would open up to her.

"Laundry," David said scornfully as Luke walked past him.

Luke winced inwardly but never faltered. And when he stepped outside he let out a long breath; he never would have thought the scorn of a fifteen-year-old could burn so deep. Maybe he had liked that hero worship idea more than he'd realized.

Chapter 8

"He'll come around, Luke. I know he will."

Amelia sipped at the soda Luke had brought along with the number five Chinese dinner for two from the Jade Garden down the street. He'd shown up just after six, startling her but making her stomach growl; she'd donated her lunch to David, who hadn't eaten since the day before, and now she was starving. She'd been startled, even flattered, when he'd arrived, but then she'd realized he just wanted a report on what had happened with David. Still, it had been thoughtful of him.

Luke leaned back in the guest chair, his feet propped up on her desk, a small white carton of fried rice with shrimp in one hand, a set of chopsticks he manipulated with surprising ease in the other.

"As long as he went home, so she doesn't call the cops on him," he said.

There was a world of bitter experience in his voice, and Amelia knew it had happened to him more than once. She set her soda down on her desk blotter. "He said he would."

She didn't add that David, still disillusioned with his brother, also said it was only because he wasn't ready to bail out just yet, he needed to save up a bit more cash, since Luke had copped out on him and he was going to be on his own. Luke was feeling guilty enough already, he didn't need that added on.

"So...what now?" she asked.

He snagged a shrimp and ate it before saying, almost wearily, "I don't know. I should probably just get the hell out of Dodge, as they say. I'm not doing any good and probably just making things worse."

"I know it seems like that now," Amelia said.

She picked at the last of her rice—with a fork, she'd never really tried to get the hang of chopsticks—wishing there was something she could say to give him some hope. He'd cared enough to come here, to the town he surely must hate; she hated to see him leave thinking he'd failed, even pushed his brother from miserable over into desperate.

She hated to see him leave, period.

She quickly turned to drop her empty carton in the trash, more to hide her suddenly flushed face than anything. What a fool she could be sometimes.

But she *would* hate to see him leave. If nothing else, she thought, she never got tired of looking at him. There was something about the barely controlled wildness she sensed, something about the way he moved, the way he sometimes looked off into the distance as if he were used to gazing on horizons much broader than little Santiago Beach, that called to some part of her she'd never known existed. Or that she'd buried so deeply she'd thought it dormant beyond revival.

And, she admitted, determined to be honest at least with herself, she did feel flattered by his attention, even though she knew full well that his concern over David was the real reason for it.

Before she could dwell on the foolishness of her own

reaction, the Enterprise computer announced a new arrival. She got to her feet.

"Be right back," she said, and Luke nodded.

But when she stepped out into the store, her heart sank. Jim Stavros had just been in the other day, and he usually came only every couple of weeks. Besides, he was in uniform. He'd never come in like this before, and it made her wonder. Especially with Luke in her office.

Steadying herself, she managed to say cheerfully enough, "Hello, Jim. I hope this isn't an official visit?"

"No. I'm working nights for a while, but not really."

Uh-oh. She didn't like the undertone in his voice, as if he were doing something he didn't want to. "Problem with your book?" she asked.

"No, nothing like that." He fiddled with the key ring on his belt. He was a big man, she'd known that, but somehow, in uniform, with his gun belt on, and inside her store, he seemed even bigger.

"What, then?" she prodded when he didn't go on.

He grimaced, took a breath, and Amelia wondered what on earth could have this big, strong, authoritative cop so nervous. Then Jim said in a rush, "Look, I heard you'd been seen a couple of times with Luke McGuire."

Oh, no, not another one, she thought. And wondered if she'd pulled the office door closed.

"I just wanted to…"

"Warn me?" she said when he faltered.

"Yeah. I like you, Amelia, and I'd hate to see you get in trouble, or hurt, or worse."

It was hard to be angry with him when he put it that way. But he was just the latest in a long line of well-meaning advice givers today, and she'd had about enough. Especially with the taste of the meal Luke had brought still in her mouth.

"Look, I appreciate your concern, Jim. But whatever

Luke did or didn't do in the past, he's been nice to me since he got here.''

"That may be true, but don't kid yourself," Jim said ominously. "It's not very likely that he's changed much."

"But it's not impossible."

"Maybe. Do you even know what he's doing now?"

"No," she said, only now realizing they'd been so wrapped up in David's troubles that she'd never asked. "Do you?"

"No," he admitted, "but I can guess."

"And you'd convict him on a guess?"

"An educated guess," Jim amended. "Look, just be careful. I know you and his brother are tight, and that that's probably all it is, but Joann wanted me to talk to you just in case."

Great, Amelia thought, a double-barreled warning. "Thank her for her concern."

After Jim had left, Amelia returned slowly to her office. And found she'd left the door wide open.

She stepped inside. Luke was finishing his own soda, the white carton he'd been working on empty and stacked with hers.

"Thanks again for dinner," she said brightly. "It's nice not to have to think about fixing something when I get home."

"You're welcome."

"I'll just clear this up. Let me get the bag, and I'll toss it in the Dumpster out back." *Lord, she was chattering now.*

There was a long moment where the only sound was the rustling of paper and the click of her plastic fork against the chopsticks as she gathered them up.

"He's right, you know."

She looked at him then. And saw in his face that he'd heard every word.

"Luke—"

"You really should be more careful. You don't know anything about me."

She straightened up, tightening her fingers around the chopsticks because she was afraid they would shake. But she had to say it.

"I know that you care about your brother, that you had reason enough to be a little wild, and have every right to hate your mother. And it's true, you *have* been nice to me since you got here."

She watched him as she blurted it all out, making herself meet his gaze, and she saw his expression change from something almost defiant to something much, much softer. And when he spoke, his voice was almost unbearably gentle.

"Is this really the amenable, quiet Amelia Blair I've heard about?"

"Maybe I've had enough of being amenable," she said snappishly.

"Digging in your heels?"

"Just ignoring unwanted advice."

He smiled, a slow curving of his mouth that did strange things to her pulse rate. And then he stood up, moving much like she would guess a wild creature would move, smooth, graceful, seemingly without effort.

Stop it, she ordered herself. *The man just stood up, that's all.*

"Been getting a lot of advice lately?"

He said it as if he knew others beside Jim had been offering their blunt opinions. And as if he knew exactly what those opinions were.

"Too much of it," she said, reining in the uncharacteristic flare of temper. It wasn't she who had to live with it, after all, it was Luke who had to walk around knowing everybody thought he was a hairbreadth away from doing something villainous.

"Didn't take them long," Luke said, in a level, undisturbed tone that sounded oddly as if it were all about someone else, not him.

"That's because most of them are apparently stuck in time a decade ago."

He walked around the desk and stopped in front of her. Too closely in front of her. She could feel his heat, could smell the faint scent of soap, and suddenly she could barely breathe. And then he reached out and cupped her face in his hands, and she forgot about breathing altogether.

"Nobody in this town ever stood up for me the way you just did."

He leaned forward and planted a light kiss on her forehead. Her blush returned twofold; she wasn't sure if it was because he was kissing her like a child or a sister, or because even this slight touch of his lips sent a rush of heat through her.

Before she could decide on that, he leaned forward again and this time gently kissed the end of her nose. Definitely sister, she thought, but again heat rippled through her.

She tried to tamp down her response, but it seemed already out of control. And when he pulled back just slightly and she realized he was staring at her mouth, it was all she could do to stop herself from closing the gap between them.

As soon as she thought it, he did what she'd longed to. He lowered his head, his mouth brushing hers, then returning, lingering. And Amelia knew that the heat she'd felt before had been a mere flicker.

His lips were warm and firm, but that alone surely wasn't enough to send this wave of sensation rocketing through her. Nor was the way he moved his mouth on hers, gently, slowly, coaxingly....

She heard a tiny moaning sound and was amazed to realize it had come from her. Luke seemed to take it as a sign and deepened the kiss. And then she felt the incredibly hot, erotic swipe of his tongue over her lips, and she gasped at the pleasurable shock. She opened for him without thought, eagerly. He probed deeper, tasting, and Amelia felt a tremor that she couldn't be sure started in her or him.

At last he broke the kiss and drew back. She smothered the sound of protest that rose to her lips; she couldn't believe what she'd done. He was staring down at her, his breath coming hard and fast, and the only thing that saved her from total embarrassment was the look of stunned wonder in his eyes.

"Damn," he muttered.

Indeed, she thought, completely incapable of forming a coherent, audible response.

She was still unable to speak as he made some fumbling excuse and escaped. Only when she heard the roar of his bike did she let out a breath and sink down into her desk chair.

So that was it, she thought, still a bit dazed. That was the attraction of the bad boy. All these years she'd wondered why she was so fascinated. Now she knew.

He kissed like a fallen angel.

Damn. Damn, damn, damn.

Luke turned his bike inland, heading for the canyon in an instinctive need to put some distance between himself and the woman who had startled him with her response to a kiss that had been supposed to be merely a token of appreciation.

He had a sneaking suspicion his own response was driving him, as well, but there was no way get some distance there. Well, there was, and once he might have resorted to it, the numbing relief of booze or drugs, but not now.

He leaned into the turn onto the canyon road, laying the bike over hard. He accelerated out of the turn, and the bike obediently snapped upright. And he kept right on rolling the throttle forward.

For a few seconds he goosed it up to mind-clearing speed, feeling the power of the wind in his face and the tug of his hair as it whipped behind him. But he knew the cops kept a close watch on this stretch of road, and he didn't really want a speeding ticket, especially coupled with a helmet violation, so after too short a time he let it edge back down.

He pulled over at the spot near the end of the road where a gap in the hills gave a view down to the Pacific. The lay of the land was such that you could see only the water, not the sprawl of civilization beside it, and if you looked from just the right spot, you could convince yourself you were the only person for miles.

He used to love that feeling and had come up here often seeking it when he couldn't stand to be closed inside his other secret refuge. Seeking just a few moments of pretending he was alone, free of all the troubles down below. The canyon had been populated with wildlife then, including his favorites, the red-tailed hawk and the clever coyote.

It wouldn't last much longer, he thought, glancing over his shoulder at the seemingly inexorable march; bulldozers and graders were already at work on the hills behind him. Another wild place lost. The coyotes would adapt, they always did. And maybe even the hawks would survive.

It was creatures like him who had the problem. Who kept having to go farther and farther out to find the places that brought them wonder and peace.

But this time he had the feeling his usual places weren't going to bring him peace. Not when he could still feel Amelia's mouth beneath his, not when the tiny cry she had made echoed in his ears as surely as the rustle of the leaves in the afternoon sea breeze.

He heard the sound of a car and turned to look. His jaw tightened slightly when he saw the marked police unit. He relaxed slightly when he saw that the woman in the uniform wasn't much older than he was; it wasn't a cop he'd had a run in with before, at least.

She pulled up beside him, looked him over, and apparently decided on a neutral approach.

"Nice view."

He nodded.

"That all you're up here for?"

He resisted the urge to ask what else it could be, in this still-isolated area. Maybe she thought he was going to steal a bulldozer. But he'd learned—finally—it was more trouble than it was worth to antagonize the police.

"I used to live down there. I just wanted to see if it was the same up here."

She looked him up and down again, then at his bike, lingering on the winged symbol on the tank. "McGuire?"

Great, Luke groaned inwardly, *even cops I've never set eyes on know me.* He felt the old feelings welling up, the defensiveness, the urge to either answer sarcastically or clam up entirely.

With an effort, he said merely, "Yes."

He waited, leaving the ball in her court. Somewhat to his surprise, she only nodded and told him to have a nice day. He watched as she drove away and wondered if she would take up a position down the hill and wait for him.

He turned to look out toward the ocean again but finally had to admit it wasn't going to work this time, that the sense of solitude wasn't enough anymore. Maybe it was the cop's visit. Maybe it was the lurking presence of the heavy equipment that would soon turn this place into just one more housing development, or maybe he was simply anxious to get out of Santiago Beach.

Maybe it was just that he was an adult now, with problems too complex to be eased by a peaceful vista. But he knew that wasn't really true; he still found peace and comfort in the new wild places he'd found. Or maybe he was restless, anxious to get back to those places.

Maybe he was just restless, period, and that was what had sent him shooting up the hill to this place.

His mouth twisted. He knew perfectly well what had sent him screaming up here, and her name was Amelia.

He reached for the helmet he'd forgone on the way up

and jammed it on, for the benefit of the cop he figured would be waiting for him. He started the bike, wheeled it around and started down the hill at a much more decorous pace than he'd come up it. And when he passed the police car, parked and waiting, pointed down the hill to come after him if necessary, he nodded and waved; it could have been worse, he thought.

It could have been Jim Stavros, who had made a special trip to Amelia's store just to warn her about him.

He smiled behind the helmet as he remembered how quiet, reserved Ms. Blair had stood up for him. It had happened rarely enough in his life, certainly not often enough for him to take it for granted. And never here.

And she hadn't even asked him, despite the pointed hint, what he was doing now.

Maybe she thought she already knew, he thought, a little grimly. Maybe she figured, like everyone else did, that he was up to no good like always.

But surely she wouldn't have kissed him then? Because she hadn't just let him kiss her; she had kissed him back. It had been hesitant and unpracticed, but she *had* kissed him back.

The heated memories stormed back into the front of his mind from where they'd been lurking not far away ever since it had happened.

So much for quiet and reserved; she'd almost fried him with that kiss.

Distance. That was what he needed, distance from the unexpectedly explosive woman who hid that fire behind a facade of reserve and shyness.

He was still pondering—dangerously, he knew—the possibilities there as he reached the bottom of the canyon road and headed back toward town. A convenience store with a boarded-up front window caught his eye for a moment—it hadn't been like that yesterday, he thought—but nothing was quite distracting enough to keep his mind occupied.

Back at the motel, he had his duffel bag inside and was dragging out the clothes he'd just laundered before he noticed the message light was lit on the telephone.

He crossed the room and dialed the office; the small motel didn't run to sophisticated voice mail. A female voice came on the line—the wife of the man who had checked him in, Luke supposed. He'd said he and "the missus" ran the place.

The tiniest hint of curiosity came into her voice when she realized who was calling. He tried to ignore it, tried not to think of what she might have heard that would make her suddenly interested in a guest who'd been there a couple of days already.

"The message?" he prompted.

"Oh, of course." He heard the rustle of paper. "Here it is. It's from Amelia Blair and says 'David went home. He's grounded for a month.' That's all."

Luke let out a sigh of relief. Grounded for a month seemed rather mild, compared to his own history with their mother's punishments.

And then his brow furrowed. "Did she say Amelia Blair?"

"Yes, that's what it is. I always make sure I get names right."

"I mean, did she say Blair, or did you ask her last name?"

"She said it. I only asked how to spell it."

"Thanks," he said, and hung up.

She'd said her last name? How many Amelias did she think he knew here? Was it simply a habit, to give her last name when leaving a message?

Or had she done it intentionally, given that formal "Amelia Blair" as if they weren't even on a first-name basis?

Irritation spiked through him at that thought. But it was quickly followed by a sheepish realization. Hadn't he just been recommending to himself that he put some distance between them? But when it seemed she might be doing the same, all of a sudden he wasn't happy with the idea.

His mouth twitched at his own rueful self-assessment. For somebody who had spent his childhood all too aware that life could be very inequitable, he'd just pulled a beaut. If he was going to pull back, then she had the same right.

If he didn't like that, then maybe he needed to think about why.

And if he didn't want to think about it, maybe he needed to figure out the why of that, too.

Chapter 9

" ——Child is going to turn out just like his brother, you mark my words."

This had to be a record, Amelia thought; Mrs. Clancy came in regularly, but never three days in one week. And this time she didn't seem interested in even pretending to look for something to buy; she'd headed for Amelia the moment she'd spotted her and started right in.

"My George spoke to Mrs. Hanson from the convenience store this morning, and she's certain the Hiller boy and his friends are responsible for that broken window. And no doubt that fire in the Dumpster behind the library and destroying the playground in the park."

"David has been grounded," Amelia said; perhaps she shouldn't let that out, but she wanted to nip this in the bud.

"Well, he hasn't let that stop him," Mrs. Clancy said with a sniff. "I saw him and those other delinquents just last night, as we came out of the movie theater. Nearly midnight, when he should have been at home."

Amelia frowned. "You're certain it was David?"

"Of course I am. My eyes are still sharp, girl."

If she was right, then David must be sneaking out, Amelia thought, stifling a sigh. And if he was, he was headed for even more trouble.

"You're not still seeing that boy, are you?"

"David?" Amelia asked, knowing perfectly well what the woman meant.

"Don't you get smart with me," Mrs. Clancy warned. "You know who I mean."

The last thing she needed was the imperious woman angry at her, so Amelia answered by stating a truth she wasn't necessarily happy with. She hadn't seen or heard from Luke since he'd kissed her, and she didn't like any of the reasons that she could come up with.

"I haven't been 'seeing' him at all, not in that sense," Amelia said, neglecting to mention that the idea of spending more time with Luke was oddly exhilarating, considering that she was spending most of her time telling herself that that kiss had meant nothing. That he was probably used to kissing women like that all the time. That he'd only meant to thank her for standing up for him to Jim, not curl her toes and very nearly her hair. It wasn't his fault if she'd...overreacted.

You reacted, she told herself wryly, *like a love-starved prude who suddenly woke up. You probably embarrassed him, that's why he took off running like that. He'd been saying a simple thank-you, and you reacted as if he'd declared undying love.*

"—of your reputation. People will talk, you know." And some of them, Amelia thought wearily, will talk endlessly. "For one thing, you must be years older than he is."

"Thank you for pointing that out," Amelia said, her tone a bit acid; she'd done the math long ago. But her sarcasm was lost amid the continuing lecture.

"And for all we know, *he's* the one behind all this vandalism. It's just the sort of thing he'd do."

What happened to your certainty it was David? Amelia wondered. Mrs. Clancy was one of her best customers, and she'd never had a problem with her before, had always thought of her as set in her ways but a good person at heart. But if the woman told her one more time what a wastrel, cad and scoundrel Luke was, she was going to say something rude.

Or at least give the woman a current dictionary, so she could pick out some new words, perhaps rooted in this century.

"Remember your gardenia, Mrs. Clancy?" Amelia said, not caring that she'd interrupted the woman's latest harangue.

"My gardenia?" the woman said, startled.

"Yes. Remember all the trouble you had when you first got it? All the books you had to consult, to get the soil and conditions just right so it would bloom?"

"Well, of course." The woman shook her head, but there was a note of pride in her voice. "Took me nearly three years to get that bush to bloom. But now it's the best in town, probably even in the county."

"Why didn't you give up on it?"

"Give up? I knew I just had to find the right combination, and with enough care and attention it would thrive."

"So you'd say it changed a great deal from the troublesome plant you first bought?"

"Well…yes."

"If a plant can do it, Mrs. Clancy, why can't a person?"

There were a few seconds' delay before the woman got her point. Then she frowned, her face as set as her mind apparently was.

"You're too generous, girl. Luke McGuire will never change."

Amelia's jaw tightened with determination. "You know, walking past your garden today, you would never know what he once did to it. I'll bet that before he came back,

even you had forgotten. But he didn't. It's been ten years,
and he still feels guilty.''

''As well he should.''

''But don't you see?'' Amelia said, sounding almost urgent, even to her own ears. ''If he was as bad as you've
painted him, he wouldn't care at all.''

Mrs. Clancy opened her mouth to retort. Then closed it.
Her frown deepened.

Amelia could only hope it was because she was having
to think about her hatred, probably for the first time in a
decade.

When the woman finally left, Amelia breathed a heartfelt
sigh of relief. She didn't know how much more of this advice giving she could take, however well-intentioned it
might be. She supposed she should be happy that people
cared enough to warn her. And she might be, were it not for
the niggling certainty that it was mainly the fact that it was
Luke who was garnering her all this concern.

Think about David, she ordered herself.

The problem was, she didn't know what else to do. To
the outside eye, the boy had a good—even enviable, if com-
forts and money were your standards—home. And his
mother had become the proverbial pillar of the community;
she might once have been the subject of gossip, but now she
was the object of admiration for overcoming a rocky start,
and even more for having done it with the drawback of a
ne'er-do-well son like Luke.

Too bad they weren't as generous when it came to that
son.

And there she was, back on that channel again. For nearly
two days she'd waited, wondered what he was thinking, if
she would hear from him, until finally she was convinced
she was either losing her mind or a fool, and she wasn't sure
which of the two she preferred.

She'd even sunk to driving by the motel this morning after
her kickboxing class—a class she'd attacked with a bit more

vehemence than usual—telling herself it was only a block out of her way. His motorcycle hadn't been parked outside his room, and she was torn between wondering where he was and wondering if he was even still in town at all.

The possibility that he'd simply left without a word to her stung. But she couldn't deny it was a possibility. He hardly owed her a formal goodbye, just because of one kiss.

David was another matter. Surely he wouldn't leave without saying goodbye to his brother?

But if David was still angry, as his actions seemed to indicate, he might well be in no mood to see his brother at all. And it was David she should be worried about, not her own silly feelings. It wasn't David's fault if she let her imagination run away with her every time she saw his brother.

It wasn't Luke's fault, either, really, she admitted wryly as she called up her accounting program on the computer, desperate enough for distraction to tackle even that. He was probably trying to be kind by staying away, so she didn't get any silly ideas. Any more than she already had, anyway.

When the door alarm activated, she instinctively smiled at the classic voice of Mr. Spock, but inside she was chanting to her heart not to leap, her eyes not to snap toward the door in hope....

It was David.

He looked ragged enough for Mrs. Clancy to have been right about him being out all night. And suddenly she didn't know what to do or say. The closer the boy got to the edge, the more afraid she was that she might inadvertently push him even further. So when he came to a stop beside the counter, the only thing she could think of to say was, "Are you all right?"

David shrugged.

She tried again. "I heard you got grounded."

He shrugged again. But this time at least he spoke. "It's not so bad, if you know how to get around it."

"Are you getting around it now?"

A third shrug. He was working awfully hard to give the impression he didn't care. "She thinks I'm in one of her stupid summer classes. And since she's off on her crusade again, she doesn't care, really."

"David—"

"And don't tell me she does. She doesn't know how."

"I won't try to change your mind about that, David," she said, not wanting to make it more difficult for the boy to get along with his mother, but not wanting to deny what she suspected was the truth, either. "But if you think you have it bad, imagine how it must feel to be the reason your mother's on this crusade. To know she blames you for ruining her life."

For a moment David's mouth tightened stubbornly. Clearly he was still angry at his brother. But then what she'd said must have gotten through.

"Yeah, I know she blames him. Like there's anything to blame him for. She's got such a tough life," David added sarcastically.

"Do you remember your grandmother?"

"Not really. I was just a baby when she died. And my mother never talks about her much. I think she was a real nasty old witch, though." He gave Amelia a sideways look. "And yeah, I know, that's probably why Mom's the way she is."

"Doesn't make it any easier to live with though, does it?" Amelia asked sympathetically.

"I think the old bat was awful to Luke, too."

Well, Amelia thought, if he realized that, maybe he was coming around as far as his brother was concerned.

"Why don't you ask him?" When he didn't answer, she added, "Or are you still not speaking to him?"

David took a deep breath. He stared down at the counter. "I thought he'd understand. I thought he'd get me out of here."

"He does understand. But unfortunately, everything he

said was true. No official agency would let you live with him over your mother. He didn't make the laws, David.''

His head came up then. ''No, but all of a sudden he's living by them?''

''Is that what you want, for him to break the law for you? End up in trouble all over again?''

David didn't answer, but he did look uncomfortable. So he wasn't *that* angry with Luke. She decided to press the point and maybe wake him up a little about his own actions, as well.

''Or maybe you'd just rather get in trouble yourself, so he can feel even more guilty about the example he set for you?''

His eyes widened slightly, then his gaze darted away, and she knew she'd struck a nerve. With a sinking feeling inside, she realized Mrs. Clancy was probably right about what he'd been up to.

''You know,'' she said, ''there are some people in town who are blaming your brother for what's going on, all the vandalism and break-ins. Don't you think he's taken enough heat around here without taking yours, too?''

''I can't help who they blame,'' David said; it wasn't quite an admission, but it was close. She changed tacks.

''Maybe your mother doesn't care like she should, David. Maybe she never learned how. But you know I care. And your brother cares, too.''

''Yeah?'' It was disbelieving, but not sarcastic, giving Amelia hope.

''Yes. He told me you were the only good memory he had of this place.''

David looked startled at that. ''He did?''

She nodded. ''He came a long way, just to see if he could help. He probably already knew he couldn't do what you wanted him to, but he came anyway. Because he cares.''

David studied her for a moment. ''How come you're not

like the rest of them? You don't hate him for what he did back then.''

"Well, I wasn't here then. I didn't know him—"

"A lot of them didn't, either. But they heard bad things and they believed them, and hated him even though he never did nothing to them.''

"I try not to judge people on hearsay," Amelia said, realizing even as she said it that she sounded a bit self-righteous. So she added, with a smile, "And I guess maybe I've always had a thing for the underdog."

Or bad boys, she admitted silently. For whatever reason, it was true. Maybe because she'd always been so blessed good all her life, people who weren't fascinated her. Of course, it didn't hurt that this one looked like something from that slightly wicked, wrong kind of paradise.

Mr. Spock spoke again, and this time she looked up eagerly and with hope. David was feeling much more favorably toward his brother now; if it was Luke...

It was Snake. And entourage.

Amelia went instantly on guard.

"Hey, Hiller-man, what're you doin' in this place?"

"Just hanging out," David said, and already Amelia could see the change in him. He was suddenly slouching, and his entire expression had changed to one of cocky insolence touched with chronic anger.

"She's a little old for you, isn't she?" one of the other boys said, with a snicker.

"And boring, like these books," Snake said, giving Amelia a look that reminded her rather forcefully of the knife he no doubt had in his pocket. But he turned back to David then, and Amelia cravenly let out an inaudible breath of relief.

"You want to hang with us," Snake said, "you can't keep comin' here. Makes you look like a wimp, you know?"

"Yeah, sure," David said with a shrug.

"C'mon, man, we got plans to make before midnight."

"Sure," David said again.

And just like that he walked out with them, leaving Amelia stunned anew at the power of peer pressure.

And more worried than ever that David was headed for serious trouble.

"Going to be with us much longer?"

Luke grimaced as he handed the motel night manager another day's rent for tomorrow. "I don't know."

He hadn't intended to be here this long. And for the past two days, he'd just hung around doing not much of anything, except going through the money he'd allotted for the trip.

He should have just kept right on going, he thought as he headed back toward his room, after he'd left the bookstore that evening. Should have pointed the bike north, and by 3:00 a.m. he would have been home. Back in the mountains, the river country, where he'd finally found his life.

And only the fact that it would look like he was running from Amelia had stopped him from doing just that.

Oh? And wouldn't you have been?

He'd been hearing way too much of that little voice in his head lately. Once it had encouraged him to take the chances that most of the time landed him in trouble, now it just seemed to nag him. Hoping to shut it off, he retreated to his room, picked up his book, and settled in to read.

He finished the book all too soon, freeing his mind to wander. Except that it didn't; it went straight back to exactly where he didn't want it to go.

It was only a kiss, for God's sake. What was wrong with him? He'd kissed lots of women before. Just because he hadn't meant to kiss this one but hadn't been able to stop himself didn't have to mean anything. Just because he'd only meant to make it a quick, brotherly kiss and had lost control of it didn't have to mean anything.

The instant fire that had blazed along his nerves was a bit harder to explain away.

He glanced at his watch. Not yet midnight. Maybe he would go for a ride, blow out the cobwebs.

Then again, he thought, maybe not; it might not be late to him, but to most of Santiago Beach it was the middle of the night, and he didn't want to add fuel to the fire by waking up the whole town snarling up and down their streets. Time was that would have been his sole goal in life, but things had changed.

But he could take a walk, as he often did when he couldn't sleep at night. It wouldn't be at all the same here, but maybe it would help.

Or maybe, he thought after he'd been tramping a half an hour along a sidewalk that seemed to him too level and civilized for a real walk, it would make things worse.

He hadn't intended to do it, but he'd been so busy fighting off the persistent thoughts of Amelia and memories of that kiss that he hadn't paid much attention to where he was going. And now he was here, as if his feet had remembered the way and forgotten to mention to his mind where they were going.

He stopped at the corner, under the big hibiscus tree, staring down at the big white house in the middle of the block. His mother had been so proud of that house. No doubt she still was. The new husband she'd acquired when Luke was ten would have preferred something less grand, something designed a bit more with children in mind—he'd wanted lots of them, Luke remembered now. But then as later, Jackie got what she wanted. So Luke had spent eight years in that house, afraid to touch anything outside his own room and aware that his mother begrudged him even that much space.

She'd even resented the time Ed Hiller had spent with Luke, and sometimes Luke thought she'd had David partly to cut down on that as well as to insure that Ed stayed in line. The other part was the fulfilling of the one desire her husband had expressed; she'd presented him with a son of his own and expected him to be happy with that.

And Ed had been. He'd loved David with all his heart and still had enough left over to give his stepson a little. He'd wanted more children, and Luke knew he would have loved them all, but his wife had said one was enough. Even then, he hadn't counted.

He watched the darkened house and wondered if everyone who came back home felt this odd sense of distance, as if what had happened here had happened to someone else. It wasn't that it was any better, looking back, it was simply that it didn't matter as much as it once had. Once it had been the core of his life, fueling his anger and drive to make as much trouble as he could. Now…now it was cooling embers, requiring intentional stirring and added fuel to produce any heat.

A movement at the side of the house yanked him out of his reverie.

He leaned forward, eyes narrowing as he looked into the deep shadows along the four-car garage. He'd just about decided he'd imagined it when something moved again, low down, next to the white wall. It was awfully big for a local animal, unless the Langs still lived down the street and still fancied Newfoundlands.

And then the shape stood up, and he knew from the height, the baggy cargo pants and the backward baseball cap that it was David.

He wondered if his brother had taken the same way out he always had, through the bathroom window that opened over the garage roof, then down the back side, where you could just reach the edge of the patio roof. He'd never taken the boy with him, but he supposed he could have watched. And remembered.

David moved stealthily toward the sidewalk, then up the street, away from where Luke was hidden in the shadow of the hibiscus. As David neared the corner, Luke saw two more figures appear, carrying backpacks. The three waited, and a few minutes later three more arrived. Then the six took off with purposeful yet furtive strides, heads swiveling as they checked their surroundings constantly.

Luke knew that look. He knew exactly how it felt to be constantly on the watch, ready to run if you were spotted by the wrong person.

He also knew what it meant. He'd done it too often himself to forget; David and his buddies were up to something they shouldn't be.

He waited until they were just out of sight, then started after them. He wasn't sure what he was going to do, but he couldn't not go.

He hadn't gone far when he realized the follower himself was being followed. A car was behind him, a small black coupe, keeping its distance, but never so far that the driver would lose sight of him. He wondered if maybe it was an undercover police car, but it looked pretty racy for that, unless things had changed mightily at Santiago Beach PD.

His attention now split between the boys up ahead and the car behind, he kept going. It was an odd sort of real, physical flashback to a time when skulking along darkened streets had been a regular habit of his.

They reached Main Street, and Luke knew he would have to be careful now. There was too much open space, too many places where his quarry could spot him. If they turned north, there wasn't much cover; if they went south, there was an occasional recessed doorway in front of the businesses along the block that would afford some cover, and the courtyard of the community center, with all its trees and benches.

He got lucky, they went south.

He'd been so focused on them for the moment that he didn't realize the car had stopped until he paused at the corner to let the boys get far enough away. He glanced back; the black coupe was parked now, and just as he looked, the headlights went out. He turned back and leaned to look

around the corner; the boys were walking slowly, watch-
fully, and he knew he had to give them more space.

"Luke!"

The whisper was just loud enough for him to hear, but
still he nearly whacked his head on the sign advertising
T-shirts at the corner tourist trap as he whipped around at
the unexpected sound of his name.

Amelia. Of all the people he might have expected to come
across prowling around in the middle of the night, she would
have been the last.

"What are you doing here?" he asked, still shaking off
the vestiges of the alarm she'd given him.

"The same thing you are, I think," she whispered back.
"I heard David's...friends talking about something happen-
ing at midnight tonight, so I followed him."

He stared at her. "You came out in the middle of the
night, following that pack of kids, when you know at least
one of them is carrying a weapon? And you think you're
not brave?"

"I'm just trying to help David. That's not bravery."

"The heck it's not," he said softly.

He leaned back to glance around the corner of the building
again. The boys were three blocks down, heading toward the
beach.

"Much farther and they'll be out of sight," he said, giving
up on the whisper but still speaking quietly.

"Then let's go."

He looked back at her. "I suppose it's useless to say let
me handle this?"

"I can help," she insisted. "David's still a little angry
with you, but I don't think he would do anything...stupid
in front of me."

"I hope you're right," Luke muttered.

They started down the street. They had to be careful, because every few minutes one of the boys would look around;

they were obviously worried about being followed or spotted.

"You're good at this," Amelia said when Luke pulled her into the doorway of what had been a jewelry store but was now a surf-wear shop, the third time they'd dodged out of sight.

"I did enough sneaking up and down this street at night myself," he told her. "The names have changed, but the terrain hasn't."

A half block later, when the whole group of boys stopped and looked around carefully, Amelia said rather despondently, "They really are up to no good, aren't they?"

"Looks like it," Luke said, feeling rather grim himself.

"Then they really are the ones who broke that window and vandalized the playground."

Luke twisted around to look at her. "What?"

"The front window at the convenience store up on the highway was shattered, and all the gym equipment on the playground at the park was broken up."

"I saw the window boarded up," Luke said, turning to look back down the street. The boys hadn't moved. "Uh-oh."

"What?"

"They've stopped moving."

"Maybe they've changed their minds," Amelia said hopefully.

"That optimism of yours again." Luke wondered if he'd ever been that upbeat in his life. He doubted it. "They're being careful so they don't get caught."

"Then...shouldn't we stop them?"

"How?"

"I don't know. Talk them out of it or something."

Luke shook his head wryly. "Those boys aren't listening. To anyone. If they were, they wouldn't be here."

"But we have to try, don't we? David might listen to me. He always has."

"He might, normally." When he saw her brow furrow in puzzlement he tried to explain. "Normally he might listen, and I know you're a good persuader...you could sure talk me into or out of about anything. But he's in front of his friends right now. And with a guy that age, he'd sooner die than go against them or let some girl talk him out of their macho plan."

Amelia just looked at him for a long, silent moment. Even in the faint light he could see her big eyes widen even further, and only when she finally spoke did he realize what part of what he'd said she had fixated on.

"I...could?"

It took him a moment to figure out what she meant. And then he was grateful for the dim light, because he was sure he was blushing as his own words came back to him. *You could sure talk me into or out of about anything....*

Especially out of my clothes, he added to himself, bracing himself against the rush of heated sensation that rippled through him at the thought of being naked with her. A mere kiss had been like shooting class-five rapids; anything more would be like going over the falls. Or running a river everyone said was unrunnable.

The problem, of course, was living to tell about it.

"Luke?"

Her soft voicing of his name sent another burst of heat through him. With an effort he beat it back and leaned out to look down the street once more.

They were gone.

Luke swore under his breath, then held up a hand to forestall Amelia's natural query. He listened, and in the night air could hear the sound of movement and, once, the clank of metal on metal.

"Whatever they're going to do, they've started."

They began to hurry, still maintaining as much cover as he could. But he doubted the boys were looking now; they'd obviously decided they were clear.

The Silhouette Reader Service™ — Here's how it works:

Accepting your 2 free books and gift places you under no obligation to buy anything. You may keep the books and gift and return the shipping statement marked "cancel." If you do not cancel, about a month later we'll send you 6 additional novels and bill you just $3.80 each in the U.S., or $4.21 each in Canada, plus 25¢ shipping & handling per book and applicable taxes if any.* That's the complete price and — compared to cover prices of $4.50 each in the U.S. and $5.25 each in Canada — it's quite a bargain! You may cancel at any time, but if you choose to continue, every month we'll send you 6 more books, which you may either purchase at the discount price or return to us and cancel your subscription.
*Terms and prices subject to change without notice. Sales tax applicable in N.Y. Canadian residents will be charged applicable provincial taxes and GST.

Play The Lucky Hearts Game

and get...

FREE BOOKS & a FREE GIFT... YOURS to KEEP!

Yes! I have scratched off the silver card. Please send me my **2 FREE BOOKS** and **FREE MYSTERY GIFT**. I understand that I am under no obligation to purchase any books as explained on the back of this card.

Scratch Here!
then look below to see
what your cards get you...

DETACH AND MAIL CARD TODAY! (S-IM-OS-10/00)

345 SDL C6KG   **245 SDL C6KC**

NAME   (PLEASE PRINT CLEARLY)

ADDRESS

APT.#   CITY

STATE/PROV.   ZIP/POSTAL CODE

Twenty-one gets you
2 FREE BOOKS and a
FREE MYSTERY GIFT!

Twenty gets you
2 FREE BOOKS!

Nineteen gets you
1 FREE BOOK!

TRY AGAIN!

Visit us online at

www.eHarlequin.com

Offer limited to one per household and not valid to current Silhouette Intimate Moments® subscribers. All orders subject to approval.

"It's the community center," Amelia whispered when they got close enough to see exactly where the boys had stopped. "I wonder—"

He stopped her with a sharp gesture as he spotted one of the boys as he crossed in front of a light patch of wall. Then he swore again, low and harsh.

"He's got a gas can."

"Gas—" Amelia began, breaking off when the obvious answer came to her. "Oh, God, no, they wouldn't."

"Don't you doubt it," Luke said grimly.

"Luke, we've got to stop them! If they burn down the community center... I've got my cell phone."

He knew she was right. And for the first time he considered actually calling the police. But he knew too well what would happen to his brother if he did.

"Maybe I can scare them off," he said.

"Maybe *we* can," Amelia corrected. He started to protest but saw by the set of her jaw there was no point. He gave in, making a mental note to discuss her supposed timidity later.

"Dial 911 and keep it in your hand, ready to send," he said. Amelia did as he said, and then they began to move again.

The boy with the gas can spotted them first. He yelled a warning, and the other boys whipped around. David was the first to recognize them. He let out a string of curses that would have done Luke proud at that age.

"Evening, boys," Luke drawled. "Planning a weenie roast?"

"They'll tell my mom," David said rather desperately, and not to anyone in particular. "She'll lock me up for the rest of my life!"

And then, before anyone could react, he whirled and ran, darting through the alley. He was out of sight in seconds.

And Luke and Amelia stood facing five very angry young men, one holding a gas can that was leaking, the fumes getting stronger as he sloshed it around menacingly, and one flipping open his deadly blade.

Snake took a step toward them, knife at the ready. His eyes narrowed as he looked at Amelia.

''You do anything with that phone, bitch, and I'll cut your throat.''

Luke's jaw tightened as the boy threatened her. And he wondered if he remembered enough about knife fighting to keep her alive.

Chapter 10

"Look, why don't we all just go home and forget about this?" Amelia said. It took every bit of control she had to keep her voice from shaking with fear.

"Why don't you just go on back to your books?" Snake said with a sneer. "Leave the real life to us. You can't handle it."

Amelia nearly gasped aloud. How had he done it, this angry street kid? How had he seen through her, down to the depths of her frightened soul, to the basic fear she lived with every day, that she was too much of a coward for real life, that that was the basis of her love of books and her faint-heartedness everywhere else?

"Don't," Luke said, "bite off more than *you* can handle."

As shaken as she was, Amelia couldn't miss the quiet warning in Luke's voice. She glanced at him, and there was not a trace of the fear she was feeling. She could see the faint glint of the gold earring and thought inanely of pirates repelling boarders.

"I keep hearin' what a tough guy you are," Snake said, waving his knife for emphasis. "But I don't think I believe it. I think you're all talk, like that mommy-whupped little brother of yours. Poor little rich kid."

Amelia forced herself to focus; her own pride didn't matter right now. And she didn't like the way Luke moved, the way he shifted his weight, the way he was standing there eyeing the five of them as if fighting were an option. "Luke, let's get out of here."

Snake laughed. "Yeah, you listen to the book lady here. Run, like your brother did."

"There's five of them. Come on," Amelia insisted.

"That's the way it works," he said to her, although he never took his eyes off Snake and the others. "Guys like this don't have the guts to stand by themselves, so they have to travel in packs."

Snake stiffened and muttered a name involving Luke's mother that make him laugh ironically. That was the last straw piled on Snake's uncertain temper; he leapt at Luke, knife at the ready.

Amelia smothered her instinctive scream. She stared at the oddly graceful dance that was unfolding. Snake stabbing, Luke dodging. The others closing in around them. Snake had the weapon, but Luke was bigger. Stronger. And, oddly, quicker.

The two circled. Feint, feint, stab, dodge. Seconds passed before Amelia remembered.

"Idiot!" she snapped at herself. And lifted her cell phone.

The next thing she knew was an explosion of pain through her wrist. She cried out, unable to stop the sound. The phone clattered on the ground. Her attacker, the one with the gas can, stomped on it with a booted foot.

Luke's head whipped around at the sound of her cry.

Snake attacked.

Luke went down under the rush, and the two rolled on the asphalt.

My fault, my fault. The words rang in her head, the power of the guilt shoving aside even the pain of her wrist. Luke could be killed with that wicked knife, and it would be her fault.

And then they were up again. Luke broke free, seemingly unhurt. Snake, however, had a bloody nose. And he was no longer cocky; she could see in his face that he was enraged.

"Watch her!" Snake said to the boy with the can. "We'll take him!"

Warily, one of the others began to circle Luke. Frantically Amelia looked around for a weapon, anything. There was nothing nearby except for the gas can abandoned when the boy carrying it had seen her try to use the phone.

The two boys answering Snake's order lunged. Luke ducked. The two collided, one of them going down. Luke let momentum carry the other boy stumbling over him, careening into Snake. They both went down, the one swearing a string of curses as Snake's blade sliced him. Luke spun around just as a fourth one leaped. He drove a shoulder into the boy's belly and dropped him breathless to the ground.

Her guardian forgot all about watching her. He started toward the fray.

Stop him, stop him, stop him!

Desperate, Amelia grabbed the gas can and swung it in an arc toward the boy. The handle was slippery with the oily contents, and the pungent liquid sprayed out, drenching him. He staggered back, screaming as he rubbed at his face and eyes.

Snake was up. He came at Luke furiously. The vicious blade glinted. The boy who had merely collided with the other one and wasn't winded started toward Luke from behind.

Amelia ran toward them. It was as if her body had taken over from her paralyzed mind. It went into the movements so often practiced, the muscles moving in a way they knew well. Her mind seemed to be reacting, recording, rather than initiating.

One. Two. Three. Up. Snap. Kick. Contact.

She wasn't sure what she connected with. Harder than a stomach, softer than a joint. But it gave.

Leg back. Tuck. Land. Flex. Balance.

She overbalanced and had to catch herself. She took a deep breath, trying to steady the shaking that had begun. By the time she recovered, Luke was beside her. He had Snake's knife in his hand.

She lifted her head and saw the boy she'd hit disappearing around the corner of the building. The smell of gasoline permeated the air. And they were alone.

She blinked.

"—all right?"

Luke had been talking to her, she realized suddenly. "I...yes."

"You're sure?"

She nodded. She gave herself a mental shake. "You? Are you all right?" When he nodded in turn, she pressed the matter. "Are *you* sure? That knife..."

He lifted the blade and flicked it shut with a quick motion that spoke of familiarity. "Did some damage to my shirt and nicked a knuckle, but that's about it."

She looked at his hands, saw the tracing of blood down his right index finger. It didn't look serious, and he was upright and talking normally, so with relief she accepted his assessment. And with that relief came a sudden weakness in her knees.

She almost fell, but he caught her. He moved until he was leaning against the wall, the yellow light from an outdoor wall sconce spilling over them. She shivered despite the warmth of the summer night. He pulled her against him, and she instinctively snuggled into the warmth of his body.

"Thanks," he said.

"What?" She was puzzled, but unwilling to part with his warmth even long enough to look up at him.

One of his hands came up to stroke her hair. It felt as good as his warmth. "If you hadn't taken those guys out, I would have been dead meat."

"Too slow," she said with a sigh, knowing it was true, she'd waited a shamefully long time before reacting. Fear, her old nemesis.

"Slow? Man, that flying kick move of yours is really something. You'll have to teach it to me."

"I'd rather," she said frankly "just avoid situations like that one."

She felt him chuckle before she heard it. "As I recall, you jumped into this one with both feet well before you saved my butt."

She drew back then, looking up at him. "What else could I do? David was headed for trouble. I had to do something."

His arm tightened around her. "I'm glad for his sake there's someone here with the nerve to care that much."

"Nerve? No." She lowered her head and finished sadly, "I'm the world's biggest chicken."

She felt his arm move, then his finger under her chin, gently lifting her head. There was something in his eyes that warmed her as much as his body heat, but in a very different way.

"You've got a very mistaken idea about nerve," he said.

She shook her head. In the aftermath of a confrontation that had left her feeling utterly drained, she didn't have the energy to dissemble or deny. "I'm always afraid. Of anything new or the least bit risky."

"So is that really why you have all those posters up in your office?"

"Maybe I'm hoping some of it will rub off," she said, knowing how silly it sounded.

"Amelia, Amelia," he said, shaking his head, a small smile lifting one corner of his mouth. "Any fool who's too dumb to be afraid can wade into the middle of a fight. That doesn't take nerve, that's just stupidity. Now somebody with the sense to be afraid but who tries anyway…that's courage.''

She wanted to accept his words, but the memory of how she'd stood frozen while he'd been fighting for his life made it hard.

''And that,'' he said, ''you've got. Lots of it.''

He believed it. She could see it in his eyes, in his face. But her own doubts must have shown, because he went on.

''And you do something that takes even more nerve, Amelia. You care. I wish I'd had somebody like you when I was David's age.''

Moisture brimmed in her eyes at this unexpected declaration. ''Luke,'' she breathed, unable to say anything more.

''But,'' he added, his voice suddenly thick and husky, ''I'm glad I'm my age. That way I won't feel guilty for this.''

He lowered his head and took her mouth, suddenly, fiercely. It was aftershock, she told herself, all the while knowing that what it was didn't matter, only *that* it was, that *they* were, in this moment, in this place.

She wasn't shocked this time, but that didn't lessen the effect of his kiss. It didn't lessen the heat that shot through her, didn't lessen the sizzling tingle that raced along every nerve. She was more aware this time, and she liked the hot, male taste of him. So much that she ran her tongue over his lips as he had hers, then probed deeper, over the even ridge of his teeth. He opened for her eagerly, and Amelia savored his groan of pleasure.

When at last he broke the kiss, Luke sagged back against the wall. Amelia could hear his quickened breathing, could feel the hammering of his heart, and this physical proof that she wasn't alone in this did much to ease her qualms.

It was a long time before the absurdity of it hit her; here they were, the reek of gasoline all around them, having just survived what could have been a deadly altercation, in the middle of downtown, the most public place possible, kissing like a couple of teenagers with no place else to go. It was a miracle that no one had come upon them, not even a police car.

A police car.

"We should call the police," she said reluctantly.

Luke stiffened. She felt it, and went on in a rush.

"I know you don't have fond memories of them here, but we should still call them. I mean—" she made a gesture that included both the building and the abandoned gas can "—this could have been arson."

Luke let out a long, audible breath, and she felt him, if not relax, at least become less tense.

"Look, I know there are good cops out there. Real good ones. Maybe even some here. But David's headed for real trouble. Criminal trouble. Like you said, this could have been arson."

"And?" she prompted, sensing that he hadn't finished.

"And he's already got a strike against him, simply for being my brother."

He sounded...not angry, not even upset, but there was that weariness she'd heard before. She wondered if just being here had that effect on him.

"Give me another chance," Luke said, "to try and turn him around before he winds up, if not in handcuffs, at the least etched permanently in the minds of all the cops around here."

Amelia hesitated. She didn't want David in criminal trouble any more than Luke did, but in fact, he already *was*. At least, he was involved in criminal acts; he just hadn't gotten caught yet.

But she couldn't deny he was right, she'd seen too much evidence that everyone remembered Luke McGuire chiefly for getting into trouble. And she'd wondered herself if that wasn't a factor in David's problems, either him trying to live up—or down—to his brother's reputation, or everyone expecting him to.

"At least wait until morning. After some sleep, maybe things will be clearer," Luke urged.

Whether it was what he said, that it was Luke saying it, or the pleading note in his voice, Amelia gave in.

"All right," she said. "But I at least want to tell somebody about this gasoline, before somebody comes along and tosses a cigarette out and blows up half the block."

"The fire department," Luke suggested. Then, with a lopsided grin, "I never pissed any of them off, that I know of."

"You're—" She broke off. She'd been about to say "incorrigible" but had suddenly realized it was very close to true, legally speaking. He was lucky his mother hadn't tried to have him declared so.

Probably would have taken too much of her time, she thought sourly.

"Let's get out of here," Luke said, "and stop breathing these fumes."

"Yes, please," she agreed.

She went over to retrieve what was left of her cell phone. She picked it up, then looked at Luke. "In a way, he helped you out. I would have called 911 if he hadn't hit my wrist and made me drop it."

"He hit you?" Luke said with a frown. "Hard enough to make you drop it? I thought he'd just scared you."

"It's all right." She held out her right hand, flexing and curling her fingers. "Everything still works."

He took her hand in his and gently turned it, inspecting the wrist in the yellow light. She knew there was a red mark over the knobby bone below the thumb, but there was no other sign of injury.

"It could still be pretty bruised by tomorrow," he said. "You should ice it as soon as you can."

"I'll do that."

They headed back up the street toward her car, taking

deep breaths of clean, summer-warm air. Amelia stopped at a pay phone to make her call to the fire department. When they at last reached where she'd parked, Luke looked over the low-slung, expensive black coupe.

"Nice," he said.

"It was my father's. He bought it just before he died." She smiled sadly. "I pushed him to it, I'm afraid, trying to nudge him out of his apathy after my mother died. It's far too extravagant for me, but it seemed too much to start car shopping all over again when I don't drive that often."

"So you picked it out for him?"

She shrugged. "I guess you could say that. I tried to pick something racy, that would...energize him or something, I guess. It didn't work. He only drove it a couple of times."

"Does it energize you?"

She considered that. "I've driven it faster than any other car I've ever had. Does that count?"

He grinned. "It counts."

"Is that what does it for you? Fast cars?"

He gave her a long, steady look that made her suddenly nervous, wondering what he was thinking. But when he answered her, the answer was innocuous enough.

"I'll admit to a certain addiction to speed," he said. "But I don't play with that particular fire that much anymore."

The words *What fire do you play with?* rose to her lips, but with the old adage of not asking questions you don't want the answer to in mind, she held them back.

"Where's your bike?" she asked instead.

"I walked." That surprised her; it was a good two miles to the motel. It must have shown, because he shrugged and added, "I like to walk at night. Call it an old habit I never broke."

She wondered if that meant he wanted to continue to walk. But he had just been in a fight....

Just then he twisted slightly, as if testing for pain, and that decided her.

"Would you like a ride?"

After a bare moment's hesitation, he nodded. "Thanks." He nodded at the car. "Never even ridden in one of these."

"Do you want to drive it?" she asked impulsively. Then, embarrassed at herself, she stammered, "No, of course not. It's probably boring, after your motorcycle. That was silly. I—"

He cut across her nervous chatter. "I'd love to."

"I... All right." She handed him the keys.

He took a moment to familiarize himself with the controls, then settled down into the leather seat. "Any quirks?"

"No," she answered, then smiled. "Except it slides up to eighty real easy."

He laughed. She liked the sound of it and couldn't help thinking that he'd probably had little reason to laugh when he'd lived here. And wondered how long it had taken him to learn after he'd left.

"Mind if we take the scenic route?"

It was late, and she should be exhausted, especially after what they'd been through, but instead she found herself oddly exhilarated. "No, go ahead."

Somewhat to her surprise, he kept it well under eighty. They went rather sedately down the hill to the beach, where the pier stretched out to the ocean and the palm trees seemed to emphasize the balmy summer air. She rolled down her window to smell the salt air.

"I keep meaning to take my lunch and come down here to eat it," she said, gesturing at the picnic tables set up in the grassy park next to the sand. "But something always seems to come up. Odd to think that people travel days to come here, and I can't even make it for lunch when I'm a few blocks away."

He made the turn onto the loop that rimmed the pier area, with its tourist shops and restaurants, then started down the coast road that ran along the long stretch of sandy beach the town was gifted with. "I'll bet people who've lived a long time in Anaheim don't go to Disneyland much, either,'' he said.

"You think you ignore what's in your own backyard simply because it's in your own backyard?" she asked.

He shrugged. "I think if it's always been there, you sort of...overlook it. You don't go there because you always can. Maybe, to really appreciate something, it has to have been a dream you had to work to get."

"That's rather...profound."

He made a sound that seemed almost embarrassed. "Must be the adrenaline ebb." He gave her a sideways glance. "You do know that a crash is coming?"

He said it like someone who was very well acquainted with high-adrenaline situations and their aftermath. "So I've heard," she said.

Do you even know what he's doing now?

Jim's words came back to her. It seemed foolish, to be riding alone in a car—her car, which she'd turned over with barely a thought—with a man whose reputation in this town hadn't faded much in eight years of absence, when she knew so little about him.

But what was she supposed to do, just ask? With anybody else it would be a simple, reasonable question. But to the bad boy of Santiago Beach, it could sound like she thought the same thing the rest of the town did, that he was still up to no good.

But surely they'd passed beyond that, hadn't they? After all—

"Damn."

She snapped out of her indecisive wanderings. Immediately she saw the cause of his exclamation: flashing lights directly behind them. Startled, she asked, "Where did he come from?"

"Beside the Mexican restaurant." Luke's jaw was set as he slowed, then pulled over into the beach parking area.

"You weren't speeding," she said. "I wonder why he's stopping us."

He gave her a look that was ancient in its weariness. "In this town, I'm the only reason they need."

Amelia had her mouth open to protest that when the shout came from behind them for Luke to turn off the engine. She'd only been pulled over once in her life, but she was fairly certain this wasn't standard procedure; didn't the officer simply walk up to the car and ask to see your license?

It wasn't until Luke turned the ignition off that she realized the officer had called him by name. She twisted around to look, and to her shock saw that it was Jim Stavros.

And he was approaching with his hand on his weapon.

Luke looked at her. She wasn't sure if he looked angry or ill. Amelia swallowed tightly. Then her breath left her in a rush as she heard words she thought only happened in the big city or in the movies.

"McGuire! Out of the car. Slowly. And keep your hands where I can see them!"

"Welcome to my world," Luke said.

He got out of the car with his hands up.

Chapter 11

It was like living a flashback.

At the cop's order, Luke turned and put both his hands on the roof of the car. Next would come the pat-down search, then the handcuffs and finally the interrogation. It was old news, he'd been here before. It was beyond bothering him.

At least, it had been.

But now it was all going to happen in front of Amelia, and that made him queasy. It had been a long time since he'd felt utterly humiliated, but he had a feeling he was about to be reminded what it felt like.

Just as he thought it, Amelia leaned toward the driver's side and called out. "Jim?"

Great. She knew the guy.

It hit him then that this was the same cop who'd warned her off him the other day in the store. Did the guy work twenty-four hours a day or what?

"Are you all right, Amelia?" the cop asked.

Not daring to look at her, not wanting to see her face,

Luke stared down at the roof of the car as she opened her own door and got out. "Of course. What's wrong?"

"I saw your car. You're not usually out at this hour, so I took a look. Saw him—" he nodded at Luke "—driving, so I figured I'd better check."

"In other words," Luke said dryly, finally looking at her, "he thought I'd stolen your car and kidnapped you."

Amelia's eyes widened in shock.

"Still got an attitude on you, don't you, McGuire?" the cop said.

Amelia was gaping at them both. Luke knew this was probably utterly foreign to her; he doubted she'd ever been stopped by the police in her innocent life.

"This place just brings out the best in me," Luke said, knowing he sounded bitter but unable to help it. *Time to shut up,* he told himself, *when you start sounding like that.*

"We're keeping an eye on you," Jim warned. "Some people don't think it's coincidence that you arrive back in town and we start having a rash of crimes."

"Jim, no!" Amelia exclaimed. "You can't really believe that!"

"Didn't say I did. Just that some do."

"Mrs. Clancy, you mean," Amelia said. "And you know she's got it in for Luke."

She knew? Luke wondered. She'd heard suspicions that he might be involved, but she'd never said anything? And apparently never believed them? Something warm and unfamiliar expanded inside him as he looked at her.

Jim, his attention completely on Amelia now, said, "You're awfully quick to defend him."

"Maybe because everybody else around here is so darn quick to want to hang him! I think they all need to find something else to fixate on."

Jim drew back slightly, and Luke saw Amelia suddenly realize she'd nearly shouted her words. Luke, stunned at her fierce defense of him, shook his head in wonder. Clearly embarrassed, she flicked a glance at him, and when she saw his expression her chin came up determinedly.

"Well, well," Jim said after a moment. "Maybe you've got a point there, Amelia. But if you're wrong, expect to hear a lot of 'I told you so's.'" The cop turned to go, then looked back. In that same warning tone, he added, "Assuming you're still around to hear them."

Luke didn't move until the marked police car began to pull away. He kept his eyes fixed on Amelia, who was staring after her friend in uniform in shock.

As well she might, he thought cynically, considering he'd just implied rather strongly that she could be in danger just being with Luke.

"Guess that makes up for your father not being here to warn you off the town scum."

The words came out sharply, rising out of his own pain, and he said them before he realized they might cause her pain, as well. Her head snapped around, and he saw what he'd feared there in her eyes.

"I'm sorry," he said quickly. "I didn't mean that, about your father."

He shoved away from the car. Instinctively, his hands curled into helpless fists, so he jammed them into his pockets. He stared out toward the water, as if the row upon row of breakers, eerily white in the silver moonlight, held some kind of answer for him.

"That was out of line. I'm just..."

Words failed him. Suddenly exhausted, he let his head loll back on his shoulders and closed his eyes.

"Angry?"

"I don't have the energy to spare to be angry about this anymore. I was just...embarrassed."

"At being treated like that?"

His mouth tightened. He didn't want to say it, but hadn't she earned it, by leaping to his defense like that? He lifted his head, opened his eyes and let out a compressed breath.

"At being treated like that in front of you," he admitted tiredly.

He walked slowly toward the water, only vaguely aware when the surface beneath his feet changed from solid to sand. But after a few yards his legs knew, and his body, now depleted from the adrenaline rush of the fight and the encounter with the police, didn't have the energy to compensate. He fell as much as sat down.

He didn't hear her move, didn't hear her footsteps on the sand, but suddenly she was there beside him. And instead of turning away from him, as he'd half expected, her arms came around him in a comforting hug. He was shocked at how fiercely he responded, how desperately he seemed to need this contact with her, need this reassurance. He didn't know what she was thinking, or if she had come to him simply out of the goodness of her too-kind heart rather than any deeper feeling. He only knew that right now he needed her there, and beyond that, he didn't question.

It was a very long time before he spoke, and when he did, he surprised himself by letting out something he hadn't thought about in a very long time.

"When I was about David's age, I came out here one night. It was a night like this one, warm, quiet. I stood here and wondered if I should just start swimming, and tried to guess how far I would get before I couldn't swim anymore. Then all my troubles would be over."

Amelia's arms tightened around him. "I'm glad you didn't let her win," she whispered.

He stared down at her, wondering how she'd known. "That's the only reason I didn't do it. I knew she'd be glad to be rid of me."

He heard her sigh. "I wish she *had* given you up. Then you'd have known the kind of love I knew, from parents who would have treasured you. Your whole life would have been different."

He couldn't even conceive of what that would have been

like. "So…you don't think it's all heredity? That I was doomed to trouble from the start?"

She leaned back and met his gaze. "I think it's pretty clear you were driven to most of what you did."

"Don't sugarcoat it," he said. "Maybe she pushed me to it, but once I got started, I'm the one who kept going."

She looked thoughtful for a moment. Then, with a glint of humor in her eye, she said, "Okay. So maybe you did inherit a little of that hell-raising Irish blood."

A short chuckle escaped him. She had such a different way of looking at it. "Maybe."

"Did you ever try to find him?"

"My father? Once. When I was about twelve. I had some crazy idea that if he didn't know about me, and I found him, he'd want me."

"You don't know it was crazy. Maybe he would have."

"A kid's fantasy," he said, as he had before.

"What happened?"

He shrugged. "I found out there are a hell of a lot of Patrick McGuires out there."

"But you never found the right one?"

"Not before my mother got the phone bill," he said wryly. "I paid for that one for a long time."

"Maybe you should try again."

"It doesn't really matter, not anymore."

It felt odd, even thinking about it. He'd put it behind him long ago. Talking about it—any of it—was even stranger; he never did, to anyone. Was it being back here, in this place, or just Amelia, who had opened up this torrent of long-unspoken words and memories?

"I'm sorry," she said suddenly.

"For what?"

"Everything. Your mother. Your brother. And," she added, "for leading such a dull life that the sight of my car out after midnight brings the police down on us."

He had to laugh at the wry, self-mocking tone in her

voice. And then she started to laugh, too, and it sounded good. Very good. The smile on her face as she looked up at him made him feel warm inside, and he couldn't help contrasting it to how he'd felt the last time he'd been here on this beach.

Before he even realized he was going to do it, he was kissing her. And this time there was no hesitation on her part, no little start of surprise. This time she gave him pure eagerness, and the feel of her lips parting for him, her tongue stroking his lips, then slipping into his mouth, set up a roaring in his ears that blotted out even the crash of the surf only yards away.

His hand went to the back of her head, holding her as he matched her eagerness with his own, probing deeply, tasting. Her tongue brushed over his, and a shiver rippled through him. She did it again, lingering this time, and he couldn't stop the groan that broke from him.

He went down to the sand, pulling her with him. He muttered her name as he pulled her tight against him, suddenly needing the feel of her body more than he needed his next breath. He shifted one leg over her, to hold her close, expecting her to push him away; instead she slipped her arms around him and pulled him even closer.

The last of his hesitation vanished. He took her mouth again, urgently, fiercely, the fire already licking along his nerves fed by the little sounds of pleasure she made and the way she moved, twisting against him. Her hands slid up under his shirt, over his back, and he nearly lost it at the feel of her fingers caressing his bare skin. He barely resisted the urge to strip off his clothes and then tackle hers, to hell with where they were, in a totally public place.

He couldn't remember ever being this hot this fast. This woman had a fire he never would have guessed at first glance. He doubted she even realized she had it herself; somehow she'd decided she was a meek, timid thing and wasn't about to be convinced otherwise.

Sometime he was going to make her see exactly how wrong she was.

But not now.

He shifted his weight, nearly crying out as she moved at the same time, capturing painfully aroused flesh in a sweet, exquisite vice. His hand slid slowly down her side, then over, and he cupped the soft weight of her breast in his hand. He waited, already-scant breath held, for her to pull away. But she leaned into his touch, the rounded flesh now full and hot against his palm. He could feel the tight, hard jut of her nipple, and this time the guttural cry escaped him.

He wanted that nub of flesh, wanted it naked in his hands, wanted it in his mouth, wanted to suckle it until she cried out as he had, from the gut, from deep inside, from that place his own fiercely hardened flesh wanted to be.

He fumbled at the buttons of her blouse with hands that were none too steady. Her bra was simple, white, but satin trimmed with a tiny bit of lace. Utilitarian, yet feminine. A very Amelia garment, he thought through the haze that was enveloping him. She moved, and for an instant he froze, afraid she wanted him to stop. But then he realized she was trying to make it easier for him, and the growing heat turned into a pulsing, leaping blaze as he reached behind her and fumbled for an embarrassingly long time with the hooks. But at last they gave, and he tugged the garment away from her breasts.

He sucked in a sharp breath; she'd hidden a lot behind those severe, businesslike blouses. Full and beautifully curved, her breasts were tipped with nipples that in the moonlight appeared a soft pink. More importantly, they were already aroused to tight little peaks, and the sight of them was like a kick in the gut, stealing his breath. His body surged, hard and ready, and his hands shook with the force of it as he reached out to her.

His fingers brushed over those taut crests, and when she cried out in shocked pleasure, the need that had been expanding inside him ratcheted another notch tighter. He thought—no, he knew—he was going to explode, but he couldn't help himself, he had to touch her again. And again, this time capturing her nipples between his fingertips and plucking them gently.

"Luke!"

The cry of his name broke from her on a gasp, and it was a spur he couldn't resist. He lowered his head and fulfilled the fantasy that had been torturing him, taking one begging nipple with his lips and flicking it with his tongue.

Amelia arched in his arms, thrusting herself upward to his mouth, crying out his name once more. The awe in her voice was yet another goad to his urgency; she sounded as if she had never felt this before, and that thought was enough to send him perilously close to the edge. He wondered if quiet, reserved Amelia had any idea what she was doing to him.

Quiet, reserved, Amelia.

He felt like he was caught in a swift-running river and headed for the drop. With an effort as great as trying to steer through heavy rapids, he pulled back.

For a long moment he couldn't get enough breath to speak. And looking at her only made it worse; she was looking at him with eyes that seemed dazed, drugged with passion, not even aware that she was half-undressed, her breasts bare to the sea breeze, the moon and his gaze. He felt that breeze on his back and realized he was a bit disheveled himself, thanks to her questing hands. He made himself look away.

He shivered, not from the coolness of the breeze but from the memory of her shy yet eager touch. He wanted more of it, wanted it all over him, and most of all he wanted it now. Already he was hard almost beyond bearing. He shifted on the sand, trying to ease the ache. He needed a pair of those baggy pants his brother wore, he thought ruefully, if he was going to spend much more time around Amelia.

And he wanted that time. A lot of it.

She moved then, drawing his gaze back to her. She was covering herself, her eyes downcast. In the faint light of the half moon, he could see her expression. All her tangled emotions were showing in her face, uppermost a stunned sort of shock, no doubt that she had let this happen outside on a public beach where anyone could have come by and seen them.

He felt a sudden panic rising in him at the thought that her shock would turn to shame the moment she had recovered enough.

"Don't," he whispered. "Don't feel that way."

"I don't know how to feel."

He sighed. "Exactly. That's why we're stopping, before we do something you'll regret."

Even if it kills me, he added silently,

She was very quiet as they tidied their clothes and returned to the car.

"You'd better drive," he said.

She nodded silently and went around to the driver's door and got in. When she began to turn the car to head back toward downtown and the motel, he stopped her.

"Head to your place." That earned him a startled glance. It took him a split second to realize what she was thinking. "I'll walk from there. I just want to be sure you get home okay."

"Seems to me you're more likely to have trouble than I am," she said.

He wasn't sure if it was meant to be sarcastic or just an observation on the way things were, but in either case, he had no rejoinder.

Her home was about what he'd expected: a neat, tidy little cottage. What surprised him was the garden. He couldn't really see it, not the colors anyway, but he could tell flowers abounded. And many of them had obviously been planted for night scents; the air was redolent with a sweetness that made him want to breathe deep.

For a moment after she parked the car in the small attached carport and they got out, he stood there doing just that.

"You don't have to see me to the door. I'll be fine."

"I won't be fine until I see you safe inside," he returned.

She gave him an oddly intent look but didn't protest as he went with her. She seemed to have a little trouble opening the door, but after a moment it swung inward.

She turned then, and he felt an incredible urge to go right back to what they'd been doing on the beach.

"I'd really like to kiss you good-night," he said huskily, "but I'm afraid we'd end up going a lot further. And I don't think you're ready for that."

"Thanks for deciding that for me," she retorted, a little sharply.

He winced. "Amelia, listen. It's been a hell of a night. Some crazy things happened, you're not sure how you feel, this is not the time to make a decision like this."

"Like what? Whether to leap into bed with the notorious Luke McGuire?"

He felt as if she'd punched him, and he wasn't sure if it was the appellation or just the image her words brought to vivid life in his mind. An image that lingered long after she shut the door.

He was going to need that walk back.

Amelia didn't know how long she'd stood leaning against the inside of her front door. She only knew that it seemed to take forever before she could move. And that although she should be dead on her feet—it was after two in the morning—she was strangely wired.

You do know that a crash is coming?

Luke's words came back to her almost tauntingly. She knew he'd meant the post-adrenaline crash, but now it seemed to her to be fraught with many more meanings.

He was right about one thing. She was definitely confused

about her feelings. How could she be so terrified and yet so attracted at the same time? How could she have let things go as far as they had with a man everyone said was pure trouble, a man who had a long history of run-ins with the police, a man her friend Jim was suspicious enough of to suspect him of trying to kidnap her? And be contemplating letting them go even further?

This was not what she had envisioned for herself, this radical slipping out of the quiet groove of her life. And certainly not with someone like Luke. Not the scapegrace of Santiago Beach.

It wasn't until she finally crawled into bed, at last feeling the ebbing of the emotions that had kept her on edge, that it struck her, an obvious fact that she knew she should have realized sooner.

If Luke was as bad as he was painted, he would never have cared that she was confused, hesitant or anything else. Not when she had virtually melted in his arms, beneath his kiss. He would have simply continued to seduce her as he so easily could have. Stopping him, there on the beach, had never even occurred to her passion-drugged mind, and he must have known that. She hadn't been thinking at all. Not when he was kissing her, not with his hands caressing her, and certainly not when he'd put his mouth to her breast and sent her reeling.

And she knew he'd been there with her; she might not be very experienced, but she knew there were some things that couldn't be faked, and the kind of arousal she'd felt in Luke was one of them.

But he'd managed to think. And he'd thought of her. He had been the one to call a halt, not her. For her sake.

It's been a hell of a night. Crazy things happened, you're not sure how you feel, this is not the time to make a decision like this.

He'd had more concern for her than she'd had for herself. Hardly the actions of a dissolute bad boy.

She wasn't sure if that made things better, or worse. If it made things easier, or more complicated.

Her last thought, before she finally drifted off, was that a groove was just a shallow rut.

Chapter 12

Luke paused just outside the bookshop door, thought a minute, then pulled it open.

"Oh well," he muttered a second later.

Amelia, who had been setting out new issues in her small, specialized-for-Santiago-Beach magazine section just inside the door, turned quickly. "What?"

His head snapped around, and he gave her a sheepish grin. "I lost."

"Lost?"

"I've been trying to guess ahead of time who it will be on the door. Today I guessed Captain Kirk, but it was Mr. Sulu."

She'd looked ill at ease at first, but she was smiling now. At least, she smiled until a woman in the back of the store gave him a wary, sideways look, glanced at Amelia and then scurried past them out the door.

Great, I'm driving her customers away, he thought. But she went on as if it hadn't happened.

"Right version, anyway. Are you a big fan?"

He shrugged. "I watched them all, but I'm not rabid about it. I think the attraction for me was just the idea that we were still going to be around that far into the future."

"That's the attraction for a lot of people," she said.

For a moment he just looked at her. And gradually her smile faded altogether. Then she looked away, and he felt his stomach knot. He'd tried to give her time, he'd stayed away all day yesterday, had spent his time haunting all the kids' hangouts and then all the places he used to hang out, hoping to spot his brother. He knew she'd been rattled by the fire that had flashed between them, and he thought she—and he, to be honest—needed time to deal with it.

But he'd been wrong, it seemed. Maybe she felt like he'd abandoned her after that night on the beach. She wouldn't even look at him. She was probably regretting that night, regretting that she let him kiss her, touch her, even look at her.

He saw her draw a deep breath, get ready to speak, and braced himself for the letdown, the rejection she would manage to word very gently, but that would still sting like crazy. It was his own fault; he'd left her alone to brood when he should have been reassuring her, or something.

She'd taken over most of his waking hours, and finding out she wanted nothing more to do with him was going to hurt. But he'd been hurt before and lived. He'd—

"David's missing."

He blinked. "What?"

She lifted her head, and he saw that her expression was troubled, not embarrassed. "He never came home...after that night. His...your mother called me this morning, to find out if I'd seen him."

Luke tensed, as he always seemed to when his mother came up. It was gut-level, like knowing how to read a river, so deeply ingrained an instinct he doubted he would ever beat it.

"What did you tell her?"

''The truth,'' Amelia said.

Luke exhaled audibly; David was in big trouble now.

''Sort of,'' she amended.

He looked at her quizzically. ''Sort of the truth? You sound like I used to.''

''I mean I told her I hadn't seen him the last couple of days. That's the truth.''

''Ah. Selective truth-telling.''

She blushed, and he suddenly had an inkling of how against character it was for her to have seen what she'd seen that night and not report it.

''I'm sorry,'' he said quickly. ''I shouldn't be joking, not when David's been gone this long. He really hasn't been back home?''

''She says no.'' She looked at him straight on then, her golden brown eyes wide and worried. ''That's over thirty-six hours.''

''Maybe he sneaked back in and she didn't know it. I used to.''

''She says no. She was working at home.''

His mouth quirked. ''Well, I guess she'd know, then. She never hung around waiting for me. What's she going to do?''

''She only knows he's been gone overnight. She doesn't realize he's been gone since the night before. But she's going to report him missing if he's not home by dark. She says she's given him all the slack she can.''

Luke had an opinion about her idea of slack, but it was pointless to dwell on it now. ''I've been looking. Hit all the places we used to hang out when I was here, and a couple others I heard about from whoever I found. No luck.''

''I...didn't realize that was what you'd been doing.''

He nodded. And then, driven by the urge to be honest with her, he added, ''I thought you might...need some time. To think and all.''

She lowered her gaze again, but only for a moment. Then

she met his eyes straight on. "Oh, I've been thinking, all right."

"Amelia," he began, not liking the way that had sounded.

"No," she said, holding up a hand. "Right now we have to focus on David. He needs help."

His mouth twisted. "Problem is, he doesn't want it. At least, not from me. You might have better luck with him."

"You can't give up on him, Luke. Not like everybody gave up on you."

"What do you want me to do? I've looked everywhere I can think of."

"And I've talked to all of his friends that I know," she said. "Maybe somebody else knows some other places he might be. Places he's been found before. Or talked about."

"If his friends don't know, who—" He stopped abruptly as he saw where she was headed. "Oh, no. No way."

"Luke—"

"You want to ask her, you go right ahead."

"I will, if you won't. But...don't you think you should?"

"Should what? Go give Mom a hug and a kiss and tell her how much I've missed her?"

"No. Tell her you care for your brother and are trying to help him."

"Uh-huh. And after that you can sell her the bridge."

"What do we do, then? Try and talk to Snake?"

"Apt comparison," he muttered. "And preferable."

Amelia sighed. "All right. I'll go."

He shook his head. "I'm sure she's heard about you—" *Being seen with me? Kissing me? Darn near having sex on the beach with me?* He fought down the heat that seemed to be at her beck and call and went on. "—associating with me by now. From Mrs. Clancy, if no one else. You'll be an enemy in her eyes."

"Maybe not. She did call me, after all. But so what if it will be uncomfortable. I'll bet David is more uncomfortable, wherever he is."

Shame welled up in him. She was right. He was dodging his mother because he didn't want to deal with things, while his brother, who had no choice, was out there somewhere, hiding, thinking everybody in the world had let him down.

"I'll close up for lunch as soon as I finish this," she said, picking up the last stack of magazines in her cart. "I just spoke to her, so I'm sure she's still at home."

She wasn't even going to call him on it. Wasn't going to try to embarrass him into going. She was just going to handle it. So he didn't have to.

Nobody had ever stood up for him in this town. Amelia had. Nobody had ever taken over an unpleasant task so he could avoid it. Amelia had.

The child who remembered so well the acid damage his mother could do screamed at him to let her do it.

The man he'd become knew he couldn't.

"Never mind," he said tightly. "I'll go."

She gave him a startled look. "Why? I said I'd—"

"And I said I'll go."

"But you don't want to see her. And you have every right."

"What I don't want," he said, "is for her to still have this much power over me."

"You're an adult now. She can't do anything to you."

"So I keep telling myself."

Amelia looked at him thoughtfully. "You're in control, Luke."

He blinked. "What?"

"You don't have to live with her, or deal with her, when this is over. You'll walk away. So you control how much effect she has on you." She gave a negligent half shrug. "She's only as real as you let her be."

He stared at her. He'd never thought about it like that, that now he had the power, that she had no authority over him, no recourse at all.

"How'd you get to be so...wise?"

"Age," she said dryly. "I am, as was recently pointed out to me, older than you."

The thought that the difference in their ages, slight as it was, might have bothered her pleased him. It meant she was thinking about it.

"I know," he said.

She drew back, startled. "You do?"

"David told me you were thirty before I even met you."

"Oh."

"If you're thinking four years makes you the boss, forget it."

He said it with all the mock sternness he could managed. It worked, she smiled. It did funny things to his insides, and he wanted to reach for her. He stopped himself, knowing that if he didn't get moving it was only going to get worse. Or better, he amended, as his body clenched at the memory of that night on the beach.

"I'd better go before she heads out again to save the world from disasters like me."

"We'll both go," Amelia said, quickly and efficiently sorting the last of the magazines into their slots.

"You don't have to go."

"I know. I'm older than you. I don't *have* to do anything."

She said it so deadpan that he didn't realize for a moment that she was teasing. When he did, he couldn't help laughing out loud. She looked up at him then, and he saw that glint in her eyes. She might be quiet and reserved, but a devilish sense of humor lurked behind the calm exterior.

Along with a passionate fire that was hidden even deeper. A fire that had, from what he could see, surprised even her. And he couldn't deny how that that made him feel, to think that she'd never felt that way before, that it was him, and his touch, that had startled her with her own response.

"—easier that way."

With an effort, he quashed his unruly thoughts and his

body's response to them, and tuned back in to what she was saying.

"Easier?" he asked, hoping the fact that he'd just zoned out wasn't obvious.

"I can be sort of a buffer. People usually stay calmer if there's someone else there to...referee."

"You sure you want to be in the line of fire?"

"No," she admitted. "But there's always the chance she might tell me something she might not tell you."

Boy, did she have his mother's number. And the thought of having someone standing beside him when he confronted her was more appealing than he ever would have imagined.

Or maybe it was just the thought of that someone being Amelia.

He felt a sudden urge to see her take his mother on; he had the feeling Amelia would find even more of that strength that she didn't seem to realize she had.

"Want to take the bike?" he asked. "I'd hate to disappoint her by showing up any other way."

Amelia looked startled. "I...don't know. I've never been on one."

I'll bet you never made out on the beach before, either, he thought, but wisely decided to keep the words to himself.

"You can have the helmet," he offered.

She eyed him suspiciously. "So you don't have to wear it?"

"Only partly," he admitted with a grin.

For a minute he thought she was going to refuse. But she found the nerve, and moments later they were on the bike and he was giving her some quick instructions. "Keep your feet on the pegs, even when we stop. And if I lean, stay with me, don't try to sit upright."

The black helmet bobbed once. She was nervous, clearly, but also determined.

"And," he added, "hang on tight."

She hesitated, and he reached for her hands and pulled

her arms around him. Before she could protest he started the bike, felt her jump as the Harley came to life. Her embrace tightened, and he grinned; this, not being free of the helmet, was the benefit he'd been after.

He wasn't surprised at how quickly she learned; by the third turn she had the hang of it and quit instinctively trying to stay at ninety degrees from the ground when they rounded a turn. But her embrace stayed tight, and he could feel the heat of her as she clung to him, could feel the surprising strength of her legs as she gripped him.

That gave rise to a riot of thoughts and images that soon had him reassessing the wisdom of this; he was hard and aching, and it was taking every bit of his concentration to just keep going, and to do it at a sedate enough pace not to scare her.

But it had a bright side, too. By the time they reached the house, he realized he hadn't dwelt very much on what was coming: a confrontation with the woman who had made him feel like a charity case, a child kept out of duty, his entire life. The thought took the edge off his arousal, and that particular ache faded. Another, much older one, tried to rise in its place.

Setting his jaw, he gunned the motor a couple of times as he rode up into the driveway, then again before shutting it off.

Take that, he thought, realizing even as the words formed how childish they sounded.

You control how much effect she has on you.

Amelia's words echoed in his head, and he tucked them away to be used as a shield in the next minutes. He had a feeling he was going to end up chanting them like a mantra.

He turned to her then, guessing that she would be a bit wobbly on her feet, as most people were after the first ride. She swayed slightly as she slid off the bike, and he steadied her. She fumbled with the D-ring fastener on the helmet, and he reached beneath her chin to help release it. He hoped she hadn't been frightened by the ride.

She lifted off the helmet. Ran a hand through her hair to lift it after the compression of the headgear. Shook her head. And then she looked up at him.

The exhilaration fairly radiated from her, and her eyes sparkled golden brown.

"That was...incredible!"

He let out a long, relieved breath.

"No wonder people get addicted to it! It's like flying."

He decided now was not the time to tell her they'd never gone over forty-five. Instead he grinned at her, took the helmet and hooked it onto the back of the bike, took off his sunglasses and hooked them on the neck of his T-shirt.

"Next best thing to shooting the rapids." She looked ready to ask about his comment, and he hastily forestalled her. "Let's get this over with."

She nodded, turned and then stopped. She was looking at something past his right shoulder.

"I think she heard your...announcement."

"You don't miss a thing, do you?" he said, keeping his back to the house. "On the porch?"

Amelia nodded. "Put on your flame-retardant suit."

"Breathing fire, is she?"

"Looks that way."

He drew himself up straight, determined not to betray his inner turmoil. But before he could turn around, Amelia put a hand on his arm.

"Think about it," she urged. "*She's* upset. *She's* lost her cool. *You've* done that to *her*. You're in control."

The revelation was simple, but profound. For the first time he believed it, really believed it. He wanted to kiss her. But he wouldn't, not here, not now. Instead he lifted two fingers to his lips, then pressed them to hers.

"Remind me to deliver that directly later."

Amelia blushed, but her gaze didn't waver.

He took a deep breath and let his mouth curve into the cockiest grin he could manage.

He turned around.

"Hi there, Mom!" he called out cheerfully, even waving as he walked up to the porch steps. She'd always hated that. From David she would accept "Mom," from him she had required "Mother." And had preferred nothing at all that mentioned the connection.

"What are you doing here?" She looked down at him as if he were a slug she'd discovered on her roses. "Haven't you caused enough trouble already? Humiliating me in front of an entire room of people and inciting David to act so irresponsibly?"

Well, that set the tone, Luke thought. No fence-mending going on here. And an interesting order she put his offenses in. "I heard you lost another son," he said brightly. "How'd you drive this one away?"

If his mother were the kind of woman who spat, Luke knew he would be wiping his face about now. He hadn't really meant to start out this way, but just the way she looked at him triggered old, knee-jerk responses he had to fight to control.

"Luke," Amelia said softly.

He reined in the raw temper his mother brought out in him. "Yeah, okay. Look," he said to the woman glaring at him from the porch, a bare second, he knew, from ordering him off her property, "I didn't come here to fight with you. I want to find my brother, just like you do."

"He's not your brother, and I'll thank you to stay out of this. Just go back to wherever you crawled out from and leave this to me."

"Leaving it to you is why Davie's gone."

"His name is *David.*"

"Please!" Amelia said. "It's silly to argue about names when David could be in trouble, or hurt!"

It *was* silly, Luke realized. Was that all his mother could fixate on? Her son, the son she supposedly cared about, was missing, and all she could get upset about was that he'd used a nickname she'd never liked?

He saw in that moment how truly narrow her world was, how the only things that mattered to her were those that directly affected her. And in that moment he realized how truly far behind he'd left her.

"She's right. Forget how much you hate me for a minute and tell us if you have any idea where he might have gone."

"If I had any idea, he would be home now," she snapped.

"Has he ever talked about any place he liked to go, or wanted to go?" Amelia asked, her voice more conciliatory than Luke liked, but he understood what she was trying to do.

"No. He's full of stupid ideas about doing reckless things just now, most of them *his* fault."

She didn't need to point to make it clear who she meant.

"With all due respect, Mrs. Hiller," Amelia said, startling Luke with the sudden ice in her tone, "David hasn't seen his *brother* in eight years. Any stupid ideas he might have, have been nurtured and fed here."

Jackie Hiller's nose shot upward. "As if I'd encourage such irresponsible stupidity."

"Look, Mother," Luke began, willing to be at least that conciliatory if it would help find David. She ignored him. Nothing new there.

"I've tried to overlook the gossip about you, Amelia," Jackie said, her voice now stern, condescending. "No one knows better than I what a charmer he can be when he chooses to be. It's how he wiggled out of a lot of the trouble he caused. But you must remember, he's no good and never will be."

"We're not here to talk about me," Amelia retorted.

"You should listen to me," Jackie said, almost urgently. "I was like you, once, Amelia. Young and foolish, quiet and shy. And I, too, was taken in by a handsome face, a devilish smile and an attitude. His father had all of that, and he passed it on. Along with the knowledge of how to use it,'' she ended ominously.

Luke stared at his mother; he'd never heard her so much as mention his father, not once in his life. Whenever he'd brought it up, her answer had always been ''The less you know about him, the better.'' And that had been the end of the topic, as far as she was concerned. He'd even searched the house once, looking for some clue to the man whose name was all his son had of him. He'd found nothing, and when his mother realized what he'd done, she'd locked him in his room for two days, telling him he'd wasted his time, she'd destroyed anything connected to Patrick McGuire long ago.

''Believe me,'' Jackie said, ''I know how exciting a bad boy can be, especially to a sheltered girl like you, like I was. But it's no good, Amelia. They're trouble, through and through, and you'll only be hurt in the end.''

Was this one of her speeches? he wondered. Did she use his father as well as himself to frighten young girls? Was this her platform, using not fire and brimstone, but her own flesh and blood as the example of the wages of sin, as her mother had always put it?

It suddenly occurred to him to look at Amelia, to see how she was enduring this unexpected turn in his mother's tirade. For the first time since he'd known her, her face was expressionless, and he was unable to read even the faintest clue to what she was thinking.

His stomach knotted. What *was* she thinking? Surely she wasn't buying this garbage?

''Thank you for your concern,'' Amelia said. She sounded stiff, formal and utterly unlike herself. Luke's stomach began to churn.

''I do understand, dear.'' His mother's voice was suddenly kind, coaxing, leaving Luke reeling a bit from the swiftness of the change. ''To a good girl, a boy with a reputation is fascinating. There's a certain…cachet I can't deny. I fell victim to it myself. That's why I'm trying to save you, and others, from the same fate.''

Spoken like the heroine of some tragic melodrama, Luke thought.

"I've heard enough of this," he ground out. "She's not going to be any help. Let's get out of here, Amelia."

"Yes," she said. But she didn't look at him. And when he leaned over to look at her face, her expression was still that blank, concealing mask.

He would have bet anything that she wouldn't go for his mother's invective. That if there was anyone in Santiago Beach who wouldn't believe it, it would be Amelia. He just couldn't believe that five minutes with his mother would have changed how she thought about him.

When they got back to the store and got off the motorcycle, she still wouldn't look at him. She pulled off the helmet, fastened it to the back of the bike as he had at his mother's and tidied her hair, all without a single glance his direction. It took him three tries before he could even get out her name.

"Amelia? Are you all right?"

She nodded. "I was just…thinking."

He had to force the words out past the sudden tightness in his throat. "About…what she said?"

She nodded.

"You know she hates me," he said, hating the note of desperation that had crept into his voice.

"Not what she said about you," Amelia said, her voice oddly flat. "What she said about me."

Chapter 13

I know how exciting a bad boy can be, especially to a sheltered girl like you.... To a good girl, a boy with a reputation is fascinating. There's a certain...cachet....

His mother's words rang in her head as she unlocked the door and went into the store. Luke followed her, and she sensed his tension, but she didn't dare look at him. She had to think, and she couldn't do that under his steady blue gaze.

She was a little wobbly and having trouble convincing herself it was just the ride back that had her off balance. She'd gone there expecting to hear a tirade against Luke; what she'd gotten was a rather devastating suggestion about her own attraction to him, spoken by a woman who had, for all her faults, clearly been there.

He followed her into her office; she didn't try to stop him. She couldn't even think about his presence now, while her mind was spinning, trying to process the assessment Jackie Hiller had hung on her.

She dropped her keys on her desk, pulled up her chair and sat down, needing to.

Was that it? Was that why she'd responded to him, why she'd done things she'd never done before? Was his reputation, that cachet his mother had spoken of, at the root of her attraction to him? Was she simply a good girl drawn to the thrill of being with a bad boy?

But he was so much more than that. She knew he was.

No one knows better than I what a charmer he can be when he chooses to be.

Was that it? Had she fallen for an admittedly gorgeous face and an easy charm? She had so little experience, it was only to be expected.

Am I really a thirty-year-old naive fool? she wondered.

She cringed inwardly at the thought and wished she was home in her favorite overstuffed reading chair, where she could curl up, like an animal protecting itself. Hoping for distraction, she glanced over at her answering machine, but there were no messages needing her attention. Too bad the mail hadn't come yet; maybe there would be something there that—

"Amelia." It was a whisper, barely audible. She didn't lift her gaze. She stared down at her desk blotter, stared at the notes scribbled here and there without really seeing the words.

"You can't really think you're anything like her?" He sounded almost desperate. "That's what she's saying, isn't it, that you're a fool, like she was? You're no fool."

She supposed it *was* rather insulting for his mother to assume that, at thirty, Amelia was being as blind as she herself had been at sixteen. She might not have much experience, but despite her own doubts, she was, as Luke had said, no fool.

"If you think she's right, if you're going to believe what she said about you, then you might as well believe what she said about me."

At that she finally looked up at him. What she saw in his face wrenched her soul.

He was expecting her to turn on him.

Everything he'd ever told her about his life, everything David had told her, all the snide, nasty remarks she'd heard from his mother, came rushing back. Did she really want to believe the vitriol that woman poured out on the head of her own son? Whatever her mistakes had been, what right did she have to blame her child for them?

She supposed the converse of what Luke had said was also true; if Amelia didn't believe what his mother said about him, then why believe what she said about her?

"It's not true," he said, for the first time since she'd known him actually issuing a denial. "I mean, what I did when I was a kid, a lot of that's true, but—"

"Luke, don't," she said. Until she spoke, she hadn't realized she'd already decided. "I don't believe her, not about you. But she made me think, made me wonder, about me."

"Don't let her do that," he said, and it warmed her that he sounded as disturbed by the possibility of her taking his mother's word about herself as he had been for himself.

"I don't know what to believe," she said honestly. "Jim was right. I don't even know who you are now. But I do know what I don't believe. You're not what she says you are."

He let out a long, audible sigh and sank down on the chair opposite her desk, as if his legs would no longer hold him. Elbows on his knees, he buried his face in his hands, rubbing at his eyes as if he hadn't slept in days.

"I'm sorry, Amelia," he said.

She'd never heard a more heartfelt apology. But she had to ask, "For what, exactly?"

"Being an idiot?" he suggested ruefully.

"I see."

She didn't, but she wasn't sure what he was referring to and thought it best to just let him get it out. And after a moment he lowered his hands, lifted his head and looked at her. He seemed to be trying to decide what to say, and finally she simply suggested the truth.

"The truth?" he said with a wry chuckle. "The truth is, when I got here, when I realized everybody in this place figured I'd spent the last eight years in jail, or worse, I...got mad. I figured to hell with them, if that's what they want to think, let them. And I didn't do anything to try and change their minds. In fact, I kind of...I..."

"Played to their expectations?"

"Exactly. I fed them. Said things that only made them believe it even more." He grimaced. "I got defensive and decided to let them believe the worst, told myself I didn't give a damn what anybody in this town thought of me." His mouth tightened then. "That was before I got to know you."

She considered that. "But you still didn't tell me the truth. Whatever that is."

"By the time I...wanted to, I wasn't sure you'd believe me. Sometimes it seemed like you believed all the gossip, that you were just...dealing with me because of David. And...you never asked."

"First I was too worried about David to think about it much. Then, when I realized how bad it was here for you, I was afraid you'd think I thought what everyone else did. That I asked just to find out if it was all true."

"Or afraid you'd find out it was?"

"Maybe," she admitted. "I can't deny it's not easy swimming upstream in this town."

His mouth twitched. "Interesting you should choose that figure of speech."

She blinked. "What?"

He let out a compressed breath. "You sure you're up for a long story?"

"The Closed sign is still up."

"I'll take that as a yes," he said wryly. For a long moment he didn't go on. Then, with an awkward laugh, he said,

"I've never really told anybody all this. I'm not sure where to start."

"I've already got a pretty good idea of what your life was like here."

He grimaced. "Yeah. Well." He sighed audibly. "First things first, I guess." He looked up then, met her gaze and held it steadily as he admitted, "I did a lot of the stuff they accused me of. But there was a lot I was accused of I didn't do. I did my share of smoking, drinking and reckless driving. I trashed more than Mrs. Clancy's garden. And every once in a while I'd rip something off."

Amelia wrapped her arms around herself, as if his words could hurt her, even though she already had guessed as much. The words came rapidly, as if he wanted to get them all out before he ran out of nerve. His confession was clearly painful, but it was equally clear he was going to be honest even if it hurt.

"Most people around here wouldn't believe it, but I did have a line, Amelia. I never intentionally hurt anyone. Except maybe myself. But finally I realized that if I was ever going to find my way, I had to get out of here."

"So when you left...you were eighteen?"

"Barely. I stuck around long enough to graduate high school, more for David's dad than anything. He was a good guy." A shadow flickered across his expression, but he kept going. "I left the next day. I wanted to be gone before she threw me out, like she kept saying she was going to do."

Irritation stirred in Amelia, not at Luke, but at herself, irritation that for even a moment she'd let Jackie Hiller sway her. With an effort she stayed silent.

"I'd like to say I turned my life around the minute I walked out of her house," Luke said, his tone rueful, "but it didn't quite happen that way. I headed for L.A., figuring a big city was going to solve all my problems. I tried, but I kept...backsliding." He gave her a sideways look, as if wondering how she was taking this all in. "I spent a couple of months locked up. It seemed like trouble was all I was good at.''

"All you had practice at,'' she murmured, and he gave her a flicker of a smile. This wasn't coming easily for him, and she knew he hadn't lied when he'd said he'd never told anybody all of it before.

But he was telling *her*. She relaxed her defensive posture and sat up a little straighter. "What happened?'' she asked softly, letting the warmth she was feeling creep into her voice.

"I got into some serious trouble. Not like here. I got tied in with some guys who were into…selective car procurement.''

"What?''

"You pick your car, they go out and get it for you.''

Understanding dawned. "Oh. And never mind that it happens to already belong to someone else?''

He nodded. "Anyway, when I realized what they were up to, I tried to back out. But I knew too much and they…convinced me to stay quiet.''

"Convinced?''

"They beat the crap out of me,'' he said, gesturing at the scar she'd noticed the first time she'd seen him. "A local cop found me in an alley. I figured he'd run me, expected the worst, but…''

"But?'' she prompted, trying not to think how scared he must have been, how much pain he must have suffered.

"Turned out he was one of the good guys,'' Luke said softly. "Rob Porter wasn't in it just to throw people in jail, he wanted to help. He really wanted to help.''

"And he helped you?''

Luke nodded. "I didn't make it easy on him, either. He took me to the hospital, then took me home with him afterward. He set me up with a counselor, but I bailed after two sessions. He signed me up at the boys' club, but I was so much older—in more ways than one—than most of the kids,

I didn't last there, either. I don't know why he didn't give up.''

''He obviously saw something in you that made it worth it,'' she said.

''So *he* said later. Anyway, he set it up so I could go on a river-rafting campout with some other kids who were all in the system in various stages. I was technically an adult and too old, but he got them to bend the rules.'' He grinned suddenly. ''I have a feeling Rob does a lot of that.''

She smiled. So he knew all cops weren't out to get him. She supposed she couldn't blame him for thinking the Santiago Beach ones were, considering. ''What happened?''

''I...fell in love.''

She blinked. ''What?''

He sat up straight, gesturing in the general direction of outside, then went on earnestly. ''I grew up here, where rivers don't really exist unless there's flooding. The trip was up to the Kings River. I'd never seen anything like it. It's the whole idea of it. The power, the rush, the rapids.''

''And you...fell in love with the Kings River?''

''Not that one. Nothing wrong with it, but—except during spring runoff, that's when you can get ten foot waves and really intense water action—it's pretty mild. Kings, the Merced, the American, the Klamath, the Stanislaus, they're all great rivers, but...it's the Tuolumne that's home.''

''Sounds...invigorating.''

It sounded terrifying, but she wasn't about to admit that. But he clearly had found something that he loved—she couldn't miss the glow in his eyes—and if it had straightened him around... She leaned forward herself; his energy was hard to resist.

''It...I know it sounds corny, but it...called to me. There's nothing like it. The river is...impartial. It doesn't hate you. If it hurts you, it's because you made a mistake. It's...clean, I guess, fighting something that doesn't have a motive. And if you're good enough, you can win.''

She wondered if he realized how much he was betraying, how much of his battered soul he was revealing, in his words about the love he'd found. She couldn't have spoken, even if she had the words.

"Gary Milhouse, the outfitter from up on the Tuolumne who ran the Kings River trip, was a friend of Rob's," Luke continued, "and he offered to teach me in exchange for me working on those trips for the city kids. So when the kids left for L.A., I went back with Gary to Whitewater West."

"Teach you?"

Luke nodded. "We started with class-one water, the easy stuff. I wanted to jump ahead, of course, but he made me take every baby step along the way. Took me three years to get to where I handled class-five to his satisfaction."

An adrenaline rush, Amelia thought suddenly, can be sparked in many ways. If you don't live on the edge of trouble anymore, there's always another way. Like a wild river. Another thought hit her; now she had the answer to the little gold paddle earring.

He paused before going on, and Amelia sensed he was getting to the crux of his tale. "And then?"

"I learned the Tuolumne, and that was it. I was hooked. I've been working for him ever since. He sent me to school to learn how to handle big rafts and people, and he paid for it. Then he gave me a job. He knew about my...history but said it didn't matter. Said Rob vouched for me, and so did the river."

What a...fanciful way of putting it, Amelia thought. But an unmistakable warmth filled her; while everyone here was convinced Luke was in jail somewhere, he'd in fact been working a steady job for years. And judging by his face, there was more. She waited in encouraging silence.

"And last year...I became a partner."

Her eyes widened. "A partner? In the business?"

He shrugged. "I'd saved most of what I made. Not a lot of places to spend it up there, and besides, I just wanted to be on the river. Last year Gary wanted to expand, add more equipment, and he needed the cash. He owns his property free and clear and didn't want to mortgage it, so I offered to just loan it to him. He took it, but insisted that made me a partner.''

He said it as if it were in name only, but Amelia sensed a deep feeling of pride beneath the offhand story. And rightfully so, she thought.

''So...now you help other kids like you were?''

''We do a weeklong trip every month during the summer, before the season ends in August, and one at spring break, for the more experienced kids. We teach them rafting, river safety, rescue skills, camping skills. Gary's wife, Diane, handles nature tours and interpretation. The trips are always full.''

''You love it, don't you?''

He nodded. ''It's the only job I can imagine having. I get to do what I love, and I get time to do some solo runs.''

''Why do I get the feeling,'' she said wryly, ''that your solo runs are a lot wilder than the ones you take other people out on?''

He grinned. ''Because you're very perceptive?''

She laughed. He laughed with her. The pressure she'd been feeling since they'd left his mother's house slipped away.

''Your partner sounds like quite a guy.''

He gave her a lopsided smile. ''Gary likes to use me as his proof that no kid is too far gone.''

Amelia felt a tightness in her chest that brought tears to her eyes. They'd all condemned him, certain he had nothing to offer the world, written him off as a lost cause. And how very, very wrong they all were. His mother most of all.

''He must be proud of you. And of himself, for seeing you weren't a lost cause.''

''Yeah. I think he is.''

She looked at him thoughtfully. ''Did you ever think

of…coming back? Just to show them how wrong they were?''

"The prodigal son bit? Yeah, it occurred to me. But I had a feeling they wouldn't believe me. And I'd have been right, obviously. In the end, I decided it wasn't worth it.''

For a moment silence spun out. She might be feeling an easing of pressure, but Luke suddenly looked as if he might be feeling some of his own. He stood up, stepped away from her and walked around her office, as if looking at her posters, but she didn't think he was really seeing them. She was about to ask him what was wrong when he stopped and turned back to face her, and she saw that he was working up to saying something. And from his expression, she wasn't sure she wanted to hear it.

"Does it make a difference?'' he asked finally, from safely near the door.

Not sure exactly what he meant, she lifted a brow. "A difference?''

"I'm not the nefarious, infamous scandal of Santiago Beach anymore. I'm not the guy who made the good girls whisper, the guy they used to use to get back at their parents. I'm just a guy who goes to work most days, gets a paycheck, pays taxes. Boring. Predictable.''

When it dawned on her what he was getting at, her eyes welled up again. Boring? She knew in that moment that Jackie had been utterly, totally wrong.

"Not to me,'' she whispered.

He took a step toward her, then stopped. "You're sure? You don't think she was right?''

He didn't have to explain what "she'' he meant. She got to her feet, leaving the safety of her chair and desk, and closing the distance he'd put between them. She didn't stop until she was barely a foot away from him. She had to swallow tightly before she could speak.

"I wasn't drawn to you for your…bad boy reputation, Luke. I was drawn to you in spite of it.''

She heard him let out a long breath, as if he'd been holding it. He was quiet for a moment, and she wasn't sure if she'd said the right thing or not. And then, huskily, he asked, "Just how drawn are you?"

She looked up at him, saw the flare of heat in his eyes. "Maybe drawn isn't the right word," she said, barely aware her own voice had taken on a husky note, as well.

"What is?"

"Attracted? Captivated? Fascinated?"

She thought she saw him shiver slightly. "Any of those will do. For now."

Amelia knew they were hovering on the edge of a turning point, that whatever she said now would determine which way they would go. He hadn't let her make this decision before, when she'd been rattled by their encounter with Snake and his troop and then Jim's suspicions. But he stood silently, waiting, and she knew he was going to let her make it now.

If she decided yes, she would probably pay for it in very painful coin; there was no way he would stay in this town, and she was settled here, without the daring nature it took to leave. Not to mention that it seemed to her that anyone who liked suicidal runs through raging rapids wasn't the type to settle down.

But if she said no...

She looked up at him, at the heat glowing in his eyes, at the tightness of his jaw as he waited. She realized with a little shock that while she still got a case of the shivers whenever she was close to him, it wasn't for at all the same reasons anymore.

Luke McGuire was many things. He was reckless, still a bit wild, and dangerously good-looking. But he was also kind, caring and, to certain extent, noble.

What he wasn't, was a bad boy.

And if she said no, she would wonder for the rest of her life.

"Those are perfectly good words," she said, barely managing to get the words out, knowing what would happen next. "But I just thought of another that's better."

"What?" His eyes never left her face.

She lifted her hands and placed them on his chest. "Hungry," she whispered.

He definitely shivered then. He grabbed her upper arms in a grip that was just short of painful. He took a gulping breath, and his eyes closed. "You're sure?"

"I'm sure," she said.

And she was. It didn't matter that she'd only known him for a matter of days; it didn't matter that her parents would have been scandalized; it didn't matter what price she might pay later. Right now, in this moment, looking up at the man who had moved her as no other in her life ever had, the only person she had to answer to was herself.

And her answer was yes.

It must have shown in her face, because when he opened his eyes again and looked at her, the heat in his eyes flared higher, and a low, guttural sound escaped him.

"No woman," he said hoarsely, "has ever looked at me like that before."

She didn't try for sophistication, or to sound blasé; she knew she couldn't carry it off. "It's the way I feel," she said simply.

"I can't find words for how I feel," he said, as if explaining. Then he pulled her into his arms and took her mouth, and she knew what he had meant.

She slipped her arms up around his neck, knowing she was going to need his strength; when he kissed her, hers seemed to vanish.

She trembled as he deepened the kiss, tasting, probing, urging. And she responded, kissing him back, wanting more of that hot, exotic male taste of him. And more, and more.

Her hands slid upward, into his hair. It slipped like warm, dark silk over her fingers, and she realized suddenly why one of the things all the uptight gossips said was that he needed a haircut; it was luxuriantly, dangerously sexy.

Luke moved his hands down her back, slowly, caressingly, to her hips. He pulled her against him, and she nearly gasped aloud at the feel of him, of ready male flesh pressing against her. Tentatively she moved, twisting, stroking him with her body, just to see what would happen.

He groaned, a low sound that she felt rumbling up in his chest before she heard it. He jerked slightly, pushing himself harder against her in response.

She wasn't sure how she ended up backed against her desk, but she was there. And Luke was leaning over her, pressing her backward, his mouth never leaving her, his hands moving over her as if he couldn't get enough, as if he wanted to touch her everywhere at once. The idea of being the one who made him feel that way thrilled her, and a delicious shudder rippled through her. He seemed to feel it, because he lifted his head, looking at her.

She felt bereft, already missing the sultry heat of his mouth. That made her think of that night on the beach and his mouth at her breast, his tongue on her nipple, and she almost cried out at the memory, wishing he would do it again, right here, right now....

"How much do you trust that Closed sign?" he asked, his voice thick.

It took her a moment to fight through the golden haze and realize what he meant. When she realized why he was asking, that he apparently had every intention of fulfilling the wish she'd just silently made, her breath left her in a rush. It was as if he'd read her mind.

Right here, right now...

Right here, on her office desk. Right now, in the middle of the day.

She shuddered in his arms, some wild part of her that she'd never even known existed screaming out yes. She felt the heat pooling low and deep as her body readied for him, readied for the consummation of the shocking, overwhelming urge to let Luke McGuire make love to her this instant. To let him peel away her clothes until she was naked in this place that, until now, had only meant her world of books to her. To strip him naked, as well, so that she could look her fill under the bright office lights that would let her see every beautiful male inch of him.

An image of them together flashed through her mind, more erotic than any of the imaginings she'd become prey to since he'd arrived.

"Damn," Luke muttered harshly. "I want to know what you were just thinking, but you've got me so hot already, I'm afraid if you tell me, I'll go off right now."

Amelia moaned. Luke pushed her back to lie on the desk, and she didn't even notice the edge of her calendar digging into her back. Not when Luke stepped between her knees and began to tug at the buttons of her blouse. In moments he had bared her breasts, and Amelia could feel the cool breath of the air-conditioning over her skin. She thought of how his mouth would feel, hot and wet and delicious compared to that coolness. She nearly cried out under the force of her body's response simply to the image in her mind.

For a moment that seemed like an eternity Luke didn't move. Amelia couldn't stop herself from arching upward, offering her breasts, begging without words.

Luke move swiftly then, one hand on her left breast, his fingers rolling and twisting the nipple, while his head darted to the other, taking the nipple and suckling it deep and hard while his tongue teased the tip.

She did cry out then, and her body rippled under the wave of rich, hot sensation.

The phone rang.

Luke swore. Amelia whimpered.

It rang again.

Luke straightened up. Amelia whimpered.

The third ring. She had it set on five during the day, so she could get to it from the storage room.

Or, in this case, from where she was spread half-naked across her desk, wishing Luke would just ignore the ringing and go back to what he'd been doing.

With a whimper she smothered this time, Amelia sat up. She answered the phone.

"Ms. Blair? This is Elizabeth Adams, at Santiago Beach Bank."

Amelia tried to focus. She vaguely remembered the woman, one of the supervisors at her branch. "Yes?"

"Did you write a check today for the amount of five hundred dollars?"

"What?" she asked, tugging her blouse closed while still fighting the glorious fog Luke had put her in. "No. No, I didn't."

"Are you missing any checks?"

That got her attention. "From my business account? I don't think so, but let me look."

She sat down the phone, slid to her feet and walked around the desk, feeling herself flush as she realized how close she'd come to having what she could only call wild sex atop her desk blotter.

She shook her head sharply to clear the last of the haze. She unlocked her desk and pulled out the large, notebook-style business checkbook. Luke was watching, still clearly aroused, still breathing hard and fast. She nearly forgot the phone as she stood there staring at him. Then she flipped open the checkbook.

She sank down in her office chair.

"Trouble?" Luke asked, his voice still showing a trace of the earlier sexy huskiness.

"Five hundred dollars worth, it seems," she said, reaching for the phone. "Mrs. Adams? Yes, I seem to be missing a single check."

"Number thirty-five oh-two?"

"Yes. I gather someone used it?"

She fought the panic rising in her, wondering what else might be missing, and how this had happened in the first place. She closed her eyes, thinking.

"Tried to, this morning, at our branch at Pacific Center." Another pause. Amelia concentrated. And then it struck her. The day Snake and his cohorts had come in, the day she'd showed him his knife in the book...she had been paying bills that morning. She knew she had shoved the checkbook under the counter, but one of them had been right there; if he'd leaned far enough, he could have seen it.

"Did you hire some new help?" the woman from the bank asked.

"No, I haven't. Is that what they said?"

"Yes. Our teller caught it, luckily. He usually works here, but he was filling in at the other branch. The signature didn't look right to him, and the person was very nervous, so he asked a couple of questions, enough to scare him off."

"Bless him," Amelia said as she finished rebuttoning her blouse. "I hope he gets a raise."

Elizabeth chuckled. "I'll see what I can do."

"Do you know who it was?"

"A young man, Eric said. Not eighteen, he didn't think."

Amelia sighed. "That explains it. I had a group of rather...unfriendly kids in here a couple of days ago."

"We have his photo on our branch security video. Could you come down and take a look, make an identification for the police report?"

"I...yes, I could. When?"

"As soon as possible. We want to turn it and the check over to the police by end of business."

"All right."

She hung up. She was reeling a bit; the change from hot, eager passion to the chill of the phone call was dizzying. Then Luke was there, his hands on her shoulders, steadying her.

''What's wrong?''

She explained what had happened, and her suspicions that it was one of Snake's cohorts.

''They're stupider than I thought,'' Luke muttered.

''I have to go look at the security film.''

''Now?''

She nodded mutely. He was upset, she thought. *She* was upset. But he said nothing except, ''Let's go.''

They were ready for her, and when she sat in the back office in front of a television screen, she was thinking how to explain that she had no idea who any of the boys really were. She could identify Snake, of course, and maybe most of the others, but she didn't know their real names. She didn't think Luke did, either; they'd let him in because she'd told them he knew the boys she suspected, although he hadn't been a witness to the incident where they took the check.

The screen flickered, and she turned her attention to it. They'd cued it up right to where the boy was at the teller window with the stolen check.

It was David.

Chapter 14

Luke didn't know which made him feel the sickest, looking at his brother's unmistakable image on the videotape or at Amelia's face as she watched it.

She looked stunned.

He was furious.

Maybe David did feel let down, maybe he felt betrayed. But that was no reason for him to turn around and in turn betray the only person in Santiago Beach who had genuinely wanted to help him.

"You look surprised," Mrs. Adams said. "It's not who you expected?"

Amelia swallowed. She looked at Luke. He waited. He wouldn't blame her if she turned David in; he was halfway tempted to do it himself. She had every right; the boy had abused her trust and her friendship, and deserved whatever he got.

My, what a holier-than-thou hypocrite you've become, he said wryly to himself. That had been said more than once about him, he was sure.

But he was still angry. David had hurt Amelia, and he didn't like that. At all. His reaction was so fierce it startled him, but before he had time to analyze that, Amelia was answering the bank supervisor.

"I think...this may have been just a misunderstanding," she was saying. "Can you hold off contacting the police until I can talk to the boy?"

Mrs. Adams frowned, but after a moment agreed. "Since he didn't succeed, and he's known to you, then I suppose we can. Just please keep me posted."

"I will," Amelia promised.

They were outside, next to her car, before Luke trusted himself to speak.

"You didn't have to do that."

"Yes, I did."

He shook his head. "He shouldn't have stolen from you."

"If he did, you're right. But I don't recall David ever being around when I had the checkbook out. Besides..."

She lowered her gaze, and Luke wondered what she'd been about to say. "Besides...what?"

She took an unsteady breath. "I can't help wondering what might have changed if somebody had ever looked not at what you'd done, but why."

After a moment during which he had to blink against a sudden stinging behind his eyelids, he reached out and lifted her chin with a gentle finger.

"You," he said softly, "are amazing, Amelia Blair."

Her eyes widened, and her lips parted for a quick breath. He resisted the urge to kiss her right there on the street, although it was difficult.

"We have to find him," she said. "I just can't believe David would do that. There has to be an explanation."

She was a lot more optimistic than he was. "We haven't been able to find him yet, and he'll probably be hiding even deeper now. He's got to know the bank would report this."

"But he only tried, he didn't actually do anything."

"Only because the teller was on his toes," he pointed out. It felt odd, her being the one most strongly defending David, but he really was furious. "As far as I know, attempted forgery's a crime, too."

She looked at him curiously. "Why are you so angry?"

"You mean when it's no worse than some of the things I did?" he snapped.

"I didn't say that." Amelia's voice was quiet, making his own snarling reply sound even worse.

"I'm sorry," he said, ramming a hand through his hair. "He's my brother, and I want to help him, but damn it, why you? If he was angry enough to steal, it should have been from me. I'm the one he thinks let him down."

At first she just looked at him, but then she smiled, a slow, small smile he could only call mysterious.

"I'm sure he's not thinking that clearly," she said after a moment. "He's feeling deserted, abandoned, by his mother, then his father, and now you. So he's striking out blindly."

His mouth quirked. "Been reading psychology books?"

"On occasion. But this is just common sense. Besides, what do you have here to steal that he could get to? He could hardly ride your motorcycle away, and I don't think he's up to picking your pocket or breaking into your room."

"Yet," Luke muttered.

"We have to find him, Luke," she repeated.

"I'm open to suggestions," he said. "I've looked everywhere I can think of."

"Then we'll look again. And I'll call your mother to make sure he hasn't turned up there."

He grimaced. "You sure you want to do that?"

"No, she's the last person I want to talk to right now. But this is for David."

He had the thought later, as she was making the call from the new cell phone she'd gotten to replace the one stomped in the fight, that if she would go this far just for a boy she'd sort of taken under wing, what would she do for someone she really loved?

Just about anything, he guessed.

It was a novel idea to someone who'd lived his life as a nuisance, a hindrance and a general source of aggravation to the one who, according to tradition, should be willing to do anything for him.

He didn't dare wonder what it would be like to be one of those Amelia loved and would do anything for.

Moments later she severed the connection. "He hasn't come home. She's still going to call the police if he hasn't turned up by dark."

"Okay, Amelia," he said. "We'll look again."

This wasn't, Luke thought dryly, what he'd hoped to be doing with her all afternoon.

Of course, he hadn't expected her to say yes, either.

It wasn't that he wasn't worried about David. He'd gotten over most of his anger, except that he still wanted to shake the kid for ripping off Amelia, of all people.

It was just that he wanted desperately to explore the fire that blossomed between them every time they touched. And he felt guilty because he wanted to do that even more than he wanted to look for David. He wasn't sure they could find him, anyway; he knew that if the kid truly didn't want to be found, there were places where he could hide for days, even in Santiago Beach. He knew, because he'd done it. He'd checked all the areas he knew of, but there had to be more.

But he would look. Because Amelia felt they had to. And he supposed she was right; he was just feeling a bit cranky about it.

He followed her to her house, where he left his bike parked safely off the street, and then they took her car. She turned the wheel back over to him while she called all of David's friends she had numbers for. Sadly, as had happened before, they said only that they didn't see much of David anymore, since he'd starting hanging out with Snake's crowd.

They checked the smoothie stand at the pier, the burger place on the coast road, the pizza place by the high school, not really expecting to find anything.

They were right about that, Luke was thinking, when Amelia suddenly said, "What if we see Snake or one of his pack?"

He'd thought about that and had a pretty good idea what he would do. "Wolves have packs, not snakes," was all he said.

But Amelia studied him for a moment, then said, "Shall I take that as you planning to pry whatever they know out of them by whatever means necessary?"

He shot her a startled glance. She looked back at him with an exaggeratedly innocent expression.

"You," he said, "are dangerous."

"Me? You're the dangerous one. Just ask anybody," she said sweetly.

"Yeah, yeah," he muttered, but underneath the mock irritation, he was delighted. She was actually teasing him. It must have been true, what she'd said, that she'd been drawn to him in spite of his reputation. And once he'd explained that the reputation no longer applied, she'd relaxed.

And decided she wanted him.

He was surprised he didn't grunt at the force of the need that suddenly cramped his body. His grip tightened on the steering wheel until his knuckles were white. He felt like he did when he shot over class five-falls; he was flying and not at all sure how he would land.

Probably wrong, he thought dryly. At least on most falls he knew what he was headed for. These were unscouted rapids, and he had no idea.

He hung on as they went from place to place, but his mind was barely on what they were doing. He kept having flashbacks of those moments in her office, wondering at how swiftly he'd been out of control and seconds away from taking her right there on her desk. He was on a slow, steady boil, until he was sure one touch, one trace of an echoing hunger in her eyes, and he would lose it.

Think of something else. Anything else.

He headed toward the downtown area, driving slowly, trying to think. It had been a long time since he'd had to think like a kid trying to hide, and things had changed around here in the past eight years. The old shoe store was gone, along with the hidden space under the stairway behind it, and the old, shut-down theater that had made a good hiding place if you could get in had been razed.

Stopped at the Main Street signal, he tapped his fingers on the wheel, trying to use a teenager's logic. It hadn't been *that* long, after all. His mouth quirked. If David had been younger, he would have tried his early favorite, the place he'd had to quit using when he turned fourteen and grew nearly six inches over the summer.

Grew nearly six inches.

"Luke? Did you think of something?"

"I think," he said, "I finally thought of something I should have thought of a long time ago."

"What?"

"Got a flashlight in the car?"

"Yes, under the seat. Why?"

"It'll help," he said as he maneuvered over to the right-turn lane, thankful for once for the town's relative lack of midday traffic. He turned onto Main and headed toward the library.

Amelia looked at him as they pulled into the parking lot.

"The library? Surely he wouldn't try to hide in there, would he? He must realize people will be looking for him."

"Not in," Luke said. "Under."

"What?"

"I'm not sure if it's still there, but there was a crawl space under the building, in the back. Because it's on a hill, at one end it's high enough to sit upright. Up until I was fourteen it was, anyway.''

Amelia looked at him for a long moment. "And how much time did you spend there?"

"A lot," he admitted. "And I kept it quiet. I knew they'd close the access if they knew. But then I grew about half a foot over one summer, and it got too cramped."

Amelia thought about that a moment and arrived at the conclusion he had finally reached. "David's shorter than you."

He nodded. "I should have realized it sooner," he said with disgust. "I thought about it when I first got back in town, but I'd sort of mentally crossed it off the list because at his age, I had to quit using it. I was thinking age, not size."

"Do you think David could have found it?"

"He already knew. I forgot until just now, but...I told him about it before I left. In case he ever needed a place..." Then, regretfully, Luke shook his head. "He probably forgot all about it."

Amelia shook her head in turn. "I doubt he's ever forgotten anything you told him." She looked at him curiously. "Did he know you were leaving?"

Luke nodded. "I couldn't just go. I had to tell him. He started to cry, but...I hoped he'd understand later."

"He did. Just like he'll understand this—later."

He wished he could be as sure as she seemed to be.

They walked around the back of the library. Amelia stared at the small opening, then at Luke. "Maybe I should do it."

She stopped when he shook his head. "It isn't the Ritz in there, and unless you have a fondness for large spiders, you'd best wait here. I'll manage, it just won't be pretty."

She shivered. "Spiders have their territory, and I have mine, and as long as we each stay where we belong, I don't mind them. I'm convinced. Go for it."

"You'll have to play lookout for me," he said. "I don't want to have to explain to anybody what I'm doing."

"I'll hold the cell phone to my ear, so nobody will feel compelled to come up and chat."

He grinned at her, glanced around, and then knelt down to quickly pull the screen off the access hole. He considered whether to try feet first or headfirst; neither would be comfortable or graceful, but headfirst might make it a bit easier to get his shoulders through. It was tight—had it once really been so easy?—but he made it.

He flicked on the flashlight, sent it sweeping over the dark space. And then back, holding it steady on the spot he'd always used, where the hill dropped away and the floor was the highest over his head, making it seem more like a cave than a crawl space.

Something was there.

He scrambled awkwardly across the dirt and found an old, ragged blanket that looked a bit mouse-nibbled around the edges, and a baseball cap that looked nearly as old, if a little less dirty. A wrapper from a package of snack cakes and an empty fast-food bag completed the small stash. There was nothing else, no certain sign anyone had been there recently.

He crawled back to the opening.

"Amelia?" he whispered.

"Sure, I can hang on a minute," she said.

For a split second he didn't know what she meant, and then he remembered the cell phone. A second later he heard footsteps and couldn't help grinning at her cleverness.

He waited, the footsteps faded, and then he heard her whisper, "All clear."

He clambered out through the opening and quickly put back the screen. He dusted himself off as best he could, then stepped up to the sidewalk beside her.

"Somebody's been there. There's a blanket and a baseball cap, and some junk-food debris. But it could be old, too."

One corner of his mouth twisted wryly. "Heck, it could be mine, for all I remember."

For a moment she looked as if she were seeing the boy he'd been, compassion softening her expression until his throat tightened.

"What next?" he said rather abruptly, knowing that grabbing her right there behind the library would really set the tongues of Santiago Beach wagging.

"I thought of someplace else to look. The mall just put in an arcade. It draws a lot of kids. David isn't that into video games, but he might think it's a good place to go unnoticed."

Luke nodded, and they made the trip nine miles up the freeway to the shopping mall. They found the arcade, packed with kids on this summer day, but not, at least now, David.

From there they went to the park that had been vandalized, where kids were known to hang out behind the handball courts. They found four kids sneaking cigarettes and a couple farther up in the trees smoking something more potent, but no David. And finally they went down to the state park south of town, where there were isolated coves and places to stay out of sight along the beach. They hiked for what seemed like miles but found no sign of one particular angry teenager amid the summer throng.

"Now what?" Luke asked wearily as they sat in her car and watched the sun begin to set.

"I'm really out of ideas," she said, sounding as tired as he felt.

"So am I."

Out of ideas about David, anyway, he added with silent ruefulness. He was still full of ideas about Amelia. And before he did something stupid like voice some of them, when he had no idea if she was in the same frame of mind she'd been in at her office, he suggested they get something to eat instead.

"Good idea," she agreed. "Maybe we can think of something once we have some food.'' She hesitated, then said rather shyly, ''I have some spaghetti sauce and fixings for a salad, if you'd like to come back to the house.''

He considered that for a moment, fighting down the tide of possibilities that engendered. ''That depends on why your place,'' he said.

She looked puzzled. ''I just thought it might be...quieter.''

''Not because you don't want to be seen with me anymore?''

Her eyes widened. ''Of course not!''

It was swift enough, and just affronted enough, to reassure him. ''Just checking,'' he said mildly.

''I didn't care what anyone thought before, so I certainly wouldn't now that I know the truth!''

He wanted to hug her. But he knew if he did, they would end up doing things there in her car that you usually left behind with your teenage years. At least, he had; he doubted if Amelia had *ever* done such things in a car.

''I'd like that,'' he said simply.

It was still light enough for him to really see her home this time, and all the profuse, bright colors of her garden. He suddenly thought that the wild palette was a sign of the fire she kept hidden, and that perhaps he should have realized that.

The bright colors continued in the interior, blues, greens and bright yellow, with a touch of unexpected red that added punch. It was vivid and cheerful against the clean white of the walls, and showed the hand of someone who loved making a house a home. The furniture was comfortable and practical, very Amelia.

She seemed determine to avoid talking about David, and they said little as she fixed the meal. She put him to work shredding lettuce and slicing tomatoes, while she tossed mushrooms in the simmering sauce she'd taken from the freezer—she made huge batches at once, she told him, so she could have it whenever she wanted—gave it a stir and went back to preparing garlic bread.

When he asked, as they sat down to plates giving off an aroma that made his stomach growl, she told him about the work her parents had done on the house and the rather grim, dark little place it had been before they'd started. Between bites, it took most of the meal.

"They loved this place," she said when they were down to crumbs.

"What about you?"

She shrugged. "I like it, too. And since I was renting an apartment when my father passed, it seemed only logical to move back in. But in my mind, it's still their home."

"You must miss them."

"I do. A lot. But you go on, or you become a neurotic basket case. My parents wouldn't have liked that."

She apparently decided that was enough talk about her. After they had cleared the table, and as they moved to sit on the bright blue sofa in the living room, she asked a question guaranteed to get him talking.

"Tell me about your river."

"The Tuolumne? It's the most amazing place," he said with an enthusiasm he didn't even try to hide. "There are places where you can't see a trace of civilization from the river. It's exactly like it must have looked to the first people who saw it. Only two departures a day are allowed, which keeps it that way. On a two-or three-day trip you can camp on a white sand beach under an oak tree, hike up to a water slide or a natural swimming pool. In high summer, it's like the water's heated."

She smiled. "I expected to hear about rapids and waterfalls."

He lifted one foot and rested it on his knee. "Oh, they're there. It's one of the best all-around whitewater runs in the state, probably the country. Nemesis, Hells Kitchen, or the big one, Clavey Falls, and when you make it through, it's like no other feeling on earth.''

"I can't even imagine," Amelia breathed. "I mean, I've seen it on television, and it always looks so…crazy."

"It can be. There's a place called Cherry Creek, on the upper Tuolumne, just outside Yosemite. It's the toughest stretch of class-five rapids that's run commercially. Drops an average of a hundred and ten feet per mile, two hundred feet in what they call the 'Miracle Mile.' A rafter died there, back in 1992. Took the center chute at the end by mistake and ended up overturned against Coffin Rock.''

Amelia grimaced. "Coffin Rock? How…picturesque."

He grinned at her. "Oh, we've got better names than that. Like Gray's Grindstone. And Vortex, and Chaos, which leads into Confusion on the Kern. Insanity Falls and Rotator Cuff—because so many kayakers dislocate shoulders there—the Bad Seed and Where's Barry? on Fordyce Creek.''

She was laughing by then, and barely managed to get out, "'Where's Barry'?"

"It makes sense once you've seen somebody disappear in it, then pop out the bottom. It's a drop over a six-foot ledge that's at a forty-five degree angle from the current. It's always a class-five, sometimes a six, depending on the water flow.''

"Six?"

"Unrunnable. And there's a hole and a big cavern undercut in the rock, and you can get sucked in.''

Amelia set down her fork. "Let me get this straight. People do this for *fun?*''

"Well, they don't start out there. We start them on something easy, until they get hooked. Then we work them up, if they want. But some folks keep coming back for the same runs, which is fine. They're our bread and butter, and we make sure they have a good time. Not everybody has the need to—or should—go out and tackle fives and five pluses.''

''But you do? You've run that…Cherry Creek, was it?''

He shrugged. ''I've done it. I prefer the middle fork of the Feather, and Garlic Falls on the Kings, which are as tough as Cherry Creek but not run commercially. More remote, less crowded. And there are still a few places I haven't been that I want to. There's an inlet up in British Columbia that has the most incredible standing wave that—''

''Standing wave?''

He nodded. ''A standing wave is produced when two waves traveling in opposite directions become superimposed on one another. Like along the coast, where the tide hits a shelf. You can ride it—surf it, almost—but never move. This one in B.C. is a solid class-five for what seems like forever.''

''May I say,'' Amelia announced firmly, ''that this sounds utterly insane?''

''Wait until you try it,'' he said. ''The exhilaration is beyond description.''

She hesitated a moment, and he wondered what she was thinking. Then, tentatively, she said, ''I can't see myself ever having the nerve to even try.''

''That reminds me,'' he said, suddenly intent. ''We need to talk about this idea you seem to have about your lack of nerve.''

She blushed. ''I know what you said, but…it's so hard for me to believe. I've always been…timid.''

''Timid?'' he exclaimed. ''Timid doesn't face down a kid waving a knife at her when she's alone in a store with him. Timid doesn't take out two guys in a street fight. Besides, you've got something more important than nerve, you've got brains. That'll outdo brawn and nerve most times.''

''But I could never do the things on those posters in my office. Or your rafting. I've always been afraid of…the wilder things.''

A sudden flash of insight struck Luke—hard. She'd once

thought of him as one of the wilder things; it had been written all over her expressive face.

"Like me?" he asked, before he could stop himself.

The pink in her cheeks turned to red, and he knew he'd struck home. But she held his gaze and nodded.

It explained a lot, he thought. The way she'd seemed so jumpy at first when he was around, the tension he'd sensed in her, just beneath the surface.

"You're not afraid of me now, are you?" he asked softly.

"No," she said, her color still high. "I'm a little afraid of how you make me feel."

He smiled, letting the need he'd kept at bay all day loosen a notch. "Well, that's easy," he said, reaching out to cup her face. "That just takes practice."

She bit her lip, then traced the spot with her tongue. Luke's pulse leapt immediately into overdrive. "Like...running your rapids?"

"Exactly. The more you practice, the better you get at it. But if you do it right, the thrill never goes away."

Her blush didn't fade, but now it was matched by the heat in her eyes. Luke's body surged with a response that almost weakened his knees.

"Then...maybe we should practice," she said, her voice so husky that it was like a physical caress to his aroused senses.

"Definitely," he said, his own voice a little thick now. "Practice. Lots of practice."

He pulled her into his arms then, and she went willingly, eagerly. Within moments he was nearly as hot as he'd been in her office, and he knew that the battle he'd fought to keep this under wraps all day was nothing compared to the battle it was going to be to take this slow.

But he would. Very slow. Not just so he could savor every sweet, hot minute, but so he could see her fall apart in his arms.

And if anyone or anything tried to interrupt them this time, he swore he would do violence.

Chapter 15

Amelia shivered, half in nervousness, half in anticipation. She had shyly led Luke to her bedroom, wondering what he would say when he saw it. For it was here that she had secretly indulged, and while her elaborate framed bed swathed in yards of mock mosquito netting in a lush green and piled high with many-patterned pillows was her favorite place, it hardly fit with the rest of the house's decor.

She saw him look around, saw the surprise spreading across his face.

He laughed.

She cringed, but he grabbed her and pulled her close. "I love it. I love it, Amelia. This is the woman you keep hiding, the one you need to let out. This is the woman who stood up to Snake and takes kickboxing lessons and uses them."

She realized then that his laugh hadn't been one of ridicule but of delighted discovery, and she let out a sigh of relief. A sigh that was cut off abruptly when Luke suddenly swept her off her feet and into his arms. She stared up at him, startled.

"It seems to fit," he said, and carried her easily across the room. There was something to be said, she thought, as her heart began to thud in her chest, for arms made powerful by fighting wild rivers.

Yet all that power was leashed when he touched her, controlled when he lowered her carefully to the bed, gentled when he began to unbutton her blouse. He stroked his fingers across the swell of her breasts above her bra, and she felt her body tighten. She wanted to tell him not to go so slowly, wanted to tell him to hurry, that she was desperate for his hands, his mouth, on her again.

He unfastened the bra, and her breasts slipped free. He cupped them in his strong hands. She wasn't accustomed enough not to be self-conscious, but the thought of what he might do next, that he might actually do what she wished she had the words to beg him for, overpowered the feeling.

For a long moment he simply looked at her. And then, with an urgency that was somehow flattering, he released her, tore off his own shirt and came down on the bed beside her. If there was something to be said for arms made strong from running rivers, there was even more to be said for what it did for a chest and belly, she thought a little dazedly. He was beautiful.

That was all she had time to register before he pulled her against him. She sucked in a breath at the delicious shock of his hot, sleek skin against her bare breasts, and knew from the low, rumbling groan that escaped him that this had been what he'd wanted, the feel of her breasts against his chest.

Instinctively she twisted, rubbing herself against him. He groaned again, and rolled over until she was half under him. And then it was all she could do to remember to breathe; his hands were everywhere, stroking, caressing, and his mouth soon followed the same path. He cupped her breasts again and lifted them to his lips, drawing the nipples one at a time into his mouth where he sucked and flicked them with his tongue at the same time. Amelia cried out, was gasping under the onslaught of sensations.

He unfastened her slacks and tugged at them; without hesitation she lifted herself to help him. In moments she was naked beside him, and he began all over again, searching out every sensitive place on her body and driving her mad with the intimate attention he gave each one, first with his hands, then his mouth.

She didn't think she could bear much more. She slid her hands over his back, savoring the feel of him even as she concentrated on her goal. She found the waistband of his jeans, then slipped her fingers beneath. Her fingertips reached the high, taut curve of his buttocks and ached to go farther.

Luke moved up and tickled her ear with his tongue. "You want some more room in those jeans?" he whispered.

It took her a moment, through the shivers his nibbling on her lobe was causing, to focus on his words.

"I want them," she said frankly, "off."

She froze, not quite sure she'd really said it so baldly. She risked a glance at Luke; he was grinning, and it had the same delighted quality as his laugh when he'd seen her bed.

"I aim to please," he said. He gave her ear a final flick of his tongue, then rolled away and shucked his jeans and shorts. He fumbled with them for a moment, then dropped them on the floor. Amelia barely noticed; she was, for once unabashedly, staring at him.

Beautiful, she thought, *isn't even the word for it.*

He turned back to her, dressed in only that gold earring, and suddenly it was the sexiest thing she'd ever seen. She watched him move, fascinated by the play of muscle under that sleek skin, captivated by the way one strong line of his body flowed into the next, and more than a little awed by the blunt, rigid male flesh she was about to encounter on a very intimate basis. Her lower body clenched, as if already wishing he was there to clasp, to hold.

A shudder rippled through her, and she lifted her gaze to his face. "All right?" he asked.

She didn't know if he meant did she feel all right, or if what she'd seen was all right. It didn't matter. Either way, the answer was the same.

"Yes. Oh, yes. Very."

Instinctively her hand moved, her fingers curling, almost aching to touch him. But she pulled back, uncertain.

Luke took her hand and guided it to him, gently shaping her fingers around his own hardened flesh. "Anything you want," he said harshly.

She heard him suck in a breath as she tested the length and breadth of him, marveling at the feel, at the satin weight of him against her palm and the size of him beneath the curve of her fingers. Once she heard him make a sharp sound and stopped, fearing she'd hurt him. But he lifted himself, nudging her hand until she knew it hadn't been a sound of pain. She resumed the caress, pressed the same way, rubbed the same place, until he gasped out her name on a choking breath.

Only then did the glint of foil in his hand draw her eyes. When she saw what it was, her gaze shot back to his face.

"Funny," she said, her voice suddenly a little wobbly, "I never thought of you as the cautious type."

He went very still. "You mean this?" He indicated the condom with a nod. "If you mean am I always prepared, then yes. Not because I expect anything. Although I gotta say, girl, if I hadn't had them, I would have bought them a week ago, you wind me up so tight."

He leaned over and kissed her softly.

"I'm always prepared, Amelia, because I swore from the time I realized babies came from sex that I would never, *ever* bring an unwanted child into the world."

Amelia's breath caught, and she was furious with herself for even thinking about having hurt feelings about his advance preparation. She should have realized that he, of all people, would never take the chance of causing an accidental pregnancy. Nobody knew better than he the difficulties that could cause.

She lifted her head, slipped her arms around his neck and kissed him soundly, thoroughly. She tried to put everything she couldn't find words to say in that kiss. And when she let her head fall back to the pillow at last, she could see in his face that her message had been received.

"Are you going to use that," she asked, "or just wave it around?"

He laughed, and this time she could feel it with her whole body as he lay over her. He sat up, tore open the wrapper and sheathed himself. He did it fairly easily, but with just enough awkwardness to tell her he didn't do it every day. He turned back to her, swallowed, started to speak, stopped, then tried again.

"If you want to stop, now's the time."

She stared at him; the thought of stopping at this point had never entered her mind. He seemed to misinterpret her reaction, because he said quickly, "I don't mean I won't stop if you tell me." He made a wry face at her. "I just mean if we go any further, it'll probably kill me."

"If you stop," she said, reaching out to trail a finger down his naked chest with as much nonchalance as she could muster, "I may kill you myself."

With a sound that was half groan, half chuckle, he lowered himself to her, bracing himself with those powerful arms. She welcomed him eagerly, her hands moving as swiftly as his had, tracing the powerful lines of his body, savoring every angle, every plane, every fit, potent inch of him.

When he nudged at her thighs, she opened for him quickly, shivering in anticipation, aching in some empty place deep inside that she'd never known was there.

And then Luke was sliding into her, slowly, with exquisite care, stretching her, and the emptiness began to recede.

She felt him shudder, saw the muscles in his arms tremble. Muscles that handled raging water, that powered through impossible rapids, were trembling.

She suddenly realized why.

"Don't," she said. "Don't hold back. Not now."

"Amelia," he breathed, as if she'd released him from a penance.

He drove into her, high and hard and deep. She cried out in shock at the fierceness of it, at the marvelous fullness of it, at the sheer pleasure of his sweet invasion. Her cry melded with his throttled oath as he rocked against her, grinding his hipbones against hers, pushing harder, then harder, as if he felt the same urgent need she was feeling.

She fairly writhed beneath him, wanting more, yet certain she could take no more, that she was stretched beyond bearing. The only thing she could think of that would ease this clenching, grabbing need was for him to do what he'd just done. Again. And again. And again.

"Again?" he growled against her ear as he eased his body back, and she realized she had voiced the longing.

"And again," she whispered, voicing the rest of the wish, pushed beyond shyness by raging need.

He pulled back, nearly left her, and she whimpered at the loss. He slid his hands under her, curled his fingers back over her shoulders, and when she realized he was bracing her, holding her in place so he could thrust harder, the anticipation nearly made her cry out before he even moved.

And then he drove forward, hard and fast again, burying himself to the hilt in her with one long, swift, powerful stroke. Again and again, just as she'd begged, he hammered her body with his own, driving her up and up with each plunge, until her only grip on the world was the feel of his body beneath her hands.

She clutched at him, her fingers slipping over skin now damp with sweat. She shifted her legs, opening for him even more, as her hands cupped his buttocks and she added her own urgency to his barely restrained power.

He muttered her name, once, twice, and then again, in a low, guttural voice that only added to the thrilling pounding of his body. However wild, however ferocious, this was, there was nothing mindless about it; it was very, very specific, and it was for her. Her, and her alone. Given by a man who at this moment seemed to know her better than anyone else ever had.

She no longer knew herself at all, no longer had any connection to shy, reserved Amelia Blair. She was some wild, desperate thing, propelled higher and higher by the man in her arms, flying, spinning, rising, until she thought she would break free completely and go soaring off into some other world it had taken a fallen angel to show her existed.

With a feral-sounding groan, Luke's grip on her shoulders tightened. She felt one of his hands leave her shoulder, felt it slide between their bodies. With him above her, she was wide open to his touch, and he quickly found the tiny knot of nerve endings.

He stroked her once, then again a little harder.

"Luke!" she gasped, certain she was going to lose her tenuous grip on him, and thus the world.

He made a circular motion then, and Amelia felt an unbearable pressure. She moaned, unable to stop the sound. He caressed her again, this time slowing withdrawing. She felt her body clench, trying to keep him, trying to hold him.

He swirled his finger over that bundle of nerves one more time, and before the incredible sensation could fade, he buried himself in her once more.

She didn't lose her hold on the world, it exploded around her. Her body convulsed. It wanted to curl in on itself, so violent were the waves of pleasure. But Luke was there, buried inside her, so all she could do was curl around him, holding, grasping, calling his name as the sheer force of it—

and the sound of Luke crying out her name in turn, as he poured himself into her—drove tears from her eyes.

And when she came back to earth, it didn't matter that it was shattered, forever changed. Luke was there, and he caught her, held her, cradled her against him. Nothing could be too wrong with her world if he was with her.

Hours later Amelia stirred sleepily. She'd never felt quite this way before, never known such a delicious exhaustion.

She wasn't sure how many times they'd actually made love, was almost sure she must have dreamed some of them. Maybe the time when she'd roused to his hands on her and he'd slid into her the moment he knew she was awake. Or maybe the time she'd awakened him with unstudied but eager caresses, when he'd encouraged her to explore every inch of him with the same thoroughness he'd used on her, when she'd taken the offer of his body with an eagerness that had ended with them both crying out fiercely. Yes, that was likely a dream; she couldn't really have done that, could she?

But then again, she thought as she shifted lazily and felt the tenderness of her body in unaccustomed places, maybe she had. If this was the wrong kind of paradise, she wanted to stay here forever.

She wondered what would happen if she reached for him again; would he be as ready, come to life as wildly under her hands and mouth?

Worth finding out, she thought with a new confidence gained from knowing that this man, this wild, gorgeous creature, found her so desirable he shook with it.

She rolled over.

She reached for him.

He was gone.

He should be, Luke thought, drained. Dry. Spent. Amelia had driven him to the point of madness and then beyond. He'd never had such a wild night in his life, and that it was

COMING NEXT MONTH

#1039 THE BRANDS WHO CAME FOR CHRISTMAS—
Maggie Shayne

The Oklahoma All-Girl Brands

After one incredible night spent in the arms of a stranger, Maya Brand found herself pregnant—with twins! But when her mystery man reappeared and claimed he wanted to be part of their lives, was Maya ready to trust Caleb Montgomery with her expected bundles of joy—and with her own fragile heart?

#1040 HERO AT LARGE—Robyn Amos

A Year of Loving Dangerously

SPEAR agent Keshon Gray was on a mission that could ultimately get him killed. So when his one and only love, Rennie Williams, re-entered his life, Keshon wasn't about to let her get too close. But knowing she was near forced Keshon to re-evaluate his life. If he survived his mission, would he consider starting over with the woman he couldn't resist?

#1041 MADE FOR EACH OTHER—Doreen Owens Malek

FBI bodyguard Tony Barringer knew he shouldn't mix business with pleasure when it came to protecting Jill Darcy and her father from a series of threats. After all, Tony was around for very different reasons—ones Jill *definitely* wouldn't be happy about. So until he got his answers, Tony had to hold out—no matter what his heart demanded.

#1042 HERO FOR HIRE—Marie Ferrarella

ChildFinders, Inc.

Detective Chad Andreini was more than willing to help beautiful Veronica Lancaster find her kidnapped son—*but* she insisted on helping with the investigation. So they teamed up, determined to bring the boy back home. But once the ordeal was over, could this unlikely pair put their own fears aside and allow their passions to take over?

#1043 DANGEROUS LIAISONS—Maggie Price

Nicole Taylor's business was love matches, not murder. Until her dating-service clients started turning up dead. Suddenly she found herself suspected, then safeguarded, by Sergeant Jake Ford. And falling hard for the brooding top cop who no longer believed in love.

#1044 DAD IN BLUE—Shelley Cooper

Samantha Underwood would do whatever it took to help her eight-year-old son recover from the loss of his father. And thanks to sexy police chief Carlo Garibaldi, the boy seemed to be improving. But when it came to love, Carlo was a tough man to convince—until Samantha showed him just how good it could be....

Amelia who had done it only made it more incredible. He shouldn't even be able to move.

Yet he was strangely churned up, strung so tight that he'd had to do something. He felt like he did after taking folks on a good run down Cherry Creek for the first time: tired from the exertion, but ablaze with exhilaration. He'd tried to stay still; he didn't want to disturb Amelia, especially when she lay sleeping close against him so trustingly. But he knew from experience there was only one way to handle this state of mind, and that was to walk it off.

So here he was, wandering the midnight dark streets of Santiago Beach once more. And thinking.

He wanted to simply revel in what he and Amelia had found, that incredible fire, but he couldn't help wondering what would happen now. Walking away from such incredible passion, something he'd never thought to find for himself, seemed impossible. But so did the idea of his rough and tumble world ever melding with Amelia's quiet existence.

The river was his life. He tried to picture himself living somewhere else—not even Santiago Beach, necessarily, just anywhere that didn't have a river to run. It made him ache inside, an echo of the pain he'd battled every day before he'd escaped this place and found his life.

But picturing himself going back to that life now, never seeing Amelia again, never seeing the flashes of sharp wit dart from behind that reserved mask, never seeing that shy smile, never hearing that sweet laugh again, never having another night like they'd just had...

He shook his head sharply. He told himself not to think about it, not to tarnish the moment, to concentrate on the here and now. Just think about today, not tomorrow. Once that had been the mantra that had helped him survive; now it seemed sadly ineffective.

He couldn't come back here. He knew that. That he was even thinking about it long enough to decide that shocked him. He didn't even like the idea of coming back periodically, although if that was the only way to see her, he supposed he would just have to get over it. Sure, it was a long ride, seven hours each way, but if he had to, he had to. But seeing her once a week—less during the peak rafting season, when they were all working like crazy every day—didn't seem a very satisfying solution. Not to mention the guilt. He'd already been gone longer than he'd planned, and he knew Gary had to be doing double duty to make up for his absence.

He reached Main Street and turned south, toward Amelia's store for no other reason than that it was hers. He stopped in front of it for a moment, looking in the darkened window. The beach display looked rather eerie in the dark, as if the people who had been reading those books in the sun had vanished by nightfall, leaving everything behind.

He could just see the corner of her office from here. Heat blasted through him at the memory of what had almost happened there, which brought on an even more powerful memory of what had happened tonight, in that wonderfully wicked bed of hers.

Keep walking, he told himself, knowing that if he didn't, he was going to head back to her place at a run, slide back into bed with her and make them both even rawer than they already were from a night of making love as if the sun wasn't going to rise.

He walked on, hands jammed in his pockets.

He couldn't picture her leaving here. She was settled here, with a business, a house—her parents' house—why on earth would she leave? And even if she would, what did he have to offer? He lived in a small cabin that wouldn't hold even half of her things, and—

He stopped in his tracks, suddenly realizing what he was thinking. Was he ready for this?

He made himself start walking again.

The idea of being with Amelia day in and day out was

certainly attractive, but he knew she wasn't the type for a casual affair. When it came down to it, neither was he; he'd gone through a brief stage as a teenager when he'd mistaken sex for love, when he'd found comfort in the closeness to another person, and had hungered for it from whatever girl would give it to him. But he'd soon realized the girls who would give it to him wanted the tough, notorious Luke McGuire, not a boy looking for a comfort he'd never gotten and hadn't been sure existed.

Gary and his wife had finally shown him what real love was like, the give and take, the mutual concern, the silent communication, the laughter, the tears, the incredible closeness. He'd lived with their example before him for years now, and had pretty much decided it was a very rare miracle. He had never expected to find a woman who made him think it might be possible for him.

Love? Was that what he was feeling? He'd never really been in love before. Had never really been able to picture himself together with anyone in the way Gary and Diane were together.

But he could picture it with Amelia.

His steps slowed. His mind was instinctively shying away from this revelation, looking for something, anything, else to think about, so he could shove this back into his pack and take it out later, when he was calmer. Later, when he wasn't still humming with the pleasure of her touch.

He realized he was nearing the library. That would do, he thought. He would give that crawl space another check. He didn't have the flashlight, but he should be able to hear if anyone was there, in the nighttime silence.

He picked up his pace, glad to have the distraction of a destination. He took the shortcut, the walkway that ran between the community center that faced Main Street and the library that faced Cabrillo Street behind it. The notices posted on the community center bulletin board lifted in the slight sea breeze, drawing his eye for a moment.

His mouth quirked when he saw the flyer for his mother's speech. He let out a compressed breath, surprised at himself when he realized his main reaction was one of amusement. And for the first time he wondered how much worse his life might have been had she not found this outlet for her hatred.

He moved on, leaving the flyer behind him.

He was going to leave the hatred behind him, too, Luke determined as he rounded the corner to head for the library.

And ran head on into David.

Chapter 16

Luke expected David to run when he grabbed his arm, but the boy just stood there. He was clearly startled by his brother's sudden appearance, but he looked chastened and small somehow, his usual cocky demeanor vanished. There were smudges of dirt on his cheek and jaw, and his clothes were a bit worse for wear. He looked ragged, afraid and exhausted.

For Luke, it was like looking back in time at himself, and while he was still pretty peeved at the boy for trying to rip off Amelia, he couldn't bring himself to vent at him now. Besides, if Amelia could forgive the kid, he certainly could. He was his brother, after all.

"You win," he said.

David looked up. "What?"

"I didn't think anybody could be stupider than I was at your age. Obviously I was wrong."

That didn't even get a rise out of him. The boy just lowered his gaze to his shoes again, as if he didn't even have the energy to fight back anymore. Luke had been there, too, down, beaten, on the edge of giving up. The last of his anger died away. He reached out and put his arm around his brother's shoulders. He drew the boy over to a bench in the library courtyard. David stiffened, as if he were going to resist sitting down, but then gave in.

"Good thing being stupid now doesn't mean you have to be stupid forever," Luke said.

David shook his head. Luke sighed. "It doesn't," he insisted. "Look, Amelia was pretty upset about the check. She felt…as betrayed as you did when I couldn't take you to live with me."

David's shoulders shook under his arm. He couldn't really see the boy's face, but he could guess what it looked like. His natural urge was to comfort his brother, but he also knew that he would never have a better chance to get through to him. Knew that with all his defenses down, the boy might actually listen, and if he waited until he recovered a little, those defenses would get in the way again. So instead of easing up, he bore down.

"You know, if you'd needed money that badly and you wouldn't come to me, you could have asked her. I'll bet she'd have helped. You didn't have to steal that check."

"I didn't steal it! I didn't even know they did it!"

The words broke from the boy in a rush. He sounded desperate, the kind of desperate Luke knew too well, when nobody would believe you, even when you were telling the truth.

Maybe Amelia had been right all along about who had taken the check. He decided to push a little more.

"Then those are some friends you have there. Cornering a lone woman like that, waving a knife at her so she doesn't notice when they rip her off."

David's head snapped up. Luke saw his eyes gleam for a moment in the dark.

"At least you weren't with them then. That would have broken her heart."

David lowered his gaze once more. "I wouldn't hurt Amelia."

There was a strange, almost vibrating tension in David's voice. It made Luke frown uneasily. And again he had to force himself to be tough. If had any influence left with his brother at all, he had to use it now.

"Then why did you try and pass that check?"

"They made me."

Luke gave a disbelieving snort. "Oh, please. That's such a kid's excuse. *'They made me,'*" he repeated, in a babyish voice.

"They did!" David's voice rose. "It wasn't my fault. I wouldn't hurt Amelia! But I couldn't stop them. I tried, I really tried, but I couldn't, and now they're gonna do it, and it'll be my fault!"

Luke went very still. Something had changed here, something important. That slip of tense wasn't an accident. David wasn't just talking about the check anymore; Luke could feel it. "Going to do what?"

David didn't answer. Luke heard a ragged sniffle, knew the boy was fighting breaking down completely. He reached out and gripped his brother's shoulders, turning him to face him. He saw then, in the dim glow of the building's exterior lights, that what he'd thought was dirt were instead bruises. Fresh ones, if he was any judge, and he was.

"David!" he snapped. "What are they going to do?"

David swallowed. "I can't tell you. They'll beat me up."

"Looks like they already have."

"They'll do it worse."

"I may help them along if you don't tell me what the hell is going on."

David cringed, then said, "They're…really mad at Amelia for that night you guys got in a fight. Snake doesn't like it that a girl made them run."

"I'll bet he doesn't," Luke said, suppressing a grin at the memory of Amelia's flying kick. Then, abruptly, he made the connection. "You mean they want revenge? On Amelia?"

David didn't answer, but Luke knew. His stomach knotted.

The thought of Amelia hurt, or worse, struck a terror into him that no raging torrent of a river ever had. And in that moment he knew just how deep his feelings for her ran. He had his answer; it was most definitely love.

"And you claim them as your *friends*," he said to David acidly.

"I thought they were. But they were just using me." David did sniff this time. "I found out they only let me hang out with them because of where I live. They wanted an excuse to hang out in that neighborhood."

"So they could rip off the houses," Luke guessed, and David nodded miserably.

"I thought they were my friends," he whined. "I thought they were like you, and it would make my mom mad if I hung with them. She didn't even care that my dad died, and I wanted to get back at her—"

"Just shut up!" Luke found himself suddenly devoid of patience, compassion and gentleness. "Why don't you grow up? At least you had a dad who loved you for fifteen years. But do you appreciate that? Do you try to honor his memory? No, you go out and find a bunch of dirty, stupid losers for friends, cowards who gang up on a woman."

David was shuddering now, his shoulders heaving as he gulped back sobs. Luke was merciless, both out of his rage that anyone would deliberately hurt Amelia and his certainty that only by hitting absolute bottom could David start over, as he had.

"If they had any balls they'd come after me, not Amelia. And you're turning into one of them, a sneaking, sniveling coward who lets guys who are just using him coerce him into stealing from the best friend he has left."

David broke, tears streaming down his bruised face. Luke

felt a pang; having the brother you'd once idolized chew you to bits couldn't be easy.

"I didn't mean it," David hiccuped. "I just wanted her to care. I just wanted her to notice he was gone!"

Luke knew who he meant, but right now his mother didn't concern him. "What are they planning?"

"I don't know."

"Don't give me any bull. What are they planning?"

"I don't know!" David insisted. "They wouldn't tell me. I tried to get them to, but that's when they started hitting me."

"They must have said something. You must have heard something."

David shook his head. "I don't know anything! They beat me up and then told me to get lost, 'cuz Snake didn't want me riding in his new car."

Luke stiffened. "He was getting a car?"

David hiccuped again, then nodded. "He bought it with the cash he got from selling the VCRs and camcorders they ripped off from all our neighbors. It's not new, but he was gettin' a big stereo put in today, with a CD changer."

Luke felt a chill. A gang of thugs. Knives. A thirst for revenge. They dump the one kid who doesn't want to play.

And now they had wheels.

"Why didn't he want you in it?"

"I dunno." David wiped at his eyes. "He said something about tonight bein' a special night, with the car, I guess, and I should just wait and be quiet."

A special night...

Amelia.

"Son of a *bitch!*"

Luke's heart slammed into overdrive, and he leapt to his feet. David gaped at him.

"What's wrong?" he asked, a little timidly. Luke grabbed him by one arm and hauled him to his feet.

"Don't you get it, you idiot? They're going after Amelia

tonight! They're going after her, and I left her there, all alone."

David swayed on his feet. Luke cut him no slack.

"Your house is closer," he snapped, and started dragging the boy at a run. But as the situation penetrated David's emotionally battered mind, soon Luke didn't have to drag him; David started running on his own.

It was two blocks, mostly uphill, but Luke never let his pace falter. He had to get to Amelia, and this was the quickest way, even if it meant facing his mother again. Nothing mattered beside Amelia's safety, and he was very much afraid he might already be too late.

Amelia sat in the bed Luke had called deliciously wicked and wondered why he'd left her. She wrapped her arms around her knees, curling up against the pain. It didn't help. She bit her lip, fighting tears. She tried not to look when the bedside clock clicked over another minute; she knew it was nearly one, knew it all too well.

When she'd awakened alone, she'd hoped he was just somewhere else in the house. She could see he wasn't in the bathroom off her bedroom, but she'd waited, certain he was here and would be back with her any moment. The kitchen, perhaps, getting a drink, or maybe needing something from the saddlebag on his bike. She'd even blushed then, thinking that if they kept this up, he was going to need a very large box of condoms.

But he hadn't come back. And his clothes, the clothes she'd helped him shed so eagerly, were gone. Even his shoes, which seemed somehow the most ominous thing of all.

She'd looked for a note on his pillow, on the nightstand, the dresser, some sign, anything. She'd found nothing. And now she was just sitting here, an aching, ridiculous stereotype of a weeping, abandoned woman.

Just how big a fool had she been? Now that he'd gotten

what he'd wanted, had he just abandoned her? Was she already forgotten, nothing more than a memory among many memories? They'd never talked about that, about past lovers, fool that she was. She'd thought about it, but she'd wanted him no matter what the answer, so she cravenly hadn't asked.

I wonder where I rank on that list of memories?

It didn't seem possible. How could she doubt him, after the hours they'd just spent? He'd made love to her with a wild urgency she couldn't believe was faked. And then with a gentle tenderness that was even harder to believe wasn't real.

But she was admittedly naive, and Luke was undoubtedly gone.

Okay, she told herself firmly, he's gone. He could have a perfectly good reason. Something he forgot he had to do, or maybe he'd had an idea about David and hadn't wanted to wake her while he checked it out.

But he would have left a note, wouldn't he? Or would he? She didn't have enough experience in such things to judge. Was it asking too much to expect him to let her know? Was she hopelessly old-fashioned, or was Luke too much of a free spirit to be tied down by a woman who panicked when she woke up alone?

It hit her then, belatedly. She'd awakened alone. Luke had already been gone. But she hadn't heard a thing. She wasn't surprised, after the night they'd spent, that she'd slept through him rising, getting dressed and leaving the house.

But there was no way on earth she would have slept through the snarl of the Harley starting up.

She leapt out of bed and fairly raced out of her bedroom, across the living room and into the kitchen, where a side window looked out onto the carport, where he'd parked the bike. She leaned over the sink, peering through the darkness.

Just in front of her car's bumper, she saw the faint gleam

of a polished black fender, the slightly brighter gleam of a silver pipe lower down.

Her heels hit the floor. Her eyes brimmed and overflowed. She bit her lip, and her fingers curled into fists.

He had left her a message. The biggest one he could.

He was coming back.

She started to laugh at herself through the tears and nearly choked. Lord, if that wasn't the perfect demonstration of her idiotic state. She was a fool, all right.

But at least she wasn't the kind of fool she'd thought she was.

She went back to the bedroom with a considerably lighter step. Relief was singing through her veins, and she was a bit giddy with it. Her mind was racing wildly. What would they do now? He could never come back to Santiago Beach to live; she knew that. She couldn't blame him; she wasn't very happy herself with how he'd been treated here, so she could only imagine how he felt.

And for the first time she asked herself just how attached she was to this town.

The answer, when compared to how attached she was to Luke McGuire, was not very.

Smothering a silly giggle, she resisted the urge to twirl on one foot. She couldn't decide what to do next. She knew she wouldn't be able to go back to sleep, not until he came back. Should she just get back into bed and wait there? Pretend she'd been asleep all along? She didn't think she wanted to admit how she'd panicked. But she didn't want to lie to him, either.

Maybe she should get dressed. No, that would seem very odd, and besides, he might think she didn't want them to climb right back into bed and begin again where they had left off, which she most certainly did want….

A tremor swept through her as hot, erotic images rose in her mind: Luke naked and beautiful before her, his eyes hot with desire as he looked at her, making her feel beautiful, his body driving into her, pounding her flesh so gloriously with his own, his strangled cry of her name as he bucked hard in her arms. She wanted it all again. And again.

She compromised. She pulled out a long, soft, yellow silk T-shirt trimmed with gold satin that she sometimes slept in. The color made the gold flecks in her eyes stand out, her mother had always said. She held it up to herself in front of the dresser mirror, hoping that, whatever her mother might have thought about the precipitousness of the relationship, she would be glad her daughter was, at the moment, deliriously happy.

She pulled the shirt on, forgoing anything underneath. The thought of greeting him when he came back, covered from shoulders nearly to her knees, yet naked underneath, was amazingly arousing.

She had no sooner tugged the shirt down than she heard him coming back. Her heart began to trip in anticipation. She gave a last swipe to her hair with a brush but didn't try to smooth it completely; she hoped he would remember tangling it with his hands when she'd begun her lengthy, intimate exploration of his body. She glanced in the mirror once more, amazed at the reflection that greeted her, the reflection of a woman who had been completely, thoroughly loved. Tousled hair, kiss-swollen lips, even a reddish spot or two his emerging beard had rubbed on her skin.

And, she guessed, a few other marks in some more intimate places. The heat of remembrance flooded her again, and she turned and headed for the door, her body already humming with eagerness.

She broke into a trot as she crossed the living room. As she neared the door she noticed her keys were gone from the table. She smiled; Luke must have taken them, so he could lock the door for her safety, yet get back in when he came back to her.

The noise came from the door again, a metallic sound. He seemed to be having trouble. He was probably having to try every key on there to find the right one; one of these days she would put the store keys on another ring. She smothered a laugh at how surprised he would be when the door swung open from inside. She reached for the deadbolt and flipped it, then the knob. She yanked the door open eagerly. Something fell to the ground, something that looked like a pair of locking pliers. Amelia eyes instinctively tracked the movement, then shot back up to the startled face before her.

It was Snake.

And his friends were with him.

Jackie Hiller stood in her doorway, staring in shock at her two sons.

"I need your car," Luke said abruptly.

"How dare you!" She seemed torn, not knowing who to focus on. She turned on David. "And you! I've already reported you to the police."

"I don't care. Give him the car."

"How dare you speak to me like tha—" She gasped as Luke pushed past her into the house. "I'm calling the police right back here!"

"Yes, do that. The sooner the better." He ignored his mother's puzzled look. "Where are the keys?" Luke asked his brother.

"She keeps them in the drawer. There," David supplied, pointing at a table in the elegantly appointed foyer. She'd changed the furnishings, Luke noticed as he strode across the huge entry. All the glitter and fake gold she'd always wanted. He yanked the drawer open.

"If you so much as touch my car I'll have you put in jail and the key thrown away!"

He grabbed the keys. And then he faced his mother. Somehow, in the face of possible danger to Amelia, she seemed smaller, less intimidating, a shrewish, selfish woman not worth the energy it took to hate her.

"For once in your self-centered, mean-spirited life, shut

up. You have nothing to say that either of us wants to hear.'' She gaped at him, stunned, for once, into silence. Luke turned to his brother. ''Can I trust you?''

David drew himself up. In the light of the house his face was a sight, tearstained and bruised. Bruises his mother hadn't even asked about, Luke realized.

''Yes,'' David said firmly. ''She doesn't matter.''

His mother gasped. Luke nodded; his little brother had come a long way tonight. ''No, she doesn't. Call the police. Send them to Amelia's. Fast.''

''Can't I go with you? I want to help.''

''I need you to do this,'' Luke said.

David hesitated, then did the last little bit of growing up. ''All right. Go. Hurry.''

Luke ran for the door. The last thing he heard as he hit the front steps was David's voice.

''Get out of the way, Mom. Now. I'm calling the police.''

His brother might just make it, he thought as he raced around to where his mother's big new boat of a sedan was parked. Thing probably drives like a tank, he thought as he hit the alarm release on her key chain and the car unlocked and beeped. But it didn't matter, as long as it got him to Amelia.

In time.

Chapter 17

Amelia had never been so terrified in her life. What had minutes before been arousing was now a huge mistake; she felt even more vulnerable dressed only in the silk shirt. She was cornered, nearly naked, barefoot, without a weapon in sight. Snake was between her and the door, one of the others between her and the phone.

And bearing down on her, a malicious expression on a face that seemed decades older than his actual years, was the boy she'd hit the night of the fight.

His knife was much bigger than Snake's butterfly knife. It was also shiny new, and she wondered if he'd bought—or stolen—it just for the occasion.

Amelia suppressed a shiver, knowing she didn't dare show them how scared she was. And prayed that Luke would come back. Now.

"We saw your tough-guy boyfriend leave," Snake said, as if he'd read her thoughts. "We were waiting down the street. Isn't he going to be surprised when he comes back and finds you like we're going to leave you?"

It was on the tip of her tongue to ask what they were going to do, but she bit it back. She knew her voice would shake and betray her fear. She also sensed it would somehow acknowledge their complete control of the situation. And besides, she didn't really want to know; her guesses were bad enough.

"Do you like Fargo's knife?" Snake asked, as if he'd read her earlier thoughts. "It's just for you. You'll be its first blood."

She had to do something, say something, not let them think she was cowed into total silence. She concentrated on keeping her voice steady. "Fargo? From the place or the movie?"

The boy with the blade looked startled. Snake frowned. And it was Snake who said, "The movie. Not that it's any of your business."

Amazingly, that steadied her. They were armed; they were mean; they were dangerous. But they were also kids. Kids who took nicknames out of movies. There had to be something she could do, even if she was afraid.

You've got something more important than nerve, you've got brains. That'll outdo brawn and nerve most times.

Luke's words rang in her head. She remembered the tenderness in his voice when he'd said them, and she tried to draw strength from that. Surely she could stall them until he got here?

Unless he wasn't coming back until morning. Or afternoon.

She couldn't allow herself to believe that or she would panic. And panic was going to get her hurt, raped or worse.

With a tremendous effort she put as much amusement as she could into her voice and face and asked Snake, "Doesn't anybody else talk but you?"

"Shut up, bitch," Fargo snarled.

Amelia lifted a brow. "He does talk!"

"I do the talking because I'm the head man," Snake said, gesturing with his own knife.

Amelia looked around at the others. "You guys elected *him?* Whew. Good thing you're not old enough to vote yet."

Snake lunged toward her. It took everything she had not to recoil, not to break and run. He stopped short, looking at her with intense curiosity tinged with the slightest touch of wariness.

"Why ain't she scared, Snake?" one of the others asked. Amelia didn't see who; she never took her eyes off of Snake.

"I don't know," Snake muttered, clearly disconcerted.

You've got brains....

So use them, she told herself. "She ain't scared," she said sweetly, "because she has a silent alarm and the cops are roaring over here right now."

All of them jerked upright and looked toward the street. Amelia took full advantage. She darted back toward the hallway. The instant she was out of their sight she reached out and slammed the door to the spare bedroom shut as she passed it. She dodged sideways into the next room, the second bathroom, but left the door open. She hid in the dark behind it, holding her breath.

She heard them shouting. Heard them running. And seconds later heard them pounding on the closed bedroom door. More shouting, epithets she'd never even heard before, and threats she was pretty sure were physically impossible. She held her breath, waiting for one of them to realize the door wasn't even locked.

That it stupidly took them so long gave her hope. It was a good minute before she heard one of them yell, "Hey, the door isn't even locked!"

The slam of the bedroom door back against the wall. Rapid footsteps as they charged in. The moment she was sure they were inside she gathered every bit of nerve she had—and borrowed more from Luke's faith in her—and came out from her hiding place.

With their voices ringing from the room, she grabbed the chair from the vanity in the bathroom.

"Check the closet!"

"Under the bed!"

"Isn't no window, she's gotta be here!"

She crossed the hall to the door they'd opened in one swift step. She reached in, praying they were too occupied to see her.

She yanked the door shut.

She jammed the chair under the knob.

She held her breath as they realized what had happened and tried to shove the door open.

The chair held. She let out her breath in a nearly sobbing gasp of relief.

Don't let down now. That chair won't hold forever. Call the police.

She whirled, headed for the cordless phone that she could take outside.

She'd missed one. Snake and his knife were waiting for her.

Her relief vanished. She tried desperately to pull herself back together. Her mind was racing as Snake started toward her, his knife at the ready. She saw his gaze flick to the blocked door. There was the slightest hitch in his steps as he pondered his options.

"Think you're clever, don't you, bitch?" he snarled.

"I *know* you're a coward," Amelia said with all the cool she could muster. "Why, I'll bet right now all you want to do is let your friends out, so you don't have to face the big, bad woman all alone."

He stopped dead, and she knew that was exactly what he'd been going to do. He's a hothead, she told herself. Push him, maybe he'll do something stupid.

Yeah, and you'll be on the receiving end, the coward within told her.

Stall, at least, she thought, hating herself for her paralyzing fear. The boys in the bedroom were still pounding and yelling. They shoved against the door. Amelia held her breath, but the chair held.

"You'd better shut up," Snake said, waving the Balisong at her. She should have read that book, she thought. Maybe there was a way to disarm somebody with one of those.

Stop it, she snapped inwardly. If there was, she didn't know it, and she didn't have time to waste thinking about it.

"And don't you try one of those fancy things you did to Fargo. I'll cut your leg off."

Sticking with what had worked so far—and what had worked for Luke the other night—Amelia laughed. She leaned against the back of her overstuffed chair, trying for the most insouciant posture she could manage. "Oh, no, I wouldn't think of it. I've got a much better one in mind for you. If the cops don't get here in time to save you."

She didn't know how much longer she could keep this up. She tried desperately to think of something else to distract Snake, but she was running out of ideas and had the terrifying feeling she was running out of time, as well.

"Cops'd be here by now if they were comin'," he sneered disbelievingly, but there was just enough doubt in his face to give her the fortitude to keep going. "I didn't see no alarm."

The boys trapped in the bedroom shoved against the door again.

The chair began to slip.

God, I hope I'm wrong. I hope it's all a mistake, that their talk was all bluster, that it wasn't tonight, anything. That I'll get there and everything will be quiet, she'll be sound asleep, just as I left her, soft, warm, sexy....

Luke ignored the protesting howl of the tires as he rounded the corner. For the first time in his life he prayed for the cops to see him, chase him. But also for what seemed the first time in his life—in Santiago Beach, anyway—there were none in sight.

He had to trust David. He had to trust that the boy felt awful enough and guilty enough that he would make that call, no matter how hard his mother tried to stop him.

He barely touched the brakes as he made the turn onto Amelia's street. His eyes flicked to the little white house with the profusion of flowers.

There was an old, dark sedan parked half in the driveway and half on top of her flowers.

Every muscle in his body tightened, and Luke's heart slammed into high speed like a kayak coming out of the slot. For an instant he debated. Better to arrive with tires squealing and horn blaring, so they would know she had help now? Or would that startle them into doing something they hadn't intended? Something they might do out of panic? Something irreversible…?

He couldn't, wouldn't, take that chance, not with Amelia. He blacked out the lights, then yanked the wheel to the left, pulling the big car in at an angle that blocked the other car's exit. He got out and spent a precious second listening. That was all it took for him to hear voices yelling from inside the house.

It took every bit of restraint, every ounce of patience he'd gained in years of learning when to fight the river and when to just go with it, to stop himself from blasting through the front door. Instead he crept up to it, avoiding the sidewalk for silence, keeping to the shadows of the greenery.

He got up to the edge of the porch, beneath the window thankfully open to the summer air, just in time to hear Amelia say, "—could see it and disarm it, it wouldn't be a very good alarm, now would it?"

To anyone else, Luke was sure she would sound utterly unconcerned. But he'd come to know her voice rather well, and he could hear the undertone beneath the nonchalant words.

He heard another voice, lower, male and young. Snake, he guessed. He could hear Amelia more clearly and hoped that was because Snake had his back to the window. He risked a peek.

Amelia was leaning against her chair as if she hadn't a care in the world, facing the door. Snake did indeed have his back to the partly open door, and he was the one who looked unsteady, shifting his feet nervously, waving that damned knife around. If he was just a step closer to the door, Luke thought, he could take him out with it. Hit it full force and it would knock him sideways.

For an instant he thought he saw Amelia look toward him. Her expression didn't change, but he was very in tune with that body of hers, and he saw the sudden increase in tension. He made a quick gesture at Snake and then toward the door, hoping against hope she had really looked, had seen him and had correctly interpreted his signal.

"Don't tell me you walked right by the control pad and didn't even see it?" Amelia said to Snake with creditable disbelief. "I mean, it's right there by the door."

Snake turned to look. And took that crucial one step.

God, he loved this woman! Luke went up and over the porch railing. He never stopped. He hit the front door hard with his shoulder, felt the satisfying thud as it connected with flesh on the other side.

He heard a string of curses. Saw Snake scrambling to get to his feet. Saw the glint of metal in his hand. Luke tackled him. They went down in a pile. Out of the corner of his eye he saw Snake's arm flailing. The silver knife waved in a dangerously close arc. Luke saw Amelia move. He put into play all his considerable upper body weight and strength against Snake's struggling. With a grunt of pain, the boy gave up.

Luke rolled him over, face down on the floor. Amelia was there, armed with a formidable looking brass lamp she'd apparently been about to bring down on Snake's knife hand.

Keeping one knee in the small of his back, Luke told Snake, "You're lucky I got here. She would have busted your arm. Or your head."

In that moment he heard the approaching wail of sirens; David had come through. The pounding and shoving from the spare bedroom stopped at the sound. Amelia slowly lowered the lamp. Luke looked up at her.

She looked fine. She looked unhurt. She looked damned beautiful. He grinned at her.

"Ms. Earhart," he said, "would be proud."

"We would have been here sooner," Jim Stavros apologized to Amelia, "but we thought it was some kid making a crank call."

Jim had just arrived, now that the dust had settled; he'd heard her address go out on the radio at the station, he had explained.

"That's all right. It's over now," Amelia said.

"Yeah," Luke agreed, one arm around Amelia, holding her close. "And I don't want to hear any more about nerve or courage or any of that. I've got proof now, lady."

Amelia blushed, but she had to admit that perhaps, just perhaps, she wasn't quite as timid as she'd always thought. She leaned into him, loving that it was her right to do so. He'd explained about his leaving, castigating himself so fiercely for it that she'd silenced him with a kiss.

"Just leave a note next time, will you?"

He looked relieved that there would be a next time, then said rather sheepishly, "I'm not used to having anybody who'd miss me."

"I missed you. Even before they got here, I missed you."

She would have shown him right then how much, but it didn't seem quite right, with the police scrambling all over the place. And then Jim had arrived and taken charge, and things seemed to smooth out with only him to deal with.

Jim looked over at Luke now as two officers led Snake

and the hapless Fargo away; the others were already in the back seats of patrol cars. It seemed to Amelia that the entire graveyard shift of Santiago Beach PD must be here.

"And I should have figured you'd be right in the middle of it all," Jim said.

Luke shrugged. "Hey, I just did the clean up. Amelia handled the tough part."

Jim eyed Amelia somewhat doubtfully. She couldn't blame him; she couldn't quite believe it herself, that she'd even survived this.

"Sarge?" The voice came from one of the officers at the door. "I think our reporting party just showed up."

Amelia looked at Luke. He had related in a few brief sentences what David had told him. He'd also told her he thought his little brother had learned a very painful lesson in a big hurry, and that he'd done some very fast growing up tonight. She looked at Jim and nodded.

"Send him in," Jim told the officer.

David came in slowly, hesitantly, as if the room were mined. He looked like he would rather be anywhere else, but he kept coming, until he was standing in front of Amelia.

"I...I'm sorry Amelia. I never meant for any of this to happen. I never meant any trouble for you. I thought..." He stopped, his Adam's apple bobbing as he swallowed. "I thought they were my friends."

Amelia looked at his anxious face, saw the tearstains and his bruises. He gulped and went on.

"But they tried to hurt you, and you...you were my real friend."

"You're wrong, David." He seemed to crumple before her eyes, his shoulders sagging. "Not were. *Am.* I *am* your friend."

David's head came up. "You are? After...what I did?"

She glanced at Luke pointedly, then looked back at his brother. "I believe in second chances, David. And you did the right thing in the end."

She held out her arms, hoping that under the circumstances David wouldn't think he was too old for a hug.

He didn't. And he hugged her back, rather fiercely.

"And he's agreed to give testimony about what he saw and heard, and being coerced into trying to pass a forged check," Jim said. "Haven't you?"

David nodded; Amelia could feel the slight movement against her shoulder. She looked at Luke over David's head and smiled when she saw the look of approval he was giving his little brother.

After a moment David pulled back. He sniffed. And a tentative smile tried to surface. "Boy, is my mom mad."

"I'll bet," Luke said dryly.

Jim cleared his throat. "Does this have anything to do with the car out front registered to Jacqueline Hiller?"

Amelia blinked. "What car?"

"Yeah," Luke said. "I...borrowed it to get here."

Jim looked at Luke for a long, silent moment. "Seems to me I've heard that from you before, that you 'borrowed' a car just to get somewhere."

"You heard that from a scared, angry kid." Luke let out a weary-sounding sigh. "But I suppose that doesn't make any difference. I presume she's already reported it stolen?" He laughed sourly. "God, this'll make her year, being able to get me tossed in jail."

"As it happens," Jim said, "she did call. But with all this going on, nobody's gotten over there yet."

"Jim," Amelia protested, unable to believe what she was hearing. "He saved my life. Snake had that knife, and the kid called Fargo had a bigger one. You saw it!"

Jim nodded, but his eyes never left Luke. "I think I'll go on over there now. Somebody needs to explain to Mrs. Hiller how badly it will reflect on her if she tries to press charges against a man who was only trying to prevent assault, mayhem and possibly murder."

Luke drew back, his eyes widening as he stared at the man in the police uniform he'd learned to hate.

"There's no damage to the car that I can see, you're related to the owner, and you took it to help one of Santiago Beach's finest citizens...no, I don't think that would look very good, even if you are Luke McGuire."

Luke looked so shocked that Amelia had to smother a smile. She gave Jim a grateful clasp of his hand. He squeezed back, but he still looked at no one but Luke.

"You know, after our little encounter last night, I did a little checking up on you."

"You...did?" Luke said, his voice oddly tight.

"Uh-huh. Ran your record, got a name. One Officer Rob Porter, from the Los Angeles Police Department. He had some pretty interesting things to say."

Luke let out a long breath. His shoulders sagged, much as his young brother's had, only Amelia could see that in his case it was in relief.

"One of the best river guides in the state and one of the top ten river kayakers in the country?" Jim asked.

This time it was Amelia who was surprised; she'd assumed he was good, to be a guide, but he'd never told her just how good.

Luke shifted uncomfortably, not meeting Jim's gaze. "So they say."

"And then a couple of days ago I talked to Gary Milhouse, too. He informed me you're also certified in swiftwater rescue, not to mention first aid and CPR. And an expert on hydrotopography and river dynamics."

Amelia stared at Luke, who was studying the floor too intently; she was going to have to talk to him about this understatement business.

"Milhouse also said," Jim added, "that he'd trust you with anything he owned or anyone he loved."

Luke's head came up then, sharply. "Gary said...that?"

"He did."

Luke swallowed. "How about that," he said softly.

"I take that as a good reference," Jim said, with a rather pointed glance at Amelia. "Looks like it took the newcomer to see the truth. We were all blinded by past history."

Luke drew himself up straight. And Amelia had never been prouder of him than when he looked Jim in the eye and said, "So was I."

Jim smiled. He held out his hand. After a split second's hesitation, Luke took it. They shook, and Jim nodded. "I'll be on my way. I have some gossip to spread."

Before Luke could protest, Jim turned on his heel and was gone.

Luke swore.

Amelia laughed.

"Hail the conquering hero," she said softly. "Luke McGuire has returned."

Chapter 18

"**W**hoooooeeee!"

David's yelp carried for yards, and Amelia had to laugh; she knew exactly how he felt. She was wet, she was tired, she was a little chilled, but she'd never been so totally pumped and exhilarated in her life.

Well, she amended as she watched Luke tie up the raft they'd just taken down a section of his beloved river, maybe when they made love, but that was the only thing that even came close. The heat that thought brought on did away with her slight chill.

"That was so utterly cool!" David was practically dancing on the dock at Whitewater West. "Wasn't it, Amelia?"

"Definitely," she admitted.

Luke joined them then, smiling at his little brother. "So, you liked that little run?"

"Oh, man, yeah! This is a lot cooler even than what I thought you were doing."

Thank goodness for that, Amelia thought.

"When can we do it again?" the boy asked eagerly.

"We'll make another run tomorrow, if you want."

"Yeah, I do, a lot...but after this, I mean."

"You going to stay straight?"

"I will, I promise. She won't even recognize me."

Amelia saw Luke suppress a smile. "I know you'll try," he said.

Clearly Luke knew it wouldn't be that easy. Just like he knew he was going to have to fight to stay a part of his brother's life.

"I'll see what I can do. Sgt. Stavros talked her into this one. Maybe he can talk her into a trip every summer. And I'll go annoy her in person if I have to. Maybe she'll let you go just to keep me away."

David exulted as if it were a done deal, but Amelia knew that wasn't going to be easy, either. Jim had confronted Jackie with the truth about her son and told her that she was going to lose David if she continued to force the separation between brothers. Amelia suspected Jim had also made contact with Luke an unofficial condition of David not being charged with the attempted forgery, although Amelia had never intended to press charges anyway.

In any case, Jackie had reluctantly allowed this weekend trip. And left open the possibility of future ones.

"I don't get how she can still hate you, now that she knows the truth," David said.

"She won't change, Davie," Luke said. "I don't think she can. There's never going to be love between us. But maybe, someday, we can have peace."

"Hey, David!" came a yell from behind them. "Get on over here if you're eating lunch with us!"

"Coming! Save me a burger!"

The boy took off running to where Gary, Diane and their two girls, Jennifer and Jessica, were surrounding a barbecue. Amelia watched him go, then turned to find Luke studying her intently.

"So," he said, "are you going with us tomorrow? Or staying here with Diane?"

He was giving her, she realized, an easy way out. She and Diane had hit it off rather well, so there was a good excuse if she'd hated the river and didn't want to go back.

To her own surprise, she wanted to.

"I'd like to go with you."

"You're sure?"

She nodded. "I...it was wonderful."

He must have seen that she really meant it, because he grinned. "I knew you'd think so."

"Oh? And just how did you know that, Mr. McGuire?"

"Because," he said, pulling her into a bear hug, "underneath all that calm and cool, you're a class-five, lady." She shook her head, more in wonder than denial. Amazingly, Luke saw the difference. "It's always been there inside you, Amelia. You just buried it so deep it took a while to break loose."

She laughed. It was so insane. What she'd done today was insane. Virtually every moment since she'd met him had been insane. *She* was insane, and she was loving every minute of it.

"You know," he said, his voice suddenly husky, "David's going to be busy for at least an hour over there."

Amelia knew instantly what he meant. Heat pulsed through her. Luke had come up on his motorcycle last week, then she had driven up this weekend with David, and because of the boy's presence, they had tried to be discreet. Amelia had stayed in the main lodge, rather than being where she wanted to be, in the small cabin on the river, in Luke's bed. It had been a long week for both of them.

"Maybe longer," she said hopefully.

He kissed her then, a quick but potent promise of things to come. "I wonder how fast I can get this stuff stowed?" he muttered.

"Not fast enough," she said, meaning it, and loving the

shudder that went through him. Then he released her and began gathering the last of the gear.

"I think David likes Jessica," she said, trying to control the need that was rising in her as she watched him move with that smooth, economic grace.

"He'd better watch out for Gary, then," Luke warned. "He's like a grizzly when it comes to protecting those girls."

Amelia smiled. "I like him. He's a genuinely good guy."

Luke nodded as he stacked everything away in a locker. "He let me leave at the height of the season, when he couldn't really spare anyone, no questions asked."

"I'm glad he did," she said softly.

Their gazes locked. "And unless I miss my guess," he said, his voice rough, "once he notices we're gone, he'll keep David so occupied he won't even miss us."

"Now that's a friend," she said.

By the time they reached his small cabin, they were already at a fever pitch. Amelia began to tug at his shirt before he even had the door closed and locked; she'd lost her shyness about this days ago, when he'd told her quite bluntly nothing that turned him on more than her being so hungry for him she couldn't wait.

They left a trail of clothing across the living area, kissing each other fervently as they went, and were naked by the time they hit the door to his small bedroom, their hands busy searching out those special places they'd discovered with hungry caresses, as if they'd been apart much longer than a single week.

They went down on the bed hard, grace and care forgotten, finesse abandoned as they sought the shortest path to what they so desperately needed. In unspoken agreement Amelia lay back, pulling Luke with her, barely giving him enough time to handle protection. She moaned as he slipped between her legs and she felt the thick, blunt hardness of him and knew he was as hotly aroused as she was. She was on fire; she felt as if she'd been an eon without him, and she was in no mood to wait any longer.

Luke responded to her urgency with his own, taking only a split second to guide himself and then plunging home in one hard, swift stroke. They both cried out, and for one short, intense moment they hung there, breathless, feeling the rightness of these two bodies locked together.

And then the blaze ignited. Luke began to move, and Amelia moved with him, reaching, clawing, climbing.

It hit them hard and fast, on his third stroke. Amelia, startled by the swiftness and fierceness of it, cried out his name as her body convulsed. The moment her muscles clenched in that racking spasm of pleasure, Luke slammed into her once more, then let out a throttled groan as he clutched her so tightly it should have hurt but instead felt wonderful. Her name broke from him in a stunned voice as he exploded along with her.

He collapsed atop her, his breath coming in harsh, broken gasps. Amelia felt another echoing pulse of that eruption, her body tightening again, and Luke shuddered in response. For a long moment the only sound in the small room was their rapid breathing.

"Wow," Amelia finally managed, albeit weakly.

Luke lifted his head, looking, for the moment, as stunned as she had sounded. He swallowed; then came another set of quickened breaths. Then he closed his eyes and let out a long sigh, shaking his head.

That counted as a wow, Amelia decided.

When Luke finally rolled away from her, he did it with a jerky, awkward motion that was totally unlike him. He sat on the side of the bed for a moment, then stood. He walked over to the single window in the bedroom and stood looking out over the rushing water. Amelia watched him, loving the way the light came in the window and gilded his body, making him look like a beautifully carved statue, all gold and dark in the sun.

Slowly, as the dizzying fog lifted, she realized he'd moved in that same disjointed way when he'd walked across the room. She sat up, the tiniest of furrows appearing between her brows. She opened her mouth to speak, then shut it again, remembering lessons learned. And at last he spoke.

"This place saved my life, Amelia. Until I found the river, I was just existing. Too many times I used to wonder why, used to think both the world and I would be better off if I didn't. Every day was the same. There was nothing to look forward to, not one damn thing that made me welcome a new day."

She hurt for the boy he'd been. But beneath that ache, although his words weren't particularly ominous, an uneasiness began to bubble inside her. She grabbed for something to put on; she might be shockingly brazen with Luke, but she wasn't quite up to standing naked in front of a window yet, even if the likelihood of being seen was virtually nil. She had the T-shirt half on before she realized it was Luke's. It was still warm from his body, carried his scent, so she finished pulling it down.

"Then the river became my life. It's what gives it meaning. It's what I do. It's who I am."

The ominous feeling grew, and Amelia suddenly realized the real reason she'd felt the need for clothing: for protection. He was talking gently, almost pleadingly. As if begging her to understand.

And she did, all too well. He was making it as clear as he could that this was his life. And the next step was no doubt to explain that she had no part in it. The knowledge hit her like a blow; this was why he wouldn't even look at her. The only thing she could think was that his timing stunk, no matter how he might try to let her down easily, to do it after the kind of explosive passion they had just shared.

She sat on the edge of his bed, wishing she trusted her legs enough to move, to run, to escape what she was very much afraid was coming.

''I could live on another river,'' he said. ''Maybe not even on a river, but close. But I could never, ever live in Santiago Beach again. I just can't, Amelia. I don't ever want to go back there.''

So there it was. She should have known, she supposed. She'd been a fling, a distraction when he'd been stuck in ancient history, but now he had his old life back, and she wasn't part of it.

With an effort greater than it had taken to face Snake, Fargo and the rest, knives and all, she gathered the shreds of her poise around her. She couldn't let him see how much this hurt. She wouldn't. No matter what it cost her.

''I understand,'' she said stiffly.

He turned from the window then. For an instant she broke and let herself look at him, drinking in the sight of his powerful, beautiful body, wondering how long she could live on the memory.

She turned away, gathering up her jeans and underwear, tugging them on haphazardly. ''I'll go back to the lodge. And I'll pass on tomorrow, thank you. I'll take David home as soon as you're back.''

Despite her efforts, her voice was strained. She was no good at this. How did more sophisticated people do it, have an affair and walk away so casually? How did they hide the pain? Didn't they—

''Amelia?''

She couldn't look at him. ''It's all right.'' It wasn't. It would never be all right.

He grabbed her shoulders, turned her to face him. When she still wouldn't lift her gaze, he tilted her head back with one hand, gentle but insistent. She looked at him finally, surprised to see he looked a little disturbed himself.

''Is Santiago Beach that important to you?'' he asked. Amelia drew back slightly, puzzled. Luke let out a weary breath. ''I know you've lived there for a few years, and it's your parents' house, and you've got the store, I know all that, but…it's not like you were born there, is it?''

For a moment she just stood there, barefoot, dressed in her jeans and his shirt, looking at him. "What," she said slowly, "does where I was born have to do with anything?"

Luke released her then, grimacing disgustedly. "God, I knew I'd screw this up."

He seemed to abruptly realize she was dressed and he was not. He grabbed his jeans and yanked them on, still with that jerky, nervous motion that was so unlike him. At least now she knew why, she thought painfully.

"Screw what up?" she finally asked.

He straightened and raked a hand through his tousled hair. Tousled by her eager, clutching hands. She fought down a wave of now unwanted heat as she waited for him to answer. It took him what seemed like forever.

"I guess I should have thought more about where to start. I was going to tell you about all the people who use River Park as a starting place for backpacking or camping trips. The experienced rafters or kayakers who head out on the river on their own, because they like the solitude over a group."

He was sounding like he had with David, instructional, explaining the differences between a paddle raft and an oar raft, a hard-shell kayak and an inflatable. Or, she thought rather more grimly, like he had when warning his brother not to get cocky, that in one El Niño-driven year thirteen people had died from lack of judgment, tackling rapids they'd had no training for, or with inferior equipment. That was about how she felt right now, adrift in a raft she had no idea how to steer.

"And you were going to tell me this because…?" she prompted when he didn't go on.

"I just… I mean, these people, they're pretty much roughing it. Not the ones in the big RVs, I mean the real campers. They might have a radio, but no TV, and after a long day of hiking, they're ready to unwind and relax. And most of them do it with a book.''

Amelia went still. The point of this had something to do with her, obviously, but she couldn't for the life of her see what it was.

''Thing is, a lot of them forget about that until the last minute. They're always asking us if there's anywhere around they could get a book or two. And there's only a little rack in the grocery store up in town, and most of what's there is as old as Davie.''

Her breath caught. ''Luke—'' she began, but now that he was rolling, there seemed to be no stopping him.

''There's a little storefront that's vacant, right next to the grocery, where most people go before they start out. And rent's pretty cheap here. You could move your stock, couldn't you?''

She stared at him as it finally got through to her. He swallowed tightly and finished in a rush.

''I talked to Gary first thing when I got back yesterday. He said he'd sell me the plot the cabin's on, and I could expand it, add plenty of space, whatever you wanted. It'd take a while, but—''

''Luke McGuire!'' she nearly shouted. He shut up, startled. ''What, exactly, are you asking me?''

He let out an exasperated breath. ''Cut me some slack, will you? I'm no good at this, anyway, and I've never asked anybody to marry me before.''

All the tightness in her chest, all the emotions, all the tears that had built in her in the past few minutes, were released at once. Her eyes filled, and she sat down suddenly on the edge of the bed.

Looking worried, Luke knelt beside her to look up into her face. ''Amelia? Are you crying? I know I come with a lot of history but I didn't think that mattered to you.''

She looked at him, a slow, brimming joy welled up inside her. The adventurous spirit he had called up in her burst free of the last restraint. There were, she realized suddenly, more ways to settle down than her parents' quiet, sedate way. She knew there would be difficult times, but they would tackle them like Luke tackled difficult rapids.

She smiled at him through her tears. "Does this mean I can keep the shirt?"

He gaped at her, sitting there in his Whitewater West shirt. Then a slow, lazy grin curved his mouth. "Only if you say yes."

"I like your blue one, too," she said thoughtfully.

Luke burst out laughing. "Honey, you can have any shirt of mine you want."

"All of them," she decided, looking at his bare chest. "That way you won't have any to wear."

It became a deep, joyous belly laugh, and Amelia thought it was the most beautiful sound she'd ever heard. "I'm going to take that as a yes," Luke said.

"Oh, please do."

She leaned forward then, and kissed that spot she particularly liked, where the taut, fit muscles of his abdomen met. She felt him suck in his breath, then let it out again on a gasp as she moved upward and flicked her tongue over his nipple.

It was much, much later, as she lay sleepily snuggled next to him, that she knew they'd both found the right kind of paradise.

Epilogue

Amelia McGuire tapped the big envelope with her name scrawled on the front in a bold, looping hand against her fingers thoughtfully. When Charlie had dropped it off at the store this morning, while Luke was out on a one-day run with some return Whitewater West customers, he'd commented on the postmark, which had set her heart to thrumming.

When? she wondered. When should she tell him? He was due back any minute. Should she do it now?

She lifted the flap and pulled out the letter once more. She didn't need to read it again; she already had most of it committed to memory, anyway. Instead she pulled out the photograph and stared at it. And as had happened every time since she'd first seen it, her eyes brimmed with tears.

It had to be special, she thought. As special as this was. And she hastily began to plan.

When Luke arrived back late in the afternoon, he was startled to find their little table set up out on the porch, with tablecloth, dishes and candles.

"I thought we could enjoy the sunset," she told him.

In the year since she'd left her old life behind and started a new one with him, she'd done this periodically, both because she herself enjoyed it and to show him that she had no regrets, that she was coming to love this place as much as he did. She even made river runs with him every couple of weeks, learning from him on the water, unceasingly amazed at the depth of his knowledge and skill. And proud of him for the way he had continued to see his brother, until his mother had resigned herself to visits every few months.

And while sunsets weren't quite as spectacular here as they were on the coast—in fact, sunrises were much more amazing—they still enjoyed unwinding at day's end together like this. Soon, when the construction was finished, they would have a deck on the river to do this on, but for now, this would do nicely.

He gave her that crooked smile that never failed to make her blood heat and hurried in to clean up. Minutes later, showered, his hair wet and slicked back—she'd talked him out of cutting it, although, since he seemed to enjoy the way she played with it, it hadn't taken much convincing—he sat down at the table.

They ate the spaghetti she'd prepared in honor of the first meal they'd ever had together. He told her about the run, a breeze with all old hands; she told him about the customers she'd had, including the precocious six-year-old already reading stories way beyond his age level. But all the while she was watching the light, knowing she had to do this before it got too dark to see. She wanted to do it out here, in the place he loved. It just seemed right.

When she got out the bottle of champagne and two glasses she'd been chilling, Luke eyed first them, then her. "What is it?"

"Just open it, please?"

He did, still eyeing her warily. He filled both glasses and set the bottle down.

"Amelia…"

She took a deep breath. She took out the photograph, set aside the letter for the moment. "I have something for you."

"What?"

"Your family." She reached over and set the photo down in front of him.

"My…?"

His query died unspoken as his gaze went to the picture. She knew what he was seeing: a gathering of six people, ranging from teenagers to a gray-haired couple looking to be in their seventies. Clearly a family, the resemblance in the features of the men, the coloring, even the smiles, was unmistakable. And in the center, the one who had made her gasp. The handsome, rakish-looking man in his forties who was the living image of the man holding the photograph.

His son.

She saw Luke's eyes widen in shock, saw his lips part for breath, as if air was suddenly hard to find. His gaze went unfocused for a moment; then he lifted it to her face.

"I…what…?"

She picked up the letter. "He didn't know about you, Luke. Your mother had one of those morning-after fits of hysteria and told him to go away and never come back. He was only eighteen at the time—irresponsible, he admits—so he left, figuring he'd escaped easily enough, after a one-night stand he wasn't sure why he'd pursued in the first place."

He focused suddenly. "He…said that? That—" he indicated the letter she held "—is from him?"

She nodded.

"How?" Luke asked, sounding stunned.

"Jim helped me find him. He even pried some details out of your mother. I didn't ask how. It took until last month, since he had so little to go on. But he got me a family address in Ireland, and I wrote. I sent a picture of you. This came today."

"But...you never said a thing."

"I wanted to be sure it was really him first. And that he would...want to be found."

Luke looked at the photograph again, at the faces that so resembled his own, and the man who was showing him his own future. Then he looked at his wife again.

"And...he didn't mind?"

"They," she corrected, "are delighted." She handed him the letter. "Your father says—" she had to smother a smile at the look on Luke's face as she said it "—he was the family black sheep, but finally grew up, went home and settled down. Married a local girl, had two kids and, to be honest, never again thought of your mother."

"Well, that'd fry her," Luke said with a wobbly grin; he was starting to take it all in, Amelia thought.

"You can read it yourself, of course, but the upshot is that we're invited to Ireland to meet the whole family as soon as we can."

"Ireland..."

"I looked up where they are, near Dublin, it would be easy to get to."

For a moment Luke just sat there, looking at her. Then he looked at the photo again, then back at her. Then he shook his head. "I'm a little...overwhelmed."

Amelia reached out and covered his hand with hers. "I know. But there's even a note from his wife, assuring you that she doesn't hold any ill feeling toward a son her husband sired long before he married her. And that she'd welcome a big brother to her two girls, and Patrick will be doing right by you, or he'll answer to her."

"I..." He was still sounding a bit dazed.

"How soon can we go?"

Luke couldn't seem to speak. But he got up then, hauled her into his arms and held her so tightly she could barely breathe. And she wouldn't have moved for the world.

"I've got a father," he whispered when he finally let her go.

She grinned up at him. "And a stepmom who sounds like she's a match for him. And grandparents. And sisters, two of them. Oh, those girls are going to just die when they get a look at you!"

To her very great pleasure, Luke blushed. It seemed like a good time to add what she'd been thinking about.

"And maybe, in a couple of years, we can go back and take your sisters a little niece or nephew to spoil."

Luke went very still.

"A wanted child," Amelia said pointedly. "One with a real family now, one that will love it, treasure it, the way a child should be treasured."

Luke swallowed tightly. And hugged her again. "I...I'll have to get used to that idea."

"I know." Amelia leaned back to look at him. She gave him the decidedly wicked grin he'd said he never would have thought her capable of a year ago. "But keep in mind the joy of making your mother a grandmother while she's still trying to convince the world she's only thirty-five."

Luke burst out laughing.

He kissed her.

They toasted the sunset.

He kissed her again.

This time he didn't let go.

The rest of the champagne could wait, Amelia thought. Her husband's touch was much more intoxicating.

She was ready for another visit to paradise.

*   *   *   *   *

Silhouette invites you to come back to Whitehorn, Montana...

MONTANA MAVERICKS

WED IN WHITEHORN—
12 BRAND-NEW stories that capture living and loving beneath the Big Sky where legends live on and love lasts forever!

MM

And the adventure continues...

October 2000—
Marilyn Pappano *Big Sky Lawman* (#5)

November 2000—
Pat Warren *The Baby Quest* (#6)

December 2000—
Karen Hughes *It Happened One Wedding Night* (#7)

January 2001—
Pamela Toth *The Birth Mother* (#8)

More MONTANA MAVERICKS coming soon!

Available at your favorite retail outlet.

Silhouette®
Where love comes alive™

You're not going to believe this offer!

In October and November 2000, buy any two Harlequin or Silhouette books and save $10.00 off future purchases, or buy any three and save $20.00 off future purchases!

Just fill out this form and attach 2 proofs of purchase (cash register receipts) from October and November 2000 books and Harlequin will send you a coupon booklet worth a total savings of $10.00 off future purchases of Harlequin and Silhouette books in 2001. Send us 3 proofs of purchase and we will send you a coupon booklet worth a total savings of $20.00 off future purchases.

Saving money has never been this easy.

I accept your offer! Please send me a coupon booklet:

Name: _____

Address: _____ City: _____

State/Prov.: _____ Zip/Postal Code: _____

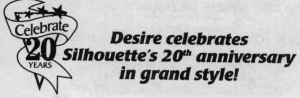